THE SORCERER'S DAUGHTER

A FIVE TOWERS NOVEL

MICHELLE MILES

Book Cover by Erin Dameron-Hill

Map Illustration by Kimberly McKelvey

First Edition June 2024

ISBN: 979-8223572329 (eBook)
ISNB: 978-1-7343068-9-7 (paperback)

Haven Island
West King Hi
White Cliffs
Loch Randoon
Five Towers
Kasari
Millhall
Littletown
Highcrest
Loch Lomar
Riverbrook
Whitefell
Innahill
Eyana Sharas
Dal Breifna
The Great Grass Sea
Raw

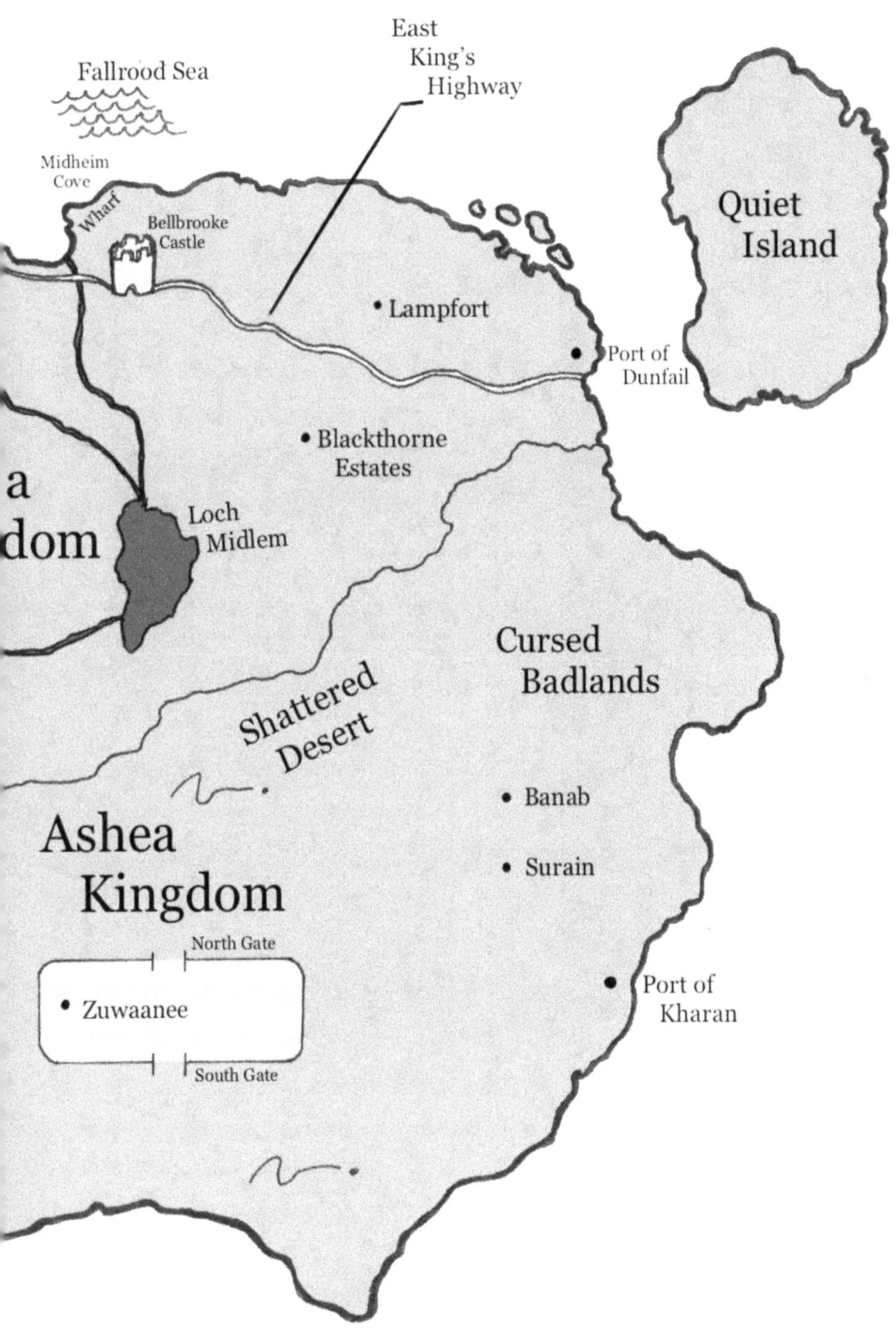

Fallrood Sea
Midheim Cove
East King's Highway
Quiet Island
Wharf
Bellbrooke Castle
Lampfort
Port of Dunfail
Blackthorne Estates
Loch Midlem
a
dom
Cursed Badlands
Shattered Desert
Banab
Surain
Ashea Kingdom
North Gate
Zuwaanee
South Gate
Port of Kharan

"I thoroughly enjoyed Sorcerer's Daughter. Michelle Miles is a bright new voice in YA Fantasy that is not to be missed. This story of a young sorceress coming into her magic is full of imaginative surprises. I loved the twists and turns that kept me reading until the wee hours of the morning. If you enjoy magic and intrigue between kingdoms, sprinkled with a light romance, you'll be delighted with Sorcerer's Daughter."

–Kathleen Baldwin, author of *A School for Unusual Girls* and a *Wall Street Journal* bestselling author

For all those who believe in the power of magic.

CHAPTER ONE

I t was a simple levitation spell. One I should have been able to do with ease. One I had memorized from the spell scroll in Papa's study.

Stretching out my hand, I closed my eyes and tried again. I imagined the large stone rising into the air and hovering over the ground at eye level. When I opened my eyes, though, the stone had barely lifted an inch from the pathway.

Dropping my hand in frustration, I blew out a heated breath. The stone crashed back to the ground with a clunk. I'd been working on that spell for months and still nothing. I should have powers like Papa, who was one of the strongest, most respected sorcerers in all the kingdom of Rovaria. And yet, I was unable to levitate a stone.

And also forbidden to attempt any type of magic. He refused to allow me to practice magic or even learn basic spells.

If Papa knew I was in his study memorizing spell scrolls...well, let's just say he wouldn't be happy with me.

I never understood why he was so adamant I stay away from magic when he had it coming out his ears.

It was hard not to resent him for that. He was, after all, the only parent I had since my mother died when I was young. I had no memory of her other than the stories Papa told me about her as I grew up. He said I had her eyes and her smile. He never mentioned how she died and I sensed something about the way she died indicated he never wanted to mention it again.

One of my earliest memories was spending time with him in his spellcasting room watching him create potions and write spell scrolls. When I took an interest in magic as well, he banished me from that room, forbidding me from ever using magic. He was vehement that I never use magic and told me often to stay away from it, though I never understood why. Sometimes, I wondered if it had to do with my mother's death.

An unwavering need to learn magic and use it burned through me. I wanted more in life. I wanted to harness the power like he did. He really gave me no choice but to sneak into his workroom and memorize spells. I had a gift for memorization—I saw words in my mind.

Now, at seventeen, he was determined to marry me off to a rich noble and, well, I wasn't having it. I rejected two suitors already. One had the personality of a wooden stump. The other had grabby hands and was determined to ruin my reputation on the first meeting.

Inhaling a deep breath, I took in the scents of the greenhouse. At this time of year, everything was beginning to bloom before being relocated to the massive estate gardens. The seeds were cultivated during the long winter and now it was time to plant. Some were flowers, while others were vegetables and fruits that would sustain the household through the next few seasons.

I didn't have much of a green thumb, but I still enjoyed spending time with my hands in the dirt. I helped the gardeners plant their seeds and take care of the fledging plants all winter. When my secret magic studies frustrated me, I came here to expend pent-up energy and calm my mind.

Some good that did. I still was unable to levitate a stupid rock.

There were days when I felt as though I was on the cusp of having a major magical breakthrough. And others where I felt as though I had not one ounce of magic within me. Perhaps Papa was right in that I didn't possess the magical ability as he did.

But, no, I refused to believe that was true. I was able to lift the rock an inch. So, there must be some deep, hidden glimmer of magic in there somewhere.

"Ah, there you are, Violet. I thought I might find you here."

Papa entered the greenhouse with his slow limping gait, an old injury that bothered him most days when the weather was foul. He paused next to me on the pathway between several of the planter's tables.

"What are you doing out here?" he asked.

Hesitation pumped through me, not wanting to tell him I'd been practicing magic because that would get me a lecture. I wasn't in the mood for a lecture.

"Just checking on the plants."

A lie. He probably knew it, too, by the sideways look he gave me. But he said nothing more about it.

"Well, I've come to retrieve you. Lord Desmond has arrived. He's waiting for you in the library."

I resisted the urge to scowl and roll my eyes. This was the third suitor in as many weeks. Lord Desmond Rothchester was the Earl of Lambridge whose first wife died childless. His second wife also failed to produce a male heir, so he cast her aside. To a nunnery. A nunnery on charge of adultery, though I suspected the adulterer was the lord himself. And now, here he was sniffing around Blackthorne Estates looking to make me his third wife.

What, then, would happen to me should I not produce an heir? Would he deposit me in a nunnery or—worse—kill me off?

"Must I meet with him, Papa?"

"We've been through this, Violet." His tone was firm.

It was a discussion we had after I refused Lord Grabby Hands. I actually couldn't recall that oaf's name and I didn't want to.

Turning away, I focused my gaze on a tiny white flower peeking through the dirt in one of the nearby pots. I said nothing as I rested my fists on top of the scarred wooden table. It was as though my life was planned for me since the moment I was born. I spent every day studying, learning the history of Rovaria from the time of the First King when he invaded a thousand years ago to the rule of today's monarch, King Jeffrey. My lessons were in the ways of poetry, literature, and art. I learned all the latest fashionable dances, how to be a proper lady, and how to run an estate. All in the name of eventually marrying a lord to rule his castle and present him with an heir.

I didn't want to marry a lord and rule his castle while he went away to war or on hunts and spent his nights with drink and wenches. I wanted nothing to do with that life.

What I wanted was to become a powerful sorceress. To use magic the way Papa did to help those around me. To become something other than a wife and mother. I didn't want that life. I wanted more out of life.

"I do not wish to marry, Papa."

I was unable to stop the words from escaping. I had, of course, told him this before and knew how the conversation would go.

"And what will become of you if you do not?" Frustration edged his words, then he sighed. It was a familiar sound. "You are a lady of the nobility. Think of all you will gain when you marry. Not only will your son inherit the title of your husband, but also Blackthorne Estate."

"Because I cannot inherit from you." A bitterness rose in my mouth as my hands tightened into a fist, my nails biting into my palm. I cut him a sharp glance. "Is that all I'm good for? As a wife and mother so Blackthorne will have an heir?"

He moved closer, placing a hand on my upper arm. "It is the way of our world, my dear. Women marry, raise children, run households."

"And yet while the men enjoy their freedoms, we are stuck with serving their needs and seeing to their households. I cannot inherit my fortune, nor can I earn it. Even you, Papa. You have the favor of the king and all the nobles. You live as you wish."

"And it is why you must marry a noble, because I have the favor of the king. He has sent his most eligible suitors to ask for your hand. Suitors which you have turned away. I will not live forever. I want to make sure you are well cared for before I'm gone."

I walked deeper into the greenhouse, my agitation crawling under my skin. My fate was sealed. I understood that at some point I would, in fact, have to choose a husband from the suitors who called on me. Lord Desmond was one who wanted my hand in marriage and to warm his bed.

There must be more to life than this.

"Your mother would have wanted you to be happy," he said.

His emotional blackmail cut deep.

"Please, Violet. At least meet with Lord Desmond." Desperation edged his voice.

I looked at him over my shoulder. Worry lines creased his face as he waited for me to acknowledge. For the first time, I noticed how much he'd aged over these last few years. How his dark hair was beginning to thin and show signs of gray at the temples. How his face was lined with constant fatigue and worry I wouldn't choose a suitable husband. Or any husband.

The stubbornness released, all the fight going out of me. "I'll meet with him."

He breathed a sigh of relief, but I held up a hand.

"But I make no other promises," I added.

His shoulders drooped a little even as he nodded, almost in defeat. "Change your dress. I will expect you in the library forthwith."

As he left, I glanced down at the plain brown smock covered in dirt over my day dress. My hair still hung in long messy waves over my shoulders. Dread filled me as I returned to my chamber to change. Sophia, my maid, was already there waiting with a gown at the ready.

"Another suitor, my lady?" She held up the dress, sympathy on her face.

I sighed. "Yes."

Sophia helped me out of the smock and dress, then assisted with the corset and voluminous hoop skirt.

Sophia was the same age as me and had been my maid for several years. Her mother had been a scullery maid in one of the nearby estates and when she'd fallen ill, Sophia had to find work. She was barely thirteen when she came to our household. Papa took her in and, though I didn't need a maid, he assigned her to me.

We were friendly, though not friends, but she shared my horror of having to meet suitor after suitor.

The gown Sophia selected was one in midnight blue with a high neck and long, lace sleeves. Once the gown was buttoned down the back,

Sophia motioned for me to sit at the dressing table. She brushed my tangled dark brown hair, then plaited it and wound it around my head in the high fashion of court ladies. Not my favorite. I'd rather wear my hair long and loose than in tight braids.

"Thank you, Sophia," I said when she finished.

"Good luck," she said.

I rose from the dressing table and stuck my feet into the slippers. I took a deep breath and prepared to meet Lord Desmond. Walking slowly through the manor would do me no good. It would delay the inevitable. Instead, I hurried down the corridor, my breath coming in short spurts due to the tightness of the corset. When I arrived, the library door was ajar. I paused and stepped aside, peering through the slight opening to see Papa sitting in one of the oversized chairs, but I couldn't see Lord Desmond.

I crept closer.

"...understand she has rebuffed several suitors," Lord Desmond said.

A thin smile slipped across Papa's face. "My daughter can be headstrong. However, I believe you would be a good match for her."

"And why do you think that?" he asked.

"I believe you'd balance her willfulness. As such, I'm prepared to offer you her dowry. Upon my death, Blackthorne will pass to her husband—you—and, in turn, her son."

"Indeed." The man's voice was thoughtful, his interest piqued.

"As well as forty thousand gold," Papa added.

Shock ripped through me so hard I stumbled back a step. Forty thousand gold? That's what my hand in marriage was worth? I was already aware Blackthorne would never belong to me. I hated the thought of

Blackthorne falling into the hands of someone else. Even if he was my husband.

"Then I accept your proposal," Lord Desmond said.

Over my dead body.

I cleared my throat loudly and stomped a few steps to make my presence known before pushing through the library door.

The library was a spacious, comfortable room that I loved despite the faded furniture and rugs. It was home and I loved it. Two walls hosted floor to ceiling bookshelves. One wall was an oversized window with a comfortable window seat perfect for lazing away the afternoons with a good book. A sofa and two wing-backed chairs were in front of the window. On the other side, Papa's desk littered with letters, scrolls, and a quill and inkpot. He spent a good amount of time here. We both did.

Both men rose as soon as I entered.

The nobleman was tall, with a full head of silver hair. His long, narrow face was ancient with age lines crinkling around his eyes and the corners of his mouth which drew down, as though he frowned a lot. He was impeccably dressed in a navy waistcoat, the ruffles at his throat hiding what was sure to be a long, thin neck. More white ruffles graced his wrists. His pants were also navy tucked into highly polished black boots, as though they had never seen a spec of dirt or dust. He must have arrived here in a coach instead of on horseback. He was too clean, too perfect, too old.

Papa gave me a nod and an approving smile as I paused in the doorway to wait for introductions.

"Ah, this must be your daughter," Lord Desmond said.

"Yes. This is Violet."

Lord Desmond moved to stand in front of me, taking my hand in his clammy one and kissed my knuckles. His lips were cold, reminding me of a dead fish. I did my best not to recoil in disgust. I lifted my gaze to his sharp, assessing blue ones and gave him my best cordial smile.

It was an effort.

"The stories are true, then. Your beauty is, indeed, exceptional, my lady." He released my hand.

"Thank you." I forced the words past my lips, dropping my hand to my side and fighting the urge to wipe my knuckles on my skirt to eradicate his lifeless kiss.

"I'll leave you to get acquainted."

Papa moved to the library door passing by in a whiff of old leather and ink, something I always associated with him. He gave me a cutting look as if to tell me to be a proper lady. When the library door was closed, Lord Desmond moved to sit in one of the oversized wing-backed chairs. He motioned for me to sit in the one next to him.

I took slow steps to the chair, my skirts swishing with the movement. Perching on the edge, I clasped my hands in my lap and waited for him to speak.

"Your father has told me quite a bit about you," he said.

I fought the urge to roll my eyes. "Has he?"

"I'm told you like to garden," he said, making small talk.

"Some, yes," I said with a slight nod.

"I have a large garden at Lambridge."

"Do you?" I resisted the urge to tell him I didn't care what he had at his fancy castle.

"It would make me happy if you would visit me there."

I cringed. The last thing I wanted to do was visit the decrepit lord at his castle. I feared I would never be able to leave. I gave him a faint smile.

"That seems rather forward of you to ask." I kept my voice neutral.

"Forward? Not at all." He gave me a faint, oily smile.

I considered his invitation with a less than enthusiastic response. I had no interest in visiting his estate now or in the future.

"I'm afraid I cannot accept your invitation." I kept my voice even and clear.

He tipped his silver head to one side. "And why is that?"

Before I answered, a servant wheeled a cart into the library. Tea cups rattled on top of their saucers as the woman moved it into the center of the room. A three-tiered server sat next to the teapot hosting tiny sandwiches and lemon cakes. She gave a quick curtsy before leaving the library.

I rose from the chair and headed to the tea cart as a distraction. I didn't want the tea, but decided it would give my hands something to do as I thought of an answer. I picked up the tea pot and poured one cup, then gave Lord Desmond a questioning glance.

"Tea?"

"Please." He eyed me as I poured, still waiting for an answer to his question.

"Cream and sugar?" I stalled.

"Just sugar."

I added a healthy dollop of cream to my own tea and a small teaspoon of sugar to his. I picked up both saucers and walked with slow, steady steps back to the chairs.

"I'm still waiting, my lady," he said as he took the cup.

I held the saucer in one hand, picking up the cup with the other. "I have duties and lessons here. I can't possibly leave Papa or the manor."

A faint smile lifted his thin lips. "It was your father who suggested it."

My heart stuttered. How could he without asking me first? "My father?"

"Indeed. As my betrothed."

My fingers tightened on the delicate handle of the porcelain as I gave him a long, hard stare. "Am I to understand you are proposing marriage to me, my lord?"

"I am." His smile widened. "Under my roof, you will find safety and security and as many comforts as you do here. And your father has already approved the match."

Of course, I heard them making plans to marry me off, but it didn't make me any less angry. Bloody hell. "Even though we just met?"

He set aside the saucer and rose, coming toward me. Everything in my mind screamed for him to stay away.

"I'm quite taken with you, my dear. You are every bit as beautiful as I've heard. I should be honored to make you my wife." He glanced at my hands holding the cup and saucer, as if he gave a silent request for me to place them aside.

I continued to hold them, refusing to move. The arrogance of this man infuriated me. The presumptuousness of Papa also infuriated me. I understood why he was here and what he wanted and I wasn't about to give it to him. No matter what Papa promised him.

"Perhaps, my lord, you are more interested in my dowry than me." It was impossible to stop the words from spilling out of my mouth. "Specifically, Blackthorne."

A dark fury passed over his features before he regained control and squelched it. "I came here with an offer of good faith."

"Ah, yes, to offer me marriage and a life of safety and security by running your castle and warming your bed in the hopes I will produce an heir for you. I must be your last resort since your other wives were unable to give you one."

This time, he did not control the fury that pinched his face. I treaded on thin ground but was unable to stop the cascade of words. How could Papa expect me to marry this man? This pompous man who had little regard and respect for women. He discarded them as though he discarded a threadbare coat.

"Perhaps, my lady, you are damaged goods."

His attempted insult did nothing but enflame my anger. I lifted by head, looking down my nose at him. "And why do you think that?"

"Why else would you refuse suitor after suitor? Or, perhaps, the suitors refused you."

"I believe it is the men who are damaged goods, my lord," I snapped. "And most, including you, are not good enough for me and never will be."

Without another word, he stalked to the library door and flung it open. As he passed through the hallway, he spoke to Papa, who must have been loitering in the foyer.

"Good luck to you finding someone to marry her."

I didn't bother to stifle the smile as I sipped my tea.

CHAPTER TWO

Papa's scorching gaze landed on me from his spot in the foyer. Instantly, I understood the calamity of my actions. Fury lined his features as he stomped into the library moments later. Turning, I calmly placed the cup and saucer on the serving cart, then picked up one of the small cucumber sandwiches.

"You have insulted the earl," he said.

"And who cares?" I snapped, turning the small rectangle around in my fingers.

"*I care.* Violet..." He said my name on an exasperated sigh. "You cannot keep turning them away. Lord after lord."

I spun to face him, still holding the tiny sandwich between thumb and forefinger. "And you cannot keep promising my hand to these pompous elitists. How can you expect me to marry someone like that, Papa? He has one foot in the grave and nothing but bad intentions."

Not to mention the forty thousand gold he'd offered up. As though that was all I was worth.

"He merely wishes to have an heir for his estate. He—"

"And we know what happened to his other wives. One died. One was placed in a nunnery. Who's to say *he* is not the one who cannot produce an heir?"

He said nothing as he pressed his lips together into a tight line. He knew I was right to refuse Lord Desmond. He just didn't want to admit it. I had one last ditch effort to implore him. One last idea that would make him see things my way. If I must marry, then I wanted it to be for love, not for a fortune. I cared not for money or land or title.

He could never know I wanted power above all else.

I put down the sandwich and bustled toward him. I gripped his hands in mine. "Papa, *please*. Allow me to make my own choice. I cannot marry someone I don't love, nor do I want to."

"My darling, you are nearly eighteen," he said.

"And is that a crime?"

"Being unwed at your age..." His words trailed off.

The punch of anger surged through me, hot and wild. I understood, then. I released his hands and stepped back.

"Is that your biggest fear, Papa? That I will remain unwed and a spinster? That I will be an embarrassment to you?"

"Violet—"

"Do not speak to me about marriage anymore." I cut him off with the acidic words.

I brushed by him in my haste to leave the library, hurrying through the hallways clutching my gown in my hands to keep from tripping. Heated tears filled my eyes. Several servants cast me a curious glance as I ran toward the kitchens and out the back door. I refused to stop until I reached the stable. Peppermint popped his head out of his stall when he heard me enter.

Blinking away the tears, I grinned. I patted him on the nose. He nuzzled my hand looking for treats.

"I'm sorry, old friend. I don't have any."

His name was Peppermint because he loved them so much. If I allowed it, he would make himself sick on them. But the stable hands were under strict instructions not to allow him the treats unless I gave them to him. I brushed his nose. The motion soothed my ragged nerves.

"How am I to make him understand?" I whispered.

Too bad the horse wasn't saddled so I could take him out for a ride. Even if he was, I doubted I would be able to ride in my voluminous gown.

I heard Papa's voice as he approached the stable asking one of the hands if he'd seen me. My heart kicked into overdrive. I didn't want to talk to him about Lord Desmond or any other suitor. On impulse, I gathered my skirts and bolted out the other end of the stable. Peppermint snorted his disappointment as I hurried away. I'd make it up to him later.

I ran toward East King's Highway with one destination in mind—the white cliffs overlooking the stormy sea. Hearing the crashing waves soothed me when I was in despair. I preferred to ride out to them, certainly, but I wanted to make haste. It did, naturally, occur to me the cliffs were too far to reach on foot in any reasonable amount of time. Even so, I continued on this fool's errand. Though Spring was near, there was still a chill in the air biting through my lace sleeves.

Tears blinded my eyes so I never saw the black horse until it reared up, whinnying its surprise. I sucked in a sharp breath as I stumbled backward out of the way.

"Whoa! Whoa, boy!" a man's voice shouted.

My heart pounded wildly as he came to a halt, turning sideways to get a good look at me. The stranger sat atop a black war horse. I was lucky I wasn't trampled.

"I-I'm so sorry!" I stammered, my cheeks hot from embarrassment.

The man was young and quite handsome, perhaps not much older than me. He had sharp blue eyes that twinkled with something between mirth and annoyance. His black hair was tousled by the faint breeze. He had a regal air about him, with a square jaw, high cheekbones, and a straight, perfect nose. His lips were thin and yet something about them seemed utterly kissable.

He was well dressed with a dark blue cloak over his shoulders pinned at the throat with a gold chain. His hands were covered in black riding gloves. His pants were the same deep blue tucked into black knee-high boots splattered with mud and covered in dirt. Clearly, he had been on the road for some time.

"What's the hurry, my lady?" he asked, a hint of a smile on his lips.

"I...I just needed some air." I cut a glance back toward the manor.

He lifted a dark brow. "Indeed?"

"I didn't see you there," I said.

"Even though I was on the road." The corner of his mouth lifted in a smile.

I knew what he insinuated—that I was not. No, I ran with reckless abandon toward the cliffs, wishing for my freedom.

"My apologies, my lord." I took up my skirts and turned back toward the manor.

He chuckled. "I am no lord, but I appreciate the sentiment."

I ignored him and continued walking, trying to put distance between us. Much to my dismay, he followed at a slow trot.

"I wish to know the name of the lady who nearly ran me off the road. May I ask?"

"You may ask," I said, without looking up at him.

"But that doesn't mean you'll tell me?" There was humor in his voice.

"I will not." I urged my exhausted legs to move a little faster.

But he and his horse easily kept up. "And why not?"

I cut him a sideways glance. "And will you be sharing your name, then?"

"Aiden Lockart, my lady. A pleasure to make your acquaintance," he said without hesitation and a little bow of his head. "And you are?"

My heart thrummed upon hearing his name. I didn't understand that reaction one bit.

"No one of consequence," I said.

He tipped his head back and laughed. "You little minx."

The rumbling of a carriage caught our attention. We both halted and turned back to see it flying down the road drawn by four black horses. I recognized the crest of Lord Desmond on the side of the carriage. A chill ran up my spine, thankful I managed to dodge marriage to that lout.

"Ah, another traveler in a bit of a hurry."

I glared at the carriage until it was out sight, mostly because I wanted to make sure he was heading away from the manor as quickly as possible.

"Good. He's not wanted here." I turned back toward the manor and started walking.

"I take it you know the carriage owner?" he called.

"Good day, Mr. Lockhart," I called back without turning.

As I hurried away, I heard him chuckle again. I resisted a glance back over my shoulder. I didn't want him to think I was interested. I mostly definitely was not interested.

When the hoof beats moved away from me, only then did I steal a glance over my shoulder to see him riding away at a very slow, very methodical pace. As though he had all the time in the world.

Maybe he did. I wondered where he was headed on the East King's Highway. Perhaps to Bellbrooke, the Rovarian capital? I'd never been but heard tales of the city with all the amazing shops. Some even lived in apartments within the city which was hard for me to imagine since I'd never actually *seen* an apartment. And there was a wharf with fisherman and warehouses and ships in the dock.

With a sigh, I headed home, walking through the manor gates.

Things were tense between Papa and me. We didn't speak much during mealtimes. I sensed he was still unhappy with me and the way I rebuffed Lord Desmond. Several days passed with us alternating between uncomfortable silence and uneasy acknowledgment of each other. I spent my mornings in my lessons and the afternoons riding my horse.

A few days after the Lord Desmond incident, I headed out to the stable. Peppermint popped his head out of his stall when he heard me enter and snorted. I laughed and pulled the bag of mints off the peg at the door. I held a handful out to him. He nibbled them off my palm while I patted his nose. He snorted his contentment.

"Your father is looking for you," the stable master said. "He was here a few minutes ago. He said it was important he speak to you."

My stomach clenched. Perhaps he found another suitor for me. Another man to offer forty thousand gold for my hand in marriage. Or perhaps he was finally going to lecture me about my behavior with Lord Desmond. I didn't want to go, but if I didn't, I'd be in even more trouble.

Peppermint nibbled the last of the mints. When all the mints were gone, I patted his nose again.

"Then I suppose I should find him."

My afternoon ride would have to wait.

With slow steps, I headed out of the stable and back into the manor. I found him in his study, his graying head bent over the desk as he quickly scrawled a message on parchment with his quill. The only sound was that of the scratching against the paper. I knocked softly on the door, preparing for the torrent of angry words.

"You were looking for me?"

He looked up, putting his pen back to the holder and nodded. "Yes. A raven came."

"A raven?"

It wasn't often a raven came to the manor. I moved deeper into the room, standing in front of his desk.

"A message from the king."

"Oh...?" My voice trailed off. I clasped my hands in front of me and waited for him to elaborate. A message from the king likely did not bring good news.

"The royal sorcerer died suddenly," he said. "And since they need a replacement in short order, my presence has been requested immediately."

My brows drew together. "Immediately?"

Questions sprang to my mind. If he was telling me, then he must intend for me to go with him. But for how long? What about the manor?

He picked up his quill and dipped it in ink. "I'm writing to my cousin in Lampfort to oversee the estates as steward until I return."

"So, it's to be a temporary situation with the king, then?" I asked.

"Yes."

I didn't like where this was going. "And what about me?"

"You are to accompany me. The king has offered us generous apartments in the castle in addition to a salary I would be mad to refuse. Aside from that, it will be a wonderful opportunity for you to meet with other ladies of the court and find a proper husband."

He gave me a pointed look, a sharp glint in his eyes. I cringed.

He was bound and determined to marry me off. I was beginning to wonder if his intentions were purely noble or if there was some other maneuvering going on that I didn't know about.

"And I will hear nothing more about you refusing to marry," he added.

I swallowed any retort I might have had. I wanted to argue, certainly, but knew it would be unwise by the hard gleam in his eyes. I'd already done enough damage.

"Yes, Papa. When do we leave?"

He returned to his scroll. "Two days. That will give Rupert time to arrive and us to pack. You may take Sophia and Peppermint with you. The king will send a garrison to accompany us on the East King's Highway."

The East King's Highway was the road into the capital. It was at least a day's ride to the manor from the castle.

At least I would have my horse. Though Sophia and I were not best friends, it would be nice to have a familiar face in a sea of strangers. I dreaded the thought of leaving my home, the only home I'd known my entire life. Of my life changing in ways I couldn't imagine.

"Thank you, Papa."

He didn't reply, effectively dismissing me as he continued to scrawl on his parchment. I backed out of the study. In the hall, I turned on my heel and returned to my chamber, my heart heavy with despair.

25

CHAPTER THREE

Two days went by in the blink of an eye. The servants packed my room, putting all my best gowns in trunks. There was no indication of how long we would be living there or even if we would return to the manor. Cousin Rupert, my first cousin once removed, wasn't someone I liked or trusted. He was probably overjoyed at the thought of moving into the manor house and running it while we were gone.

Papa and I stood outside the manor on the dirt drive as Cousin Rupert arrived with an entourage of his own in a carriage led by four white horses. Behind the carriage, a cart carried more luggage than I'd ever seen before. It was more than I was taking to Bellbrooke Castle. I shifted from one foot to the other, casting a quick glance at Papa who stood with his jaw set and his face impassive. Was he wondering, like me, if Rupert planned to move in and stay?

The footman opened the carriage door and stepped aside. A woman emerged first, which was a surprise. As far as I knew, my cousin was a bachelor. Papa emitted a soft huff, clearly just as surprised. The woman was tall, wearing a voluminous gown in a pale pink brocade. Jewels and pearls dripped around her neck, hanging over her ample bosom. Her brown hair was piled high on her head, several ringlets framing her pointed face. Soulless brown eyes landed on me with a snobbish look of disdain.

I clenched my jaw to keep from saying something I shouldn't. Who was this woman who invaded our home?

Rupert emerged next. He hadn't changed much since the last time I saw him when I was but a girl. Short in stature, his height came to the woman's shoulder as he paused next to her. I stifled the giggle that wanted to erupt. His once black hair was now peppered with gray. His once youthful face now creased with age. His once bright blue eyes now held a dull sheen. He grasped the woman's hand in his as he stepped forward with a faint, exhausted smile.

I looked from him to the woman and back again. Though he appeared fond of her, she seemed less than interested in his affection.

"My dear Cousin Simon. How kind of you to invite us to your home."

"Rupert." Papa gave him a nod of greeting as he cut a glance to the woman.

"This is Harriet." Rupert paused as if for affect. "My *wife*."

Papa remained perfectly still and stoic. "Forgive me, cousin, but I didn't realize you had taken a wife." He extended his hand to her. "A pleasure to make your acquaintance, my lady."

She gripped his hand briefly in hers and gave a nod of acknowledgement, then released it as though he carried the plague. I somehow managed to control the scowl that wanted to erupt on my face.

"We are recently married. Isn't that right, my love? A mere two weeks ago." Rupert beamed up at the woman whose face remained impassive. "It was a quick ceremony. We didn't have time for invitations."

Papa cleared his throat. "And this is my daughter, Violet," he said, motioning to me.

I gave a quick curtsey but didn't offer my hand. "My lady."

"My goodness, how you've grown!" Rupert exclaimed. "The last time I saw you, Violet, you were knee-high."

I bit my tongue before I said that was merely a year ago when I was knee-high to him. Instead, I managed a faint smile.

"Shall we?" Papa waved toward the door to avoid any more pleasantries. "I'll have your trunks brought to your room."

Harriet stepped around me, giving me a cutting look as she did so. Rupert followed. They entered the manor, moving deeper inside. My father gave me a bit of a nudge and, reluctantly, I stepped through the door.

Harriet glanced over the foyer with a critical eye, as though she had designs on redecorating the moment we departed. To one side was the parlor. To the other, the library. I watched her closely as her gaze landed on the wide staircase with the scrollwork bannisters, the faded gold and red runner going up the stairs, and then the creaking wood floors of the foyer.

"Ah, Blackthorne. The manor hasn't changed a bit," Rupert said.

"It's...old," Harriet said, speaking for the first time. Her voice was high and tinny. She pressed her pink lips together into a straight line as if living here was beneath her.

"It's been in my family for six generations," Papa said, sounding proud of the lineage.

Harriet's gaze landed on me then, sending a shiver of anxiety through me. "Six, you say?"

I clenched my fists as I read the intent in those sultry brown eyes. "Yes, six. And it will be passed down to me some day."

"Well, your son, perhaps," she said, all snooty.

My fists clenched.

Papa pressed a hand in the small of my back as a warning. "You must be famished after your trip from Lampfort. Perhaps you'll join us for dinner in an hour after you've rested?"

Rupert took Harriet by the hand once again. "We would be delighted."

The servants brought in the trunks one by one, which I was certain mostly belonged to Harriet. I frowned as they started up the stairs with them. Papa waved our guests toward the stairs.

"If you'll follow me, I'll show you to your room."

I remained rooted to my spot as Papa ascended the stairs with Harriet and Rupert right behind. As they made the curve toward the second floor, I didn't miss the look of pure animosity the woman gave me.

I paced the small area of the foyer waiting for Papa, my skirts swishing about my feet as I moved back and forth. When he finally descended the stairs, alone, I halted and waited for him. As he stepped off the last step, he continued through the manor toward the library without so much as giving me a wayward glance.

Huffing, I followed.

"Papa, you cannot think to leave our home in the hands of...of..." Words failed me as I waved toward the stairs.

He didn't pause as he headed into the library and moved to sit behind the desk. "What would you have me do? I cannot leave the manor without someone to see to the daily duties."

"Let me stay, then." It was a shot in the dark, one I suspected he'd refuse, but I had to try.

He took up his quill as he slid a piece of parchment in front of him. He dipped the tip in ink. "I cannot leave you here alone, Violet."

"But—"

"Rupert will take good care of the manor until we return." His pen scratched against the paper.

I moved closer to the desk and peered over the edge to see he wrote a letter to the king. "I don't trust them."

He paused to look at up at me. "Why not?"

I pressed a hand against my roiling stomach. "Something tells me Harriet intends to stay forever."

"Rubbish." He returned to writing his note. "She means no harm."

"I didn't like the way she eyed the place." Or me for that matter, I thought, but kept that to myself.

"Is that why you mentioned you would be inheriting the estate?" He lifted his gaze to mine, his bushy eyebrows rising as well. "Rupert understands this is merely a temporary situation."

"But does *she*?" I asked, ignoring his chastising tone. "And only two weeks married? Seems rather odd to me."

He sighed. "My darling, I do appreciate you have Blackthorne's best interests in mind, but please try to understand I have no other choice." He ran a hand over his face, sounding weary. "Rupert is my last living blood relative."

Exactly why he would be interested in getting his claws into Blackthorne. I kept that to myself as well. What I knew of my cousin was that he lived in a small row home in Lampfort. He was not well off, nor did he have the king's favor as Papa did. On the occasion he visited, he typically overstayed his welcome while enjoying our food, riding our horses—including Peppermint, much to my annoyance—and lounging about the manor reading books and living a life of faux wealthy leisure. He refused to leave until Papa gently—and sometimes not so gently—nudged him to return home. I understood from a very young age Cousin Rupert was a scrounge.

Papa was right. He had no siblings and no other family who would be able to act as a steward. Rupert was the only option. Still, I couldn't help but think *I* would make a better steward than him and his shifty wife.

"I'm sending this note to the king by raven tonight," Papa said as he continued to write. "The king sent an envoy to escort us down the main road. We will leave at first light tomorrow and be in the capital by dusk. I trust you have everything packed and prepared?"

"Yes."

"Good. Now, be a good daughter and change for dinner. I'll see you in the dining hall shortly." He never looked up from his letter as he spoke.

Another dismissal. I nodded, though he didn't see, and left the library to do as he requested. The dinner, I knew, was going to be the longest most uncomfortable one I ever experienced.

Upstairs, Sophia helped me change into my dinner gown. A pale blue one with a high neck and long, lace sleeves. This gown didn't have the numerous layers of petticoats and instead had a bustle at the back. I sat at the dressing table, watching Sophia pin up my hair. The girl had a sad look about her. It only occurred to me then she may not want to accompany me to the castle.

"Are you well, Sophia?" I asked.

Her gaze flickered up to mine in the mirror. "Aye, I am, my lady." She returned her gaze to her work, carefully placing pins in my hair.

But even as she said it, I read a sort of difference in her voice. "Are you sure you wish to go with us to Bellbrooke Castle?"

The girl's hands stopped moving and she looked up once more. "Why do you ask, my lady?"

"You seem...sad about it." I turned to face her, catching her hands in mine and clasping them. The girl's fingers were ice cold. "If you want to remain here—"

She shook her head before I finished. "No, I want to go. I do. It's just that Blackthorne is the only real home I've ever known."

I squeezed her hands. "I understand. Me, too. And I do not look forward to Papa trying to marry me off to every eligible lord." I sighed.

"Do you not wish to marry a noble?" Sophia was genuinely perplexed by my attitude.

I rose and gave my image one last glance in the mirror. I picked up a small powder puff and dotted my cheeks and nose.

"Would it be terrible of me if I said no?"

I tossed the powder puff back onto the dressing table. Sophia said nothing but I suspected her thoughts.

"I know what you're thinking. That I'm a spoiled brat for refusing the hand of a rich husband. Especially after three of them have already come to ask for my hand in marriage and I refused them."

Sophia twisted her fingers together. "Well, if I may be so bold, my lady. Lord Desmond was a bit on the ancient side."

A laugh bubbled up my throat. I was so relieved someone else saw the truth of Lord Desmond, I gave Sophia a quick hug.

"Thank you," I whispered in her ear.

"For what?" she asked when I pulled back.

"For understanding. For seeing."

We had never exchanged so many words as we did tonight. For the first time, I felt as though I might have a friend in the castle. One I could trust.

Sophia gripped my hands. "None of them are worthy of you, my lady. You deserve someone who loves you, after all."

I nodded. "We all do. Now, I must go downstairs to the dining hall and pretend to like my cousin's new wife."

"She seems a bit...odd." She immediately pressed her lips together, regret flashing over her face. "Apologies, my lady. I should not have said that."

"You most definitely *should* have said that. She is definitely odd." A pause and we both giggled. I hooked my arm with Sophia's. "Since we are to be together at the castle, I want you to tell me anything. I want you to be open with me. Gods know I need a friend there. Promise me?"

"I promise." Sophia gave me a faint smile. "I could use a friend there, as well."

"Then it's settled. I'm glad to have you with me. Now, I best go before I get into trouble for being late."

I released Sophia who gave a quick little curtsy. Taking a deep breath, I exited my room and headed down to the dining hall, steeling my nerves for what may come.

CHAPTER FOUR

Dinner was quiet and rather dreary. Thankfully, there wasn't much conversation. Harriet remained mute most of the time. Rupert went on and on about how he met her, how her late husband left her a small fortune, and how they were now looking for a new home on the upper east side of Breedon, a wealthy port city near the Rovarian capital of Bellbrooke.

I did my best to keep my thoughts to myself. Papa, too, it seemed was less than amused by Rupert's constant chatter. When the final course was served, I pushed away from the table. Rupert was saying something about something—I'd stopped listening several hours ago. In fact, I was sure my ears were bleeding by now.

"Papa, may I be excused?" I interrupted.

He stopped talking. All three of them looked at me standing next to the table.

"Are you well, my dear?" he asked.

I feigned a yawn. "Just tired."

He seemed to understand and gave a nod of approval. Without waiting for more chatter, I quickly hurried out of the dining hall. Relieved to be out of there, I headed for the stairs. But at the bottom, I halted. I took one last look at my home. And for some dreadful reason, I feared I would never be back here.

My stomach rolled. Not a good thing after having eaten a heavy meal of succulent meat in a cream sauce. As I paused there, thinking of everything I had done in this house, a pang of sadness went through me.

I'd grown up here. One of my earliest memories in the parlor on Yulemas was having hot cider and opening a shiny box with a blue ribbon. Inside was a horse carved from wood. And then Papa led me from the library to the stable where he introduced me to Peppermint. We were immediately smitten with each other and hadn't been parted since. I was relieved I was able to bring him along.

I moved to stand in the parlor doorway, remembering the large yule log that burned bright and hot all day. And how Papa seemed happy for the first time in months. I shoved away the memories. My mother had been dead for years. Papa never remarried. He hired a governess and tutors. They practically raised me as he focused his entire life on his sorcery. He had mastered his magic and garnered the attention of the king. And now, we were headed to Bellbrooke Castle to live there indefinitely while he took the position of Royal Sorcerer.

And all the while, my own magic remained dormant.

At least, that's what I decided. If I could only practice a little...learn the art of magic like Papa had, perhaps I could become a great sorceress. Perhaps I could find my own way out of a loveless marriage that was sure to happen if I did what Papa wanted.

On impulse, I hurried up the stairs and turned right down the long hallway away from the bedrooms. It was a risk, I knew, but perhaps Papa would remain at dinner with the boring Rupert and Harriet long enough for me to do what I needed.

The door at the end of the hall was closed. I paused there, glancing back down the hall with my heart beating a wicked tattoo. What I was about to do was forbidden. I wasn't allowed in Papa's spellcasting room. Not ever.

And yet, my shaking hand hovered over the knob. I was going to do it. Taking a deep breath, I twisted it and pushed the door open.

Moonlight flooded through the one window in the room, illuminating the messy desk in a blue-white glow. The bookshelf to one side was still full of all the spell books he had used throughout the years. No doubt teaching himself everything he knew. The levitation spell I had memorized was on a scroll. The scrolls were crammed haphazardly in a cubby on the left side of the room.

I approached the cubby with the scrolls. One had a long red ribbon hanging off the end decorated with what appeared to be a small gold coin. It looked interesting enough. I slipped it out and tucked it under my arm. Now was not the time to open it and try to read it. There would be time for that later.

At the bookshelf, I examined the crumbling, ancient tomes looking for...something. I wasn't sure what. What would I need to learn the ways of magic? One title leapt out at me. *Professor Quentin's Book of Magic*. I had no idea who Professor Quentin was but I grabbed that one anyway. Next to it was one labeled *The Art of Spellcasting*. I definitely needed that one.

One more and then I'd leave.

I passed by the desk to look once more at the scrolls in the cubby when something glinted in the moonlight, catching my eye. Halting, I gazed down at what appeared to be a shard of glass. I picked it up, turning it to and fro in the pale light. Not a shard of glass. A crystal. Pale pink with something glittering inside it. Something that looked like...stars? The crystal itself had a jagged edge as if it was broken off a larger piece of crystal.

Fascinating.

I tucked it into the pocket of my gown.

Two books, one scroll, and one odd looking crystal should help me find my way into the ways of magic. I hurried back to the door, closing it and then pausing. My heart pounded hard with the fear of getting caught as I stood in the darkness, my back against the door. I strained my ears for voices, but heard none.

Quick as I could, I walked down the hallway to my bedroom. I hoped Sophia wasn't there so I could stash the books and the scroll. I was relieved to see my room empty. At the largest trunk that held my favorite gowns, I shoved open the lid. I pushed aside material of several dresses and tucked both books and the scroll within the folds, then covered them up. I slammed the lid closed and stood again, my heart thrumming with excitement.

I'd done it! I managed to sneak the books out of his spellcasting room without getting caught.

As soon as I had a moment to myself, I would begin my studies. And someday, perhaps I would discover what the strange little crystal was in my pocket. I needed a safe place to hide it. I was certain I needed to keep it on my person at all times.

I pulled the crystal out of my pocket. In the lamplight of the room, I saw it more clearly. Indeed, there appeared to be tiny stars embedded in it. And, oddly, a hole at the top of the jagged piece as though it had been a pendant of some sort. It gave me an idea. I rummaged through my dressing table until I found a long pale blue ribbon. It took several attempts, but I finally managed to thread the ribbon through the small hole. I tied the ends into a tight knot, then slipped it over my neck.

Yes, that would do perfectly. From now on, I would wear the crystal under my gown. I would tell no one.

Soon, Sophia would come help me dress for bed. I slipped it off and hid it under my pillow.

As soon as I did, there was a quiet knock on my door before Sophia pushed it open. I changed into my nightgown and dressing gown, then sat at the dressing table. Sophia began to unpin my hair.

"Are you packed?" I asked.

"I am."

"Still nervous?" I asked.

The girl gave a weak smile. "A little."

I watched as Sophia brushed out my long dark locks in slow methodical sweeps. I, too, was nervous about traveling to Bellbrooke Castle, to living in a new place, and having my world upended.

After she left, I snuggled under the thick coverlet of my bed, my hand under the pillow grasping the crystal. On one side of the room was the large stack of trunks ready to make their way to the castle. As I drifted off to sleep, I thought for certain I felt the crystal warm in my palm. Falling into a dreamless slumber, though, I decided it was merely my imagination.

CHAPTER FIVE

Sophia shook me awake before dawn to help me dress for the day. I wore my riding dress and boots because I intended to ride Peppermint for most of the journey. Eyes heavy with sleep, I sat at my dressing table one last time while Sophia braided my hair in intricate weaves, letting the long plaits hang down my back.

A swift knock sounded on the door. Sophia hurried to open it. The servants entered the chamber and began moving out the large trunks. Sophia gave me a quick curtsy and was gone through the door in an instant. I didn't blame her. I was held captive by the flurry of activity until each and every trunk was moved out of my space. I kept a watchful eye on the pillow where I'd hidden the crystal.

Once they were all gone, I hurried to the bed and pushed my hand under the pillow. Grasping the crystal, I held it up to get a better look at it. The starlight inside sparkled, winking back at me. I placed it around my neck and tucked it under the folds of my gown to keep it hidden. It seemed to hum against my skin which sent a little thrill through me.

I paused in the doorway, looking back at my oversized four-poster bed with the thick quilt, the dressing table with the small round mirror which was now devoid of all my personal items, and the wardrobe standing empty. Thick velvet curtains hung at the window, blocking out the morning light. And for a moment, I worried I would never make it back here. The place where I'd grown up.

"Are you coming, my dear?" Papa's voice startled me.

I pressed a hand to my fluttering heart and glanced his way. He stood in the doorway wearing his traveling clothes. Simple brown breeches, tall black boots, a thick tunic and padded vest. His thick cloak hung over one arm.

I emitted a wistful sigh and nodded. "Yes, Papa."

As I moved toward the door, he wrapped an arm around my shoulders and hugged me.

"We will return someday," he whispered. Then kissed my temple.

I pulled back, looking him right in the eyes. "Do you promise?"

"I promise." He leaned closer, dropping his voice. "I do not wish to be in service to the king forever." He cracked a smile. "But that's between the two of us."

I giggled as we shared the secret. "Good."

Despite that, I had a clear understanding that I likely would not return to this place. If Papa had his way, he would have me married before Yulemas.

Together, we left my chamber. I closed the door behind me as if it were for the last time and refused to look back. We walked through the manor toward the stairs. He eyed my outfit, question in his gaze.

"I'm riding today," I announced, as though it were always the plan.

His brows drew together. "The East King's Highway to Bell-brooke is riddled with highwaymen and bandits. It would be far safer for you with me in the carriage."

"I want to ride Peppermint." Stubbornness was my mother's trait, or so my father said.

"It's spring. Storms are brewing to the west," he added, as though I hadn't spoken.

"*Papa*, I'm riding."

He relented with a sheepish look. "Very well."

We made it to the bottom of the stairs where the servants lined up to bid us farewell. Suddenly, it became all too real. My father, being the lord of the manor, greeted every one of them with a handshake, thanking them for their service. The cook, a robust woman who had been with us for as long as I remembered, had tears standing her eyes. Her name was Miss Morton. She tucked a wayward lock of faded red hair behind an ear as my father came to her, taking her hands in his.

"Keep that lemon cake recipe at the ready," Papa said. "I shall want it immediately upon our return."

"Of course, my lord." She kept a brave face, but sniffed back her tears.

I followed Papa's lead and bid them all farewell, too. As I came to Miss Morton, the woman surprised me by hugging me, squeezing tight.

"Now you behave yourself in the castle kitchens, Miss Violet," she chastised. "They won't allow you to filch from their pantry, I daresay."

I laughed. "I'll miss you, too, Miss Morton."

She squeezed me one last time before releasing me. As I stepped back, Miss Morton wiped her eyes with the edge of her apron. I had to admit, seeing her so teary-eyed made emotion clot in my throat. I turned away, before I allowed the tears burning the back of my eyes to cloud my vision. I followed Papa out of the manor.

Several of the king's men stood at attention waiting for our departure. I counted eight. All wore armor with a sword at their sides. The man who appeared to be the captain wore a cloak in the royal colors of deep plum and crimson trimmed in gold.

Outside, on the gravel drive, Cousin Rupert and Harriet waited to bid us farewell. No doubt Harriet was ready to start counting the silver and redecorating.

My father bid them both farewell with promises to return. But Harriet looked bored and annoyed at the very thought we might return. I refused to tell them farewell. Instead, I gave them both a jaunty wave and hurried to Peppermint, who was saddled and ready.

My father's face turned red with annoyance. He made some excuse, no doubt, as he spoke one last time to Rupert. The captain made his way to Papa, his hand on the hilt of his sword. My father bowed to him.

"I am Captain Falkirk here to escort you to the castle," he said, his voice a deep baritone. "If everything is in order, we'd like to be on our way. It's a long journey especially with—" he cut a glance at the inordinate amount of luggage piled high on the cart, "—such a large entourage."

"Yes, of course. If you'll permit me, captain, I'd like to cast a protection spell to ensure safe travels."

The captain's disdain was clear. "No sorcery is needed. I have seven of my best knights."

He started to object when the captain held up a hand. "We must be on our way, my lord."

"As you wish." He gave him a nod of acquiescence.

Papa gave me one last glance as the footman held the carriage door open for him. He climbed in as I stepped into the stirrup and hoisted myself into the saddle, taking the reins in my gloved hands. Peppermint was restless, ready to be on the way. I patted his neck in reassurance.

And then the caravan began its long journey eastward to Bellbrooke Castle, heading out of the manor gates and onto the East King's Highway. The very highway I had nearly been trampled on by the black horse. I hadn't thought of Aiden since that morning. He'd been heading up the East King's Highway, then. Was he headed to Bellbrooke Castle? Would I see him again?

I kicked Peppermint into a gallop hurrying toward the front of the line, placing myself behind several of the king's men. If they noticed, they didn't acknowledge me. Captain Falkirk trotted next to the carriage in which Papa and Sophia rode. I didn't want to be in the back at a slow trot with the carriage or, even worse, behind the cart with all the luggage.

The sun peeked over the horizon as we made our way west early that morning. By nightfall, we would be in the capital and sleep in our new apartment in the castle. Something about that tugged at me, making my stomach turn over. A little fear coupled with anticipation.

I shoved aside those thoughts as I rode, watching the sun rise. A breeze fluttered past. I hated to admit Papa was right in that the weather was starting to turn. Even so, I lifted my face to the wind, closed my eyes and inhaled. Indeed, the faint whisper of a coming spring storm tinged the air.

I clutched my cloak tighter. For now, I would enjoy it and I would be free.

We rode for hours. When the sun was high in the sky, we stopped for luncheon and to rest the horses. Though I was an accomplished rider, I was getting a little saddle sore. I was grateful for the rest.

As I dismounted Peppermint, I relinquished the reins to one of the knights who led my horse to one of the squires. He handed over the reins to the young boy, who then removed the saddle and led him to the nearby stream for water. A little twitch cut through me knowing my horse was in someone else's care. Someone that wasn't one of the stable hands from the manor.

"Come, Violet," Papa called. He held up a large basket.

Next to him, Sophia had a blanket over one arm and wore a look that pled for me to join them. With a smile, I hurried over. We headed to a small grassy area under a copse of trees out of the bright sunshine. Sophia spread the blanket and we all settled on it for a light lunch of fruit, cheese and bread.

"How much farther until we reach the castle?" I asked.

"A few more hours. We should arrive by sundown," he said.

A few more hours of freedom. A few more hours to enjoy my solitude.

"I have made arrangements for you to continue your lessons," he said as he cut into the cheese. He sliced several pieces.

Alarm shifted through me. "My lessons?"

"You will continue your education in the castle. Reading and poetry, for one. I've also made arrangements for you to take piano lessons, dancing, and singing." He handed me a small silver plate with cheese, apples, bread, and grapes.

I took it, trying to keep the frown off my face. Sophia, however, kept her wide-eyed gaze on me as she accepted her own plate of food.

"Why must I—"

"You will learn to be a proper lady," Papa said, interrupting.

I poked a piece of the yellow cheese around on my plate. He was grooming me to be a proper lady so I would, eventually, be a proper wife. I had no interest in learning the piano, or dancing, or singing. I thought of the hidden spell books in my trunk and the crystal hiding under my gown at my throat. I resisted reaching up to touch it.

As I thought of it, it warmed against my skin.

"Sophia will make sure you make it to each and every lesson," he said.

The girl's head snapped up as she looked at Papa, eyes as big as saucers. He pinned her with his lethal, fatherly gaze.

"Isn't that right, Sophia?" he asked.

The girl merely nodded agreement. I popped a piece of cheese in my mouth, but it turned to ash on my tongue.

"You will begin tomorrow morning bright and early with your first lesson in history. That will be followed by dancing lessons and then piano lessons. After lunch, you will return to your tutor for a singing lesson and then poetry. Then you and I will feast with the king and the royal family."

I sighed. He managed to fill my first day with lessons from dawn until dusk. Why must I feast with the royal family? I had no interest in that whatsoever. But I knew if I argued, I would be chastised for my insolence. Instead, I nodded.

"Yes, of course, Papa. I look forward it." The bitter lie singed my tongue but I managed to say it with a smile, even though I felt nothing.

Somehow, I would find a way to learn magic and free myself from a life of drudgery.

After the horses were rested and watered, we resumed our travel down the East King's Highway. Papa wanted me to ride in the carriage, but I stubbornly mounted Peppermint. If my life was going to be planned for me the moment we arrived in Bellbrooke, I was going to savor my last hours of independence.

As before, I trotted ahead to the front of the line, remaining behind the line of knights. Captain Falkirk was in the lead.

I spotted dark shapes coming toward us at a breakneck speed on the road in the distance. As they neared, I realized they were men on horseback. The captain kicked his horse into a gallop. I watched him on his black war horse as he hurried ahead of us, holding tight to the reins, and then turning back at the same speed.

"Trouble ahead," he said to the two men in front. "Come with me."

I wasn't sure what trouble he saw in the figures heading down the King's Highway, but I was certain it didn't bode well. Pinpricks of fear prickled the back of my neck. One of the knights trotted up next to me.

"Best get in the carriage where it's safest, my lady," he said.

Before I could reply, he moved ahead. He and another knight took the places of the ones who rode off with the captain. I focused my gaze on the figures ahead. The captain and the two knights drew their swords.

Fear clawed its way to my throat as I realized with horror we were about to be attacked by those men.

Papa's words rang back to me.

The East King's Highway to Bellbrooke is riddled with highwaymen and bandits.

I turned Peppermint around and galloped toward the carriage. But as I did, an arrow sailed past. I hunched down, my face inches from Peppermint's neck. The arrow embedded into the side of the carriage at the back of the line with an audible thunk.

It missed me and several others. I was lucky.

Sucking in a sharp breath, I snapped the reins. "Hurry, Peppermint!"

As the horse picked up speed, I stole a glance over my shoulder. The captain and the two knights were outnumbered by far. There had to be at least twenty of them. Not highwaymen, but worse. Bandits. I'd heard there were bandits on the East King's Highway—travelers were easy targets.

The other three knights drew swords and joined the fray, leaving our party unguarded. I glanced at the carriage, urging the horse to hurry. But the sound of hooves directly behind me signaled I was in danger.

The bandit emitted a high-pitched cry of what sounded like triumph. The next thing I knew, he rode next to me and reached for my reins. I jerked them to one side, batting his hand away. As I did, Peppermint veered so sharply, I nearly lost my balance. The bandit wasn't giving up that easily.

He was next to me again. This time, he reached for my braids instead of the reins. I tried to dodge, but he was quicker. His hand wrapped around the length. Holding on, he pulled himself closer to me, pulling my hair. I cried out in pain as he brought us to a halt. I nudged Peppermint with my heels, but to no avail. He whinnied and reared his head back in agitation.

Meanwhile, Papa's carriage continued on, turning off the road heading into the trees. I wasn't certain, but it looked as though one of the bandits had taken control of it. All around, the sounds of swords clanging and men shouting filled my ears. The sharp metallic smell of blood invaded my nose.

"Aren't you a right pretty thing," he said, in a gravelly voice.

Nausea burned through me. I was weaponless and had no way to defend myself while he pulled me closer.

"You're coming with me, lass," he said.

My breath hitched. He was close enough to reach, so I did the only thing I could think to do. I jerked my fist outward and punched him hard in the chest. He grunted, but still did not release my hair.

"Feisty one." He grinned, showing off yellow teeth, his weathered face wrinkling. "You'll be a fun one to break."

I met his squinting eyes. I would rather die than go with him. My fear turned to anger.

Something strange happened, then. A warming sensation went through me as I met his gaze. A bright light pulsed between us, striking him square in the chest. He released my hair with a yelp as he fell off the horse. When he landed, his head cracked on a rock. I didn't stick around to see if he was dead.

I took that moment to kick Peppermint into a gallop heading to where the carriage disappeared into the woods. What I intended to do I had no idea. All I knew was I had to get to Papa and Sophia. I had to make sure they were safe.

A deafening boom sounded followed by a cracking of light that filtered through the trees. The ground shook. Birds fled the treetops. I jerked Peppermint to a halt, my heart racing a wild beat as I stared into the dense forest. A black plume of smoke curled upward into the sky. The sharp, earthy twang of magic filled the air.

Moments later, the carriage and its horses barreled out of the trees. The carriage, though, looked as though it had seen better days. Arrows stuck out of one side. The other side was charred. The footman was nowhere to be seen. And the driver was that of Papa with Sophia clinging to him on the edge of the seat.

I blew out a relieved breath, thanking the gods they were all right. I hurried to meet them.

"I thought you were done for." My breath hitched as emotions punched through me.

Papa, however, grinned from ear to ear as though he'd had a grand time. "I am the Royal Sorcerer, my daughter. I cannot be bested."

Captain Falkirk rode up then. Blood was splattered on the front of his once-shiny armor. His blade was covered it in, too. He glanced from me to Papa. "Are you all right?"

"We're fine but I'm afraid we've had a few casualties," he said.

The captain nodded, a grim expression on his face. "As did I. The marauders killed two of my men. We managed to dispatch them, though. I've sent Fergus ahead. We need more men if we're to continue."

"We cannot delay," Papa said. "We must continue."

"There could be more of them out there," the captain nodded up the road.

"Indeed, but if you'll allow me, I can cast a protection spell over us for the remainder of the journey. Something I should have done to begin with." He gave the captain a pointed look.

Falkirk clenched his jaw, unhappy with the idea. "I'll permit it."

"Good. Gather your men. We must all be in the same area together." Then he turned his glittering gaze on me. "And you, Violet, will ride the rest of the way in the carriage."

Knowing I couldn't object, I nodded. "Yes, Papa."

CHAPTER SIX

Papa used his magic to protect us for the rest of the trip. The remaining hours of travel were hot and bumpy in the carriage. At one point, a thunderstorm erupted. It rained so hard, we had to stop under some trees until it passed. The poor knights were drenched.

One of the knights took over as driver. Papa sat across from me dozing with his head tilted back against the seat. Sophia perched next to me, sitting with her back ramrod straight and her hands clasped in her lap.

"You can relax," I whispered so as not to disturb him.

Sophia cut me a glance but still remained stiff as a board.

I placed my hand on hers, giving them a gentle squeeze. At last, Sophia expelled a breath and eased back into the cushion. Her hands relaxed, but as they did, they shook. Her eyes fluttered closed for a brief moment.

I understood, then. The raid from the bandits shook her to the core. I squeezed her hands again.

"Do you want to talk about it?" I asked.

Sophia opened her eyes and met my gaze. "It was terrifying." Her voice was low, shaky. She drew in a long breath and expelled it, as though doing that calmed her. "I heard the arrows hit the side of the carriage. Your father used his magic to try and keep the bandits away. Two still attacked.

One yanked open the door while the other killed the driver. As soon as the first one jerked open the door, your father…" She paused, cut him a glance.

"What did he do?" I said on a breath.

"A white light pulsed from his hand. It hit the man in the chest. He fell out, but by then we were careening into the forest. He ordered me to stay put. He climbed out. I don't know what happened after that, exactly. Only that there was a burst of blue-white light and then a metallic smell in the air. The side of the carriage was singed, and the bandit driving the carriage was charred—"

She clamped her mouth shut and pressed her lips together in a thin line as she recalled.

"We came to a stop," she continued. "And then your father helped me out of the carriage and onto the seat with him as he drove us out of the forest."

I looked again at Papa with his graying hair at the temples and crinkles at the corners of his eyes. I tried to imagine him using that type of magic, killing a man with what I guessed was a destroyer spell. I'd seen them written in his spell books. These spells were forbidden—a sort of dark magic. And using them to kill was against all the laws of magic. Papa knew that as well as I. But perhaps he hadn't killed him at all and used magic in a different way to defeat the bandit. Sophia wasn't clear when she told the story.

While he was stern, he was never cruel, nor had he ever scared me with his magic. I remembered several times as a child he would conjure things—flowers or ribbons for my hair.

Whatever he did, terrified Sophia. Because he was powerful. The very reason the king summoned him to be the Royal Sorcerer.

I patted her hands. "It's over now."

And yet, I was unnerved to think he killed a man without remorse or concern. Instead, he went about his business as if everything was normal.

The carriage jolted as we went from dirt road to cobblestone street. I pushed aside the curtain on the window of the door and peeked out. We were on the bridge over the creek leading into the capital. Papa roused, sitting up straight and running a hand over his dark hair.

"Have we arrived in the city?" he asked.

"Yes," I said.

I never took my gaze off the window as I watched the stone houses go by and, closer to the castle in the inner city, the shops and the apartments. In the distance, warehouses and other buildings lined the wharf. Twinkling lanterns lined the street, illuminating the cobblestone street in a pale-yellow glow from the firelight.

The closer we got to the castle, the more my gut clenched with the knowledge that my life was about to change. Starting tomorrow, I would no longer have free reign to do as I wished. My days would be ruled with lessons and, as the royal sorcerer's daughter, who knew what else.

The carriage turned up a long, wide street leading up to the castle on the hill overlooking the city. In the darkness, I made out the shape of the turrets, the heraldry flapping in the night breeze atop the highest peaks, the gate ahead that stood open to welcome us.

At the top of the hill, the road smoothed out, making the ride a little more bearable. Once we were through the gate, I pressed my face against the window to get a better look ahead. When I was unable to see anything more, I sat back into the seat, clutching my hands in my lap to wait.

We pulled to a halt. Moments later, the knight who drove the carriage opened the door. He offered his hand. I took it without thinking and stepped out, moving aside. Sophia was next, who stepped behind me, followed by Papa, who remained next to me.

Torches lined the circular drive, illuminating the small courtyard in shimmery gold light. Two large torches were in brackets on either side of the double-oak door. I glanced upward to see the height of the stone castle soaring into the night sky blotting out the stars overhead.

Movement ahead caught my eye and it was then I noticed the group who came toward us. They must have been waiting outside the castle for our arrival. The man in the center was the tallest with a full beard and broad smile. He wore a tunic with gold brocade, black trousers, and boots, and a cloak trailing behind him. I recognized the king immediately. Next to him, a young version of him who I assumed was the crown prince. On the other side, a regal looking woman with her head held high, her hair piled even higher, and her gown a stunning gold and black. Her nose came to a point, her cheekbones were high, and her hands laced together in front of her. A large ruby ring winked in the torchlight. Trailing behind her, a girl about the same age as me. The queen and the princess.

They were followed by several guards, each wearing swords and armor and scowls. Captain Falkirk and the other knights joined them, standing with the travelers facing the royals.

"Simon, my old friend, I'm glad you made it."

When the king reached Papa, he bowed low. Sophia and I curtsied.

"Get up," the king said, humor in his voice.

As he rose, the king took him in a great bear hug, the smile still on his face.

"It's good to see you again, your majesty," Papa said.

The king's gaze flickered to me then. He moved to stand in front of me, eyeing me with that same broad smile.

"This must be your daughter."

"Indeed. My daughter, Violet."

"I've heard much about you," he said.

"Thank you, your majesty." I bowed my head as I spoke.

"You and my Olivia are about the same age." He motioned to the blonde girl behind the queen. "I'm sure you'll make fast friends."

I gave a cursory glance to Princess Olivia who scowled back at me. There was nothing friendly or approachable about her. The prince, however, grinned at me with a smile that made my stomach flutter.

"My son, Philip. And of course, you remember my wife, Eleanor." The king gestured to them, respectively.

"Of course."

Papa bowed to the queen. I curtsied as I glanced up at the woman through my lashes. Her expression was snooty as she looked down her nose at us, as though we were lowly commoners when in fact my father was a member of the nobility. I tried not to be offended but I immediately didn't like the woman.

The queen stepped forward then. "You must be exhausted after your long journey. Jeffrey tends to forget his manners." She gave her husband a sly glance.

"Your pardon, my lord," the king said. "My wife is, as usual, quite right. Captain Falkirk will show you to your rooms in the east wing. You'll find the view to be breathtaking. Tomorrow night, we feast to celebrate your arrival."

When we entered the castle, the royal family departed having done their duty of greeting the travelers. I didn't miss the look of disdain Papa gave the king as the captain led us through the keep, up a curving stone staircase that seemed to go on forever, and then to a set of double doors.

Captain Falkirk made a motion for two of the knights to open the doors and stand aside. The interior chamber was well lit and looked to be furnished with a great deal of fine things. I pressed a hand against my roiling stomach to steady my nerves.

"Your luggage will be brought up soon," Falkirk said. He gave a quick bow and then he and the other knights left.

I glanced at Papa as he watched them walk away, disappearing down the shadowy corridor. He waited until their footsteps receded to enter the chamber. Sophia and I followed.

We were in a large sitting room with terrace doors to a balcony. On one side of the room, a settee to the side of a large fireplace. Two chairs were on the other. A large dining table was on the other side with four chairs. Just past the table, a narrow hallway. Papa headed for that and I followed, curious to see the bedrooms.

Down the narrow hallway, there were three rooms. One at the end of the hall and one on either side. I picked the first door on the right and pushed it open. I paused in the doorway, gaping at the room that was twice the size of my bedroom at the manor.

A large four-poster bed draped in heavy velvet curtains dominated one side. The other side had a dressing table with a cushioned stool. A wardrobe next to that. The floor was covered in a plush garnet rug. One wall hosted floor to ceiling windows with gossamer curtains.

I stepped inside and noticed a doorway to the left of the large bed. I headed there next and was surprised to see my own bathing chamber with tiled floors and walls hosting a private tub, a wash basin, and a shelf of thick towels. Unable to stop myself, I reached for the faucet and turned the knob. Water rushed out into the tub.

I stared at it, awestruck. For all the luxury we had living in the manor, we did not have running water. I definitely did not have a private bath. And I certainly didn't have thick, soft towels.

"My lady." Sophia's soft gasp behind me made me turn. "Can you believe it?" She waved her arms to encompass the entire room.

"It's exquisite," I said. "Your room?"

"It's across the hall. Just like this one. I...I have never been in such a fine place."

"Nor I," I said.

When I moved past her, I noticed her face was flushed.

"Are you well?"

"My lady, I just want to say..." She paused and swallowed hard, then reached for my hand and squeezed it. "Thank you."

"For what?"

"For allowing me to accompany you. I am...honored."

I smiled and nodded understanding. I saw how much it meant to her to be my handmaid. None of us could have foreseen coming to live at the castle.

"I'm glad you're here, Sophia." On impulse, I gave her a quick hug. "Now, we should rest. For tomorrow, we have a busy day."

She nodded and left my room, closing the door behind her. Once she was gone, I tugged the crystal from underneath my gown. Much to my surprise, the pink crystal held a soft glow and several of the starry-like objects inside appeared to be the ones emitting the faint light.

I placed it on the coverlet. When I released it, the glowing faded and winked out.

Odd.

When I picked it back up again, the faint twinkle returned.

"Fascinating," I whispered.

I didn't have much time to ponder that when there was a knock on the door. I stashed the crystal under the pillows.

"Come," I called.

Papa entered, a smile on his face as he took in the room. "How do you like your room?"

With a quirk of a grin, I gave a half shrug. "It will do."

He chuckled, then turned serious. "The trunks should be brought here shortly. Violet, I have much work to do with the king. You may not see much of me in the coming weeks."

I tipped my head to the side in question but remained silent. He reached for me, then, placing his hands on my shoulders and giving me a stern look.

"I want you to be a good girl and go to your lessons. Promise me."

"I promise, Papa." I said it without thinking, merely wanting to please him.

He kissed my forehead. "Good girl. We feast tomorrow night with the king. After that, I want to hear about your first lessons."

"Of course."

He bid me goodnight. When he was gone, I pulled off my riding boots, then fished the crystal out from under the pillows. The faint glimmer returned the moment I touched it. With a yawn, I curled up on the bed, holding the crystal tight in my fist, and quickly fell asleep.

CHAPTER SEVEN

I awoke with a start, sitting straight up. After moments of disorientation, I recalled where I was. Not in my own bed, but in the bed in the apartment we had in the castle. Faint morning light filtered through the gossamer curtains at the windows.

The crystal was still clutched in my hand.

It was humming.

I opened my fingers to see the stars inside dancing around as though they were doing a happy jig. The crystal itself glowed, illuminating my palm with pale pink light.

It mesmerized me.

A brisk knock on my door startled me out of my fascination. I quickly put the crystal on over my head, tucking it into the folds of my nightdress. Yet it continued to glow under the white fabric.

"Not now," I whispered to it.

And suddenly, the light faded.

I didn't have time to puzzle that out when the door swung open and Sophia stood in the doorway, the light from the hallway slashing inside my chamber. She lit the lamp on the bedside table.

"I suppose it's time, isn't it?" I asked with a sigh.

"Yes, my lady. I'll help you dress. While you're at your lessons, I'll unpack for you." She motioned toward the trunks on the opposite side of the room. My heart rammed hard as I thought of the hidden spell books and scroll under the folds of material.

I had a vague recollection of the trunks arriving sometime in the night. The servants apologized profusely for disturbing me as they made quick work of arranging them in my room. I merely yawned and went back to sleep.

"Oh, that's not necessary," I said with a wave of my hand. I did my best to sound nonchalant. "I can handle it. You should unpack your trunks."

She gave me an odd look, tipping her head to the side. "I only have one trunk, my lady."

I flushed hot. "Well, there's no need to trouble yourself with my things."

One blonde eyebrow raised. "Are you certain?"

"I'm certain."

I sprang from the bed with a smile I didn't feel was genuine. I didn't want her to find the books or the scroll. While I trusted Sophia, I wasn't sure *how much* I was willing to trust her. I didn't want to risk her telling Papa about the items I'd filched from his spellcasting room.

"Well, in the meantime, you need something to wear today."

She moved to the first trunk, the one that had the petticoats and the hoop skirts and the corsets. I bustled around her and shoved open the lid to the one with all my gowns. Perhaps if I picked one before she did, then she wouldn't go digging and discover the stolen property. The first one on top was a dark blue gown embroidered with white roses along the skirt from waistline to hem.

I pulled the gown out with a flourish. "How about this one?"

My voice was too high, too tinny, too forced.

She eyed it, then gave me a look as though I'd grown a second head. "That's not a day dress, my lady. You should save that one for the feast with the royal family tonight."

She was right, of course. I nodded and tossed it aside. "Quite right."

Then I dug back into the trunk and pulled out a gown with a high neck that had a white ruffled collar and long sleeves. It was a pale pink gown with a print of tiny lavender roses.

"Much better," Sophia said with a nod.

"I'm going to wash up," I said, thinking of the crystal around my neck.

I didn't want her to find it. The only place to stash it was in between the thick towels. I hurried into the private bath. A ewer of water sat next to a porcelain bowl. I poured water into it, then slipped the crystal off my neck and stuck it between two of the thick towels. It hummed at me, as though displeased.

"Shh," I whispered, leaning over to it. "It's only for a moment."

The humming stopped. How odd that it seemed to respond to my commands.

I splashed cool water on my face and it made me shiver. When finished, I exited to see Sophia had my clothing laid out on the unmade bed. She helped me dress with all the proper layers, then motioned to the dressing table. My reflection showed my messy hair and the braids that had come loose during the night. My scalp was still sore from the bandit grabbing it.

"No braids today."

Sophia began to release the plaits, running her fingers through the strands. "Then how would you like it?"

"Long and loose," I said, feeling rebellious.

Her stern look in the mirror disagreed.

"Fine, then, your discretion."

She brushed out my long hair, then pulled back the sides and did one plait down the middle of the back. I kept the wincing to a minimum.

"I'm to escort you to your first lesson," she said.

I frowned. "Must you?"

"Your father commanded it," she reminded me.

I nodded with a sigh. "I know."

I rose from the dressing table, thinking of the crystal between the towels. "One moment and I'll be ready."

Before she replied, I dashed into the bathing chamber. I slipped the crystal from the towels. It hummed approval as I slipped it around my neck, then pulsed a happy glow.

"Stop it," I said. "No one can know about you."

The pulsing stopped. I tucked the crystal under the neck of my gown, pushing it down between my breasts so there wouldn't be an odd bulge at my throat. The crystal was cool against my skin.

Now ready, the two of us left my chamber and headed for my first lesson in history.

The history lesson was a dull affair. I wasn't the only student, either. There were three other noble children in the class with me. One was a tall lanky boy who was all arms and legs. Freckles dotted his nose and cheeks. He kept his brown eyes downcast and followed along with the lesson in silence. His auburn hair fell over his forehead, hiding most of his face. He was, apparently, very shy. He barely gave me a glance when the teacher, Mr. Martin, introduced me to the others. His name was Jacob.

Eliza was also tall with auburn hair and freckles dotting her delicate face which resembled Jacob's. They were siblings. She was, unlike her brother, not shy at all. She wore a lovely gown in pale green silk which had me envying the delicate lace at the cuffs and around the hem.

The last student was Kalen with smooth brown skin and wide, round dark eyes. His glossy black hair fell in waves to his shoulders. He carried a mysterious air about him and gave me a faint smile as our eyes met.

Mr. Martin, who was a stern-looking man with thick, bushy eyebrows, made us each read a stanza from the epic poem *The First King* describing how he descended upon Rovaria with his armed forces and invaded, taking what he wanted and proclaiming himself king. It was a long, drawn-out poem that told the story of his rise to power and, ultimately, his own death by his son who had betrayed him and took the crown for himself.

And so began the reign of the Second King.

I was already familiar with this poem. It took much effort not to yawn with boredom.

When we were released, the four of us left Mr. Martin's school room with explicit instructions to memorize the first one hundred lines of the epic poem and recite them in two days.

"Can you believe we have to *memorize* that? How boring!" Eliza said as soon as we were out of the room. She turned to me and pasted on a bright smile. "Did you enjoy it, Violet?"

"No," I said matter-of-factly.

Shocked expressions from all of them was the initial response. Then Eliza laughed as though I told the best joke. But I was serious. I was bored out of my head.

"I already know the poem of the First King," I said.

"How lucky for you," Eliza said. "You'll have no problem memorizing those lines, then."

"Perhaps," I agreed. But I still wasn't interested in memorizing useless poetry.

"What about you, Kalen?" Eliza nudged him.

"I do not understand why we must perform such an exercise." He had a slight accent.

I tipped my head to the side. "That accent. I haven't heard it before."

"Kalen is from Ashea," Eliza helpfully supplied.

He shot her a look of annoyance. Ashea was the neighboring desert kingdom south of Rovaria.

"My father sent me here to learn from different scholars. To expand my horizons, he said," Kalen said. "I return home in the Fall. What about you, Violet?"

"My father is the new Royal Sorcerer," I said.

They all gave me wide-eyed silent looks. Eliza and Jacob exchanged a look I was unable to read.

"He's newly appointed then," Eliza said.

What was left unsaid was after the death of the previous Royal Sorcerer. I merely nodded.

"Then you must have magic, too," Kalen said, his dark eyes alight with excitement. "Show us something." His face broke into a wide, encouraging grin.

A cringe shifted through me. I didn't want to tell him I had no magic. The crystal must have sensed my distress for it started pulsing as though agitated. I started to reply, but Sophia arrived to escort me to my next lesson, saving me from any more uncomfortable conversation.

"Perhaps another time. I must go." I dipped a curtsy as I left and met Sophia, hooking my arm with hers. "Thank you for saving me."

"From what?"

"Horribly boring conversation with the other students from my history class."

"You don't like them?"

"It's not that. It's..." My voice trailed off.

It was the look they all had on their faces when I told them who Papa was. That exchange between Eliza and Jacob. Though Kalen had no idea I didn't possess magic, asking me to perform as though I were a trained monkey rather got under my skin.

"It's nothing," I said at last.

She looked unconvinced but didn't press the issue as we walked through the castle from Mr. Martin's room to the music room in the north tower. There were all sorts of people milling about the castle hallways. Courtiers, nobles, servants. One person in particular I recognized—Lord Desmond.

I averted my gaze but it was too late. He pinpointed me with this lethal glare. Thankfully, he kept his pace the same and didn't stop to harass me, though I suspected he wanted to speak some unkind words to me after the way we parted. Sophia appeared not to have seen him. For that I was grateful. I didn't want to discuss his presence here.

When we arrived at the music room, Sophia left me, promising to return in an hour to take me to our apartment for luncheon. Even as she said it, my stomach rumbled reminding me I didn't have breakfast.

Faint piano music was on the other side of the door. Someone was already there, playing. I rapped twice, unsure of protocol. The muffled man's voice from inside bid me to enter.

When I opened the door, I paused to take in the opulent room. The large instrument dominated the middle of the room, the lid lifted and held up by the stand. The maple was polished to a perfect, high shine bringing out the lovely wood grains. From my vantage point, I was able to see the hammers moving up and down on the strings with every note from the keyboard.

On the other side of the room were two oversized wing-backed chairs in front of a fireplace, the hearth nothing more than ashes. Between the chairs a small round table with a silver tea set on a tray as though waiting for someone to sit and have cup of tea. The scent of bergamot was redolent in the air.

But perhaps the most shocking thing was the familiar stranger sitting behind the instrument playing an unfamiliar tune.

I made no move to enter further into the room.

"Do come in," he said, never taking his eyes off his fingers as he continued to play.

I was rooted in place, though. The man behind the instrument playing beautiful music was none other than the man who nearly ran me down on the East King's Highway.

Aiden.

For a moment, I thought I must be in the wrong place for surely Aiden was not the piano instructor? His dark head was bent as he played, not looking at the music before him as though he had it memorized.

At last, he stopped playing and lifted his gaze to mine. He quickly recovered from his surprise and granted me a smile that lifted all the way to his twinkling blue gaze.

"Well, I daresay I never expected to see you here." He rose from the piano and walked around it to pause in front of me. "How lucky am I."

"Is that a jest?" I snapped, trying not to be insulted.

"Indeed, no. I had no idea you were my student this morning, but I'm delighted." He reached out a hand. "Perhaps you'll do me the honor of giving me your name?"

"Violet Winthrope." I put my hand in his.

He grasped it, turned it over and placed a delicate kiss on my knuckles. The brush of his lips on my skin sent a delicious thrill through me. Underneath my gown, the crystal came alive with a happy little vibration. I drew my hand from his with a little gasp. Glancing down, I was relieved to see the crystal was not pulsing light. Only humming what I interpreted as deep satisfaction.

"Ah, yes. The daughter of the new Royal Sorcerer." He granted me a knee-melting smile.

"I am. And what of it?" I wasn't sure why I felt so defensive. Perhaps it was due to my earlier interaction with the other students.

"I didn't realize I would be teaching his daughter. I do apologize for nearly trampling you on the road that day, my lady." He moved to stand behind the piano and waved to the bench. "Shall we begin?"

I remained where I was, my feet refusing to move as I regarded the large instrument with trepidation.

"What's wrong?" Aiden asked.

"It's just that...I have never played before."

"Ah. Then we will start with the basics." He motioned to the bench once more.

I forced my feet to move and stood behind the piano with him. He moved aside to allow me to sit. On the music stand were several sheets of music that looked far too complicated for anyone to play. I stared at all the tiny black notes on the lines with apprehension.

"Do you read music?" he asked.

I shook my head.

"Then we'll begin with the *very* basics."

There was a smile in his voice and I glanced up to meet his gaze. A daring, dazzling, blue eyed gaze that made my heart turn over with a wild beat. He reached for the music on the stand and gathered it up.

"Is that what you were playing?" I asked.

"It is."

"What is it called?"

"It's called Nocturne in B Flat by the great Rovarian royal composer Allaine."

I cocked my head to one side. "Not a very romantic name."

He chuckled. "And what would you call it, then?"

I stared at the keyboard before me. "Something beautiful to fit the way it sounds."

"How about *A Dreamy Evening in the Garden with a Girl Named Violet.*"

I cut him a sharp glance and pushed up from the bench. It scraped along the floor as I rose. "Now you're making fun."

"I am not." He looked offended.

When I started to cut around the bench to leave, he stepped in front of me. He put up one of his hands in surrender. "I meant no offense."

I relented, even though I didn't want to. I eyed the sheet music in his other hand. I only heard a muffled version of it on the other side of the door, then was too distracted by seeing Aiden to hear the rest. On impulse, I asked, "Will you play it for me?"

He stood still for a long moment, his face impassive as though he was unsure about my request.

"I would really love to hear it," I added, doing my best to sound sincere.

He nodded and walked around me to the piano and sat. He placed the music back on the music stand, arranging the pages in order. Then he began to play, though I noticed he didn't look at the music much. He had played it so much he had memorized the notes. I moved to stand beside him to watch his long slender fingers dance with grace over the ebony and ivory keys. The tune was passionate with a waltz-like tempo that made me want to sway. I closed my eyes and listened to the magical tune that seemed to sing through me. Even the crystal pulsed its humming right along with the tune as if it, too, enjoyed it.

When he finished, I opened my eyes. He sat with his hands in his lap, looking up at me with a sort of curiosity. I cleared my throat and stood straight, a flush of embarrassment creeping through me. I lost myself while he played.

"That was lovely."

"I don't think anyone has ever enjoyed it more than you. Perhaps we really should rename it in honor of you."

He was serious. I flushed hot to the roots of my hair and turned away so he wouldn't see. I ran my finger down the length of the shiny instrument, eyeing the strings and hammers along the sound board. The crystal continued to hum its apparent delight.

"Did you come to Bellbrooke to teach piano lessons?" I asked, changing the subject.

"I did," he said. "Does that surprise you?"

I glanced back at him, remembering his large war horse and the fine clothing he wore that day on the road. Would a piano teacher ride such a great beast? I doubted it, but I was intrigued by him.

"No," I said, though I wasn't sure that was the truth. I wasn't surprised and yet, at the same time, I was.

"I don't have many gifts," he said with a smile, "but teaching is one of them. Now, shall we teach you how to read music, my lady?"

He rose and gestured toward the bench once more. With a nod, I moved to sit in front of the keyboard, trying very hard not to be intimidated by the instrument or the teacher.

CHAPTER EIGHT

Try as I might, I was unable to stop thinking about Aiden or that haunting tune he played on the piano. As I moved to my next lessons, I caught myself humming it. Even the crystal nestled underneath my clothing seemed to approve.

Sophia was quiet when she escorted me from my last lesson back to our apartment. I sensed there was something troubling her. Only when I entered my bedchamber did I realize what.

She had unpacked my trunks—even though I told her not to. Shear panic struck through me as I stared at the space where the trunks once resided. She must have unpacked them and had the servants remove them.

Where were the spell books and the scroll?

A faint knock behind me had me whirling around. Sophia stood in the doorway, guilt on her pretty features. I knew at once she saw the books.

"What did you do?" I demanded.

She flushed, her cheeks turning a bright pink. "I-I'm so sorry. But your father insisted the trunks be unpacked today so they could be removed. And so, I-I did as he asked." She twisted her hands together in front of her.

I stepped toward her, took her by the arm and dragged her inside my room, closing the door behind her with a snap.

"What did you do with them?" I asked.

Guilt swarmed her features. It was enough to tell me she knew exactly what I meant.

"I hid them," she whispered.

That gave me pause. "Where?"

"Here."

She hurried past me and bent at the edge of the bed, reaching under it. She pulled out the two books and the scroll. Not a very good hiding place, but at least she thought to hide them.

"Does Papa know?" I demanded.

She shook her head wildly. "No! He was busy with his own trunks and the servants who helped him unpack." She held them out to me. "I won't tell him. I promise."

I took them from her, holding them against my ramming heart. "Thank you."

I searched for a better hiding place. I wasn't sure what to do with them at this point but I had to find a place to stash them.

"May I ask, though," Sophia said, "what do you plan to do with them?"

"The books?" I rummaged in the bottom of my wardrobe where my shoes were lined up like perfect little soldiers.

"Yes. And the scroll."

I stashed them at the back. Then straightened and found a shawl folded neatly in one of the drawers of the bureau. I tucked it around the books, arranging it so it wouldn't look as though it wasn't hiding something but rather as if it was haphazardly tossed there. When I straightened, I turned to her.

"I intend to read them."

Confusion crossed her face. "And then?"

"And then learn from them."

Surprise flickered over her face as she realized what I meant. "But I thought your father—"

"Yes, he did forbid me. But..." I paused and stepped closer to her, grasping her by the hands and holding them tight and looking her directly in the eye. "I cannot live my life for Papa or a husband I don't love."

Understanding slipped over her delicate features. She nodded then.

"I can trust you not to tell him, can't I?" I asked.

She nodded again.

"I need more than a promise, Sophia," I said. "Swear it." I glanced around the room and spied a hair pin on the dressing table. I released her hands and picked it up, holding it up. "Swear it by a blood oath."

Blood oaths were some of the strongest magic there was. If I made her swear, she had to obey.

She swallowed hard as her face paled. I pricked my thumb with the pin. A drop of blood formed on the tip. Then I held my hand out for hers. With some hesitation, she gave me her hand. I did the same on her thumb. When a drop of blood formed on hers, I pressed them together.

"Now swear," I demanded.

"I swear to you, Violet, I will not tell your father about the books or the scroll."

The crystal pumped a wild beat as she said it and suddenly there was a pulse that vibrated through our touching thumbs. She jerked back, eyes wide and round. She felt it, too.

Blood smeared her thumb as she stepped away from me.

"What was that?" Her voice was a rough whisper.

"I...I'm not sure."

That was the truth, though I suspected the crystal had something to do with it.

"I'm going to wash this off. Then you can help me dress for dinner."

She nodded as she swiped at the blood that was quickly drying. I headed into the bathing chamber to slip off the crystal and hide it between the thick towels. It glowed and pulsed as though displeased. I leaned close to the towels and dropped my voice so Sophia wouldn't hear.

"Behave, now. I'll be back for you."

The glowing stopped. It understood me which was both exhilarating and terrifying. I returned to my bed chamber where Sophia had my dress for dinner ready. It was the one I had pulled out that morning. After she dressed me and combed my hair—I refused to allow her to braid it around my head—she left. I returned once more to the bath chamber where I took the crystal and placed it once again around my neck, tucking it under my gown. It wasn't so easy with the tight-fitting bodice, but I managed to nestle it between my breasts so it wasn't obvious.

I steeled myself, preparing for the dinner with the royal family. I was not looking forward to it.

Papa knocked moments later and stood in the doorway. He was dressed in his finery. A black and gold brocade waistcoat, black pants, shiny black boots.

"Papa, you look handsome."

He kissed my cheek and stuck out his arm. "As do you. Shall we?"

I took his arm and away we went, leaving our apartment behind and heading through the castle to the royal family's private dining hall which was in the west wing. A long oak table dominated the middle of the room surrounded by high-backed matching chairs. It was enough place settings for thirty people. A gold and purple table runner—the royal colors—went down the middle. Each place setting was prepared with a silver charger and silver goblets. Steaming loaves of bread were strategically placed in the middle of the table.

Lilacs, chrysanthemums, lilies, and other flowers were in beautiful arrangements in silver vases along the table along with six-taper candelabras. Larger candelabras were in each corner, all lit to give the room a warm and inviting glow. But the best part about the room was the wall of windows overlooking a balcony with a view of the castle gardens. The doors were open, letting in the brisk evening air and fluttering the gossamer curtains. The sun was almost gone, leaving nothing but a crescent red glow at the horizon.

Other guests arrived as we waited for the royal family. One of them was Lord Desmond. My heart leapt to my throat, throbbing madly as I watched him tour the room, greeting guests. He hadn't noticed me yet. I took a step back behind Papa hoping he wouldn't.

But when Aiden Lockhart entered shortly after the earl, my heart turned into a different kind of palpitation. He spotted me immediately and granted me his knee-melting smile. He, too, was dressed in his best clothes. The dark blue velvet waistcoat he wore brought out the color of his eyes. The buttons were shiny gold. He had ruffles at his throat and wrists and carried himself with aplomb.

He approached us, pausing to give a slight bow to Papa and then me.

"We meet again, my lady."

Papa gave me a questioning look. "Apologies, my lord. Do you know my daughter?"

"This is Aiden Lockhart, Papa," I said, quickly. "My piano teacher."

"Ah." He extended his hand to Aiden. "A pleasure to meet you, sir. How is my daughter doing in her lessons?"

"She's only had one, my lord, but she is a quick student." His eyes twinkled as he glanced from me to Papa. "She'll be playing simples tunes in no time."

I flushed hot. What he didn't say was I had trouble learning to read the music, bless his soul.

"I'm glad to hear it. Now, if you'll excuse me, I have someone I must speak to."

I watched as he crossed the room and paused to speak to Lord Desmond. Likely apologizing for my abhorrent behavior when he called to offer me marriage. I clenched one fist at my side, trying not to read too much into that.

"Thank you," I said, keeping my voice low.

"For?" One dark brow lifted in question.

"For not telling my father what a horrible student I am."

He chuckled. "You are not a horrible student. I meant what I said when I told him you learn quickly."

"You're being generous." But I couldn't help but smile at him.

"I daresay I'm glad to see a friendly face among the crowd." His keen blue eyes glanced around the quickly filling room. "Here I thought I was going to be all alone at the dinner party."

"I'm glad you're here," I said and meant it. "Otherwise, I don't think I'd survive this dinner."

He followed my gaze to Lord Desmond and my father. "Oh? Someone you know?"

"Unfortunately, yes." I shifted from one foot to the other, trying to decide what, if anything to tell him. "Let's just say he is not my favorite person."

"Lord Desmond is not anyone's favorite person. Quite frankly, I'm surprised he was invited to this dinner. Perhaps the king didn't want it to be a dull and boring affair."

I cocked my head to one side. "Why do you say that?"

"Oh, the earl is a known troublemaker. My understanding is his estates are losing money and he owes the crown a considerable amount of gold. Likely he's here to negotiate with the king to be able to keep his lands and title," he said.

"Interesting."

I eyed the two of them, thinking of the offer of forty thousand gold as well as Blackthorne Estates for my hand in marriage. It made me wonder if Papa knew about the earl's troubles and he was offering him me and the money as a way to help him out of his problems. The very thought of it made me all the more angry.

"But let's not talk of such things." Aiden turned to me, giving me his full attention. "Perhaps you will do me the honor of sitting next to me at dinner."

The crystal under my clothes vibrated with a wild, happiness as if urging me to say yes.

I started to reply when the royal family arrived, fashionably late. The king entered with the queen on his arm. The prince and princess followed behind them, both of them looking bored and annoyed. As they entered the room, the prince caught my gaze and grinned as though he were happy to see me.

He didn't know me.

I inched closer to Aiden, the back of my hand brushing his. His fingers wrapped around mine and we exchanged a glance. He gave me a faint smile.

"Thank you all for joining us," the king said. "Please sit."

The king took the seat at the head of the table. The queen to his right. The prince to his left and the princess next to her brother. The other guests filled in the remaining chairs.

Papa headed for us. I quickly released Aiden's hand.

"Come, Violet. We must take our seats."

"I suppose I will sit wherever I'm told," I whispered.

He waited until we were at our chairs near the head of the table. Near the king. Lord Desmond inched his way to the chair next to mine, which made my gut clench with horror. But Aiden must have sensed my discomfort for he pushed his way between me and the earl with a cheerful smile and pulled the chair back from the table as Papa held mine out for me.

It was hard to hide my surprise as I tucked my skirts under me and sat.

Lord Desmond scowled but said nothing. He made his way to the other side of the table and took the seat across from me. No doubt to glare at me through the entire meal.

The chatter reduced to nothing as the king then rose to his full height, reaching for a loaf of bread.

"And now, my good friends, we will break bread together." He tore the loaf in half, steam rising from the fluffy white insides.

Several cheers went up as others reached for the bread and did the same, then passed it down the table. Aiden reached for the loaf closest to him and broke off a piece. He handed it to me.

"It's my honor to break bread with you, my lady."

As I took the bread, butterflies erupted in my stomach and the crystal refused to stop chattering. "And my honor to share it with you, my lord."

He seemed pleased with my response.

The first course arrived. Large platters of roasted boar and venison and stuffed pheasant arrived already sliced and ready to serve. The slabs of juicy meat were passed out to each and every diner. The venison in particular was a bit rare for my taste and I pushed it aside with my three-tined fork. But the king and a few of the other nobles had a hearty appetite for it and called for another round.

Roasted vegetables arrived next. Corn, potatoes, squash, leeks all seasoned with a healthy dose of garlic and saffron. So strong that it made my stomach turn. I pushed those to the side as well, only having one taste of each.

All the while, the talk around me dimmed to nothing more than a murmur. I was acutely aware of Aiden's existence next to me. The warmth of his body. The way he sat ramrod straight with perfect posture. The way he used his fork and knife to cut delicate, perfect bites of each item. His manners were flawless.

He leaned sideways toward me. "Are you quite well, my lady?"

"I'm perfectly fine. Why do you ask?" I shoved a pile of onions swimming in gravy to one side.

"You're not eating."

He noticed, which sent a flush through me. I stabbed a small piece of venison with my fork. "I find I'm not terribly hungry."

Even as I said it, my traitorous stomach growled in response. I stuck the venison in my mouth and chewed only to discover it was dry and tough. Even so, I muscled through and swallowed the foul meat as the next course—a broth of some sort—began to make the rounds.

The servants came around and collected half-eaten plates, dropping bowls in their place.

Next to me, Aiden tore off a hunk of bread and placed it on the edge of my charger just as the servant placed the bowl in front of me. I flashed him a grateful smile as I dipped the edge of a piece of bread into the salty broth. This, at least, I was able to eat.

On the other side of me, Papa was embroiled in a deep discussion about some foreign something that was happening somewhere on some border. Perhaps I should have listened closer because, by his body language, he was quite agitated by the conversation.

I picked up my silver goblet and drained it of the sweet wine, then waved for a servant to refill it.

"You should slow down with that," Aiden warned.

"You're right, of course. However, I find the food here to be absolutely abhorrent. The only thing to kill the taste of it is the sweet wine."

Too honest, I knew, but it was impossible to stop the words from flowing out of my mouth.

Across the table, Lord Desmond slurped his broth all the while eyeing me with callous contempt. I wasn't sure what the etiquette was for having a feast with the king, but I was sure shoving back from the table and stomping out to the balcony would be frowned upon. It took everything within my power to remain seated at the table.

Aiden must have sensed my distress, for he reached under the table and patted my thigh. I was so shocked by this, my head snapped in his direction. Our eyes met. There was a gleam of knowing in his and he gave me a discreet nod of understanding as he cut his gaze across the table to the dreadful Lord Desmond.

Then he said, "Perhaps you and I should stroll through the gardens after dinner to get some fresh air."

"I would like that."

Next to me, Papa shouted something and pounded the table with his fist, rattling the dishes and making me jump. The crystal did not like that outburst at all. It buzzed three times in succession. *Buzz buzz buzz.* I didn't understand what that meant, but if I were to guess, I would say it was unhappy.

Likely matching my own mood of unhappiness.

This feast was not fun at all.

"Tell me, Lady Violet," Lord Desmond suddenly spoke up. "Have you a new suitor?" He cut a glance to Aiden next to me.

I gaped at him from across the table, unsure how to answer. Several of those around us paused in their own conversations to await my response. Hot, pulsing fear shot through me and the crystal responded in kind with another *buzz, buzz, buzz.*

"Lord Desmond, are you inferring that *I* am her suitor?" Aiden said, speaking up for all to hear.

Lord Desmond's lethal gaze landed on him. "I would be wary if you are. She is nothing but a cunning little beast."

Aiden's brows rose to his hairline in surprise. A cold sweat broke out along my palms. The crystal did not like that response, either. It continued to buzz, as if it heard what the earl had said. But it couldn't have. It didn't understand.

Did it?

Aiden said, "I find that description to be less than kind, Lord Desmond. Especially at the king's feast. Perhaps you need a refresher course in court etiquette."

I, along with the others seated nearby, gawked at Aiden for his bold statement.

Lord Desmond's face turned red. "I warn you. She'll lead you on and then refuse you when you make an honorable offer of marriage."

"I did no such thing," I snapped, my ire rising.

Under the table, Aiden squeezed my hand. "If I am a suitor of the lovely Lady Violet, I believe that's none of your concern, is it?"

Lord Desmond shoved back from the table in a fit of rage. His dark, glittering gaze landed on me.

"This isn't over," he said.

Though he said it for all to hear, it was directed to me. The crystal stopped buzzing as a terrible cold fear took up residence in the pit of my stomach, twisting into a tight knot.

His face was flushed as he tossed his napkin on the chair and stalked out of the dining hall, the door slamming behind him. Silence descended in the hall as all eyes turned to the king.

But it was the queen who spoke.

"My goodness. Whatever got into Lord Desmond?"

Papa shifted his gaze to me, peering at me with question. I gave him a weak smile and picked up my bowl to sip my broth. Thankfully, Aiden came to my rescue.

"He has a bit of a temper," he said. "And clearly a bruised ego."

"Clearly," Papa said, then returned to his heated discussion with the man seated next to him as if nothing out of the ordinary had occurred.

Dessert was the final course and had started to make its rounds by the servants. But I had lost my appetite.

"I think I should like to take you up on that stroll through the gardens," I said to Aiden.

"Good." His smirk was conspiratorial. "Meet me there when you're able."

He pushed back from the table and rose, then addressed the king. "Your majesty, if you will excuse me. I have other matters to attend."

The king waved him off. Aiden cast me one last glance as he departed the dining hall. I watched the door close behind him with my heart stuck in my throat. I counted to ten as slow as possible and then I placed a hand on Papa's arm. He turned to me.

"I have a bit of headache. May I be excused?"

He nodded and waved me away.

I rose and looked to the head of the table. "Your majesties, thank you for a lovely evening."

The king gave me salute with his cup, then promptly instructed for it to be refilled. Once I was out of the dining hall, my hurried steps headed for the gardens.

CHAPTER NINE

I got lost on the way to the gardens. I hadn't learned my way around the castle yet and had relied on Sophia to get me from place to place. I spent precious minutes wandering around until I found a guard who pointed me in the right direction.

Finally, I exited the castle into the brisk night air, my gaze scanning the area for Aiden. I found him at the base of a set of stone steps. I realized they were connected to the Royal dining hall above.

He stood in a pool of torchlight, the yellow glow flickering over his dark hair. He leaned against the stone balustrade waiting and watching for me. When I finally appeared, he stood straight. A smile lit up his face. I hurried toward him, elation in every step.

"I was beginning to wonder if you changed your mind," he said.

"Apologies." The word came out on a breath as I paused to catch it. "I got lost."

He chuckled. "Easy to do in a castle the size of this one." He held his arm out to me. "Shall we?"

I took it. We started down the path heading into the hedge maze, walking in amicable silence as we went. There was something comforting about having him next to me. Something that made me feel calm and at ease. Even the crystal was silent when it had been a nuisance during dinner.

"I confess I've never seen the gardens at night," he said. "Have you?"

"This is my first time in the capital," I said.

"Is it?" He gave me a surprised glance. "I would have thought your father would have brought you before."

"Never," I said. "When he came to the capital on business, I was left behind with my governess."

"Then perhaps we need an excursion into the city," he said. "You will enjoy the shops."

"I've heard the dress shops are magnificent," I said with a wistful sigh.

"They are. And I'll take you to every one of them."

I gave him a sidelong glance. "Are you sure that's allowed?" I asked.

"It is if I'm to court you."

He said it so matter-of-factly, I halted and turned to face him. "You're courting me now?"

"Should I be?" His eyes shone with mirth. "Lord Desmond seems to think I'm one of your suitors."

I scoffed. "Lord Desmond can stuff it for all I care."

I started walking again, my fingers dragging down the cool hedge leaves.

"He clearly has taken issue with you, though I daresay I don't know why."

I realized this was Aiden's way of gleaning information out me. Since I really had nothing to lose, I decided to tell him. "Lord Desmond is a wretch who came to my home with the intention of marrying me."

"How dastardly." There was a note of sarcasm in his tone.

"Go ahead. Make fun. But tell me, Mr. Lockhart, how much do you know about the earl?"

"Only that he's in a bit of financial trouble. He does seem to be quite a bit old for you."

"Old isn't the half of it," I said. "His first wife died mysteriously. His second wife was shipped off to a nunnery. Neither of them produced an heir."

"So, he sought you out. A lovely young woman sure to produce one for him," he said.

I nodded. I left out the part where Papa offered him the Blackthorne Estates as well as forty thousand gold coin. Though now that I thought about it—and what Aiden told me about the earl's predicament—I wondered just how much forty thousand gold would help him. Unless he had planned to sell the estates. I had no proof, of course, but it was the only logical explanation for his interest in me.

Blackthorne Estates were worth quite a lot. If I had agreed to marry him, then there would be no stopping Lord Desmond from getting his grubby hands on it and doing what he wished with it once Papa was dead. No matter what I wished.

Once Papa was dead.

It did not escape me that Papa was filling in for the Royal Sorcerer who had died unexpectedly.

"You seem lost in thought," he said interrupting my internal musings.

"Yes, I apologize. I was..." I halted once again and turned to him. "Do you know how the previous Royal Sorcerer died?"

He seemed taken aback by the question. "I've heard the rumors."

"Which are?"

"He was fine one day and then gravely ill the next," he said. "He died within a few hours of taking ill. No healer could cure him, nor could they understand what was wrong with him." He took my hand in his. "But let us not speak of such dismal things here tonight."

"My father was called to court to replace him temporarily," I said, keeping the conversation on topic. "I fear the appointment will not be so temporary."

"You fear for your father?" he asked.

"Of course, I do. How could I not? And now with Lord Desmond here…" I let my words trail off.

He squeezed my cold fingers in his. "Is there anything I can do to help?"

I regarded him as he held my hands. His handsome face held question. Moonlight washed over his dark hair giving him the appearance of a halo. Starlight danced in his depthless blue eyes. He had teased me before about courting me, but what if it wasn't a tease?

"Yes," I said slowly. "There is."

The corner of his mouth lifted in a small smile. "And what is that?"

"I don't trust Lord Desmond," I said, thinking of his last words to me. "If he thinks things are not over between us, then I fear he will try again to get what he wants."

"He cannot force you to marry him," Aiden said.

"But my father can," I said. "Even though I refused Lord Desmond, my father can still agree to the marriage without my consent."

"If he wishes to enforce an antiquated custom, yes," Aiden agreed. "But do you really think he will attempt to do such a thing?"

I wasn't sure. I didn't know how far my father would go to be rid of me or how much influence Lord Desmond had over him. I shrugged.

"There is one way to ensure that he doesn't. And that is if someone else is courting me." I gave him a demure smile.

Shock rippled across his face as he understood my inference. "My lady, I was merely jesting—"

"If Lord Desmond already thinks you are courting me, then perhaps he will give me a wide berth. I do not wish to cross paths with him again and who knows how long he'll be here at court. And at any rate, it doesn't have to be a *real* courtship. It can be a bargain we strike between the two of us."

"A bargain? I court you in exchange for...?" His words drifted off.

I turned from him and paced the small walkway in the maze. In exchange for what, indeed? Aiden was a piano teacher, not some powerful lord who had influence in the court.

The truth was, I worried for Papa and his safety since the other Royal Sorcerer had died under mysterious circumstances. Papa was called to court only days after the man's death. If the king needed a Royal Sorcerer that quickly, then what was the king planning? Something dark and dangerous?

Or perhaps it was merely he was unable to be without a Royal Sorcerer. I halted my pacing.

"For information," I said at last. "I want you to find out how the previous Royal Sorcerer died and if my father is in any danger."

He blinked, his eyes growing large and owlish. "To what end?"

"To find out the truth. And when I have the truth, I will tell Papa and urge him to resign his appointment so we can go home."

It was a gamble, I knew, but I had to try. The sooner I had the truth, the sooner I would no longer be under Lord Desmond's scrutinizing glare.

"You do realize I am nothing but a humble piano instructor. How would I go about finding this information?"

He was right, of course. My mind worked quickly. "Surely, Mr. Lockhart, I'm not your only student."

He tipped his head to the side, his dark brows furrowed in question clearly wondering where I was going with this. "No."

"And surely you have numerous students belonging to noble parents who have seen and heard something about the previous Royal Sorcerer."

"Perhaps…" he said slowly.

"Then you can get information from them. You were a guest of the king's tonight," I pointed out. "Which means you are esteemed in the high court. You can move about much better than I can."

There was a long pause after I stopped talking as we looked at each other. Uncertainty creased his features. He swiped his hand over his smooth chin.

"I suppose it could work. And if I'm unable to gather any information whatsoever?"

I hooked my arm in his. "Then we'll have a grand time and enjoy each other's company."

He chuckled. "I suppose we will." He tucked my cold hand in the crook of his elbow. "Now, I must return to you to your apartment. The air is quite chilly this evening. I can't have you catching a cold on my watch. Can I?"

I grinned. "No, you cannot."

And with that, he escorted me back into the castle.

CHAPTER TEN

The following morning, Sophia woke me for my second day of lessons. She helped me dress. It was getting more difficult to hide the crystal from her. Papa sat in the small living area as though waiting for me to emerge. Unhappiness creased his face and I cringed. When I returned from the gardens with Aiden, only Sophia was in the apartment. She said he hadn't returned and so I took myself to bed.

But when Papa looked at me, his expression changed as he forced a smile.

"Ah, Violet. I missed you last night when I returned."

"My apologies, Papa, I went straight to bed." I didn't want to tell him I had been out in the gardens.

"How was your first day?" He made no move to rise and instead looked up at me from the oversized chair.

"Good." I started for the door, Sophia on my heels.

"It was nice to meet your piano teacher last night."

At the mention of Aiden, butterflies erupted in my stomach. The crystal hummed its happiness.

"Violet, about Lord Desmond—" As he spoke, he got to his feet, clasping my hand in his as I passed. Butterflies now gone, my stomach churned with anxiety upon hearing the man's name.

"What about him?"

"I was late returning last night because he came to see me. You have insulted him twice now."

I thought of the way I spurned him when he came to Blackthorne and again last night at the king's feast. How he'd glared at me from across the table with such a spiteful hate that it sent chills through me thinking of it even now.

"He's the one who insulted me at the dinner last night." I pulled my hand out of his grasp. "I'm going to be late."

I started for the door once again but his voice stopped me.

"He wants an apology."

At the door, I halted. Sophia, next to me, cut me a glance. I half turned to face him.

"I will not."

"Violet, please—"

"No, Papa. I have no wish to speak to him again." I gave Sophia a nod to open the door.

"He is willing to forgive all if you apologize and...agree to marry him."

That stopped me cold. In response, the crystal buzzed at a furious pace beneath my gown. Since Sophia was so near, she tipped her head to the side. She heard it and gazed at me with question written on her face. Now I fully turned to face him, the fear turning to bright, hot anger.

"Why should I marry him? So, he can get his hands on Blackthorne Estates?" I was unable to stop the words spilling out of me with such venom.

Surprise flickered over his face. "He isn't interested in Blackthorne."

"Isn't he?" I snapped, my voice hard. "I know of his financial troubles."

His eyes widened, then narrowed. "How do you know about that?"

"We're at court, Papa. People gossip. Now, I truly must go. I'm late."

I flung open the door without waiting for Sophia. My heart throbbed in concert to the constant irritated buzzing of the crystal. I stalked out of the apartment down the hallway, my skirts swishing around my feet.

Sophia said nothing. I was glad. The anger pounded through me so hard, I wasn't sure I had a kind word for anyone.

When we arrived at the classroom, I paused outside the door to take a deep cleansing breath. Sophia placed a hand on my arm and gave me a gentle pat, then she left me. I opened the door for my lesson in history. Kalen, Eliza, and Jacob were already there with Mr. Martin, who glowered at me as I entered the room late.

"Ah, Violet. Nice of you to join us. Take your seat, please," he said, his tone harsh and unforgiving.

"Apologies," I muttered as I slipped into the seat next to Kalen.

Our eyes met. His were big and round and somewhat sympathetic to my plight for being late. I gave Kalen a sheepish half shrug. Mr. Martin clapped his hands together to get my attention.

"Violet, if you please. Read the first stanza of *The First King*."

I shoved aside the conversation with Papa and began to read.

After class, the four of us filed out of the room. Eliza and Jacob first, then me and Kalen. Sophia loitered in the hallway nearby, waiting for me. But Kalen placed a hand on my arm.

"Are you well, Violet?" he asked.

"I'm fine." I managed a smile. "Thank you for asking."

"It's just you looked ghostly white when you came in," Eliza said. She didn't give me a chance to reply as she hurried on. "We're planning a picnic and a game of Bowls this afternoon. Would you care to join us?"

I stared, dumbfounded. I wanted to say yes. How I wanted to. But I had lessons this afternoon. Singing and dancing. Lessons I dreaded. The crystal hanging snuggly against my breast gave a little buzz of encouragement.

At least, that's what I perceived it to be.

"The game is much better when played with four people," Kalen added.

"And you're short one?" I asked.

"My brother had to return to Ashea a month ago," he said. "We've been looking for a new team member since."

"And, well, we think you'd make a great addition," Eliza added with a bright, happy smile.

I wondered if that were true or if I was merely a convenient addition since I was the newest member in their classroom. Even so, I was flattered they asked me. I made a snap, if perilous, decision.

"What time should I meet you?"

Eliza clapped her hands. "Oh, wonderful! We meet at one o'clock on the north lawn. I'll bring the picnic basket."

"And I'll bring the blankets," Kalen said.

I looked from him to Eliza and Jacob, who had remained silent. He merely stared at me with his wide eyes. "And what should I bring?"

"Yourself!" Eliza said. She gave a jaunty wave, then nudged Jacob.

"See you soon," he muttered.

As they departed, Kalen lingered, watching them go. "It will be good to play Bowls again."

"I've never played," I admitted.

"I'll teach you." He grinned, clearly happy about the idea of teaching me to play. "I look forward to it."

Then he gave me a bow and was gone.

Sophia approached then, a wary look on her face. "Are you *really* going to join them, my lady?"

I straightened my shoulders and smoothed my damp palms down my skirt. "Yes. Yes, I am."

"But your afternoon lessons—"

"I'll miss them," I said nonchalantly. "Come, Sophia. It's time for my piano lesson."

Truly, the only the lesson I'd been looking forward to all day. We headed through the castle to the other side where Aiden waited with his large piano. I sensed nervous energy coming off Sophia in waves.

"Don't worry," I said. "I'll make the necessary excuses to my father."

"It's not just that, my lady, it's..." Her voice trailed off as she gave me an unreadable look. Her cheeks were pink.

"What is it?"

"I don't quite know how to say this."

I halted, putting my hands on my hips. "Out with it."

"It's just that...there appears to be a faint buzzing coming from your chest, my lady."

She'd heard it. Of course, she did. She stood close to me when we were in the apartment. No doubt she heard it then. The crystal now, though, had gone silent. I decided to use that as a cover.

"Nonsense." I waved away the thought and resumed walking.

"I heard it," she insisted. "And when I help dress you now, you act peculiar."

The crystal buzzed. My heart throbbed a painful beat as my hands broke into a cold sweat. I tried to remain calm, telling myself she knew nothing. "What do you mean, peculiar?"

"You hide in the bathing chamber," she said, her voice flat as though she were speaking something I'd heard a million times before.

I halted and turned toward her, pushing her toward a corner of the castle hallway that was unoccupied and not likely to have ears that would overhear.

"All right, then," I said on my roughened whisper. "Do you wish to know the truth?"

Her eyes were wide as she nodded.

"Do you promise not to tell my father?"

Her face scrunched in a frown. "Are you going to make me swear again with blood?"

No doubt thinking of the odd thing that had happened when I made her promise not to tell him about the spell books. "No," I said slowly. "Can I trust you?"

She nodded. "You can."

I took a deep breath. "Before we left Blackthorne, I found a crystal in my father's study. I have no other explanation other than I was compelled to take it."

Her gaze went over me, as though trying to find the crystal. Her brows drew together in question. "Are you...wearing it?"

"Yes," I said, the word coming out a low hiss. "Around my neck, hidden under my clothes. It feels as though it's attuned itself to me."

"What does that mean?" she asked.

"It means," I said, "that it senses what I feel and responds in kind."

Her eyes grew large and round. "And that's what the buzzing is?"

I nodded, then gripped her arm. "Please, Sophia, you cannot tell Papa."

"I-I promise," she stammered.

Realizing my fingers were digging into her arm, I released her. "I'm sorry. I didn't mean to do that."

"It's fine, my lady. Shall we continue to your piano lesson?" She waved toward the hallway.

I nodded and we resumed walking.

But I was still troubled by her finding out about the crystal. Not only that, but also the conversation I had with my father before leaving for lessons that morning. The fact he wanted me to apologize and agree to marry Lord Desmond was still fresh in my mind when Sophia left me at Aiden's door.

I took a deep breath and glanced down to where the crystal resided hidden underneath my gown. I placed my hand over it, lightly pressing it.

"Listen here, you," I said, my voice a whisper. "You must remain quiet at all times. It won't do for others to find out about you. It's bad enough Sophia knows."

The crystal responded with a faint buzz. I took that to mean it understood, then lifted my hand and knocked with a quick rap.

"Come in," he called through the door.

I entered, closing the door and leaning against it, my nerves jangling after everything that had happened. Aiden sat at the piano, his fingers dancing along the keys playing a bright tune I hadn't heard before. When I failed to move, he stopped playing and looked up.

"Ah, Lady Violet. Do come in." He rose and waved toward the piano bench. "Shall we begin?"

"I..." My voice faltered.

Concern creased his features. "Are you quite well?"

He came around the bench and took my elbow, steering me toward one of the oversized chairs on the side of the room. I lowered down into the soft cushions while Aiden poured a cup of tea and handed it to me. The steam rose and tickled my nose.

"I'm fine," I managed at last.

"You don't look fine. You look as though something dreadful happened."

Something dreadful *had* happened. Papa insisted I accept Lord Desmond's marriage proposal and Sophia found out about the crystal. I stared into the liquid in the cup searching for answers.

"Can I help?" Aiden poured himself a cup and perched on the opposite chair.

"I don't know if you can."

I thought of our bargain, that he was supposed to court me, and yet the charade had yet to begin. How was I to repel Lord Desmond's advances if Aiden hadn't yet made it known we were to be a couple?

"Last night in the garden," I began, "you agreed to court me."

He gave a small smile and nodded over his tea cup, then sipped. "I did."

"Pardon me if this is too bold, but, when do you plan to start?"

He didn't bother to hide his shock as he looked at me, then placed the tea cup on the table between us. He reached for me, holding out his hands. I leaned forward, placing the cup next to his, and gave him my hands. His warm fingers clasped my cold ones.

"My lady, it's only been a few hours since we made our bargain."

"But—"

"It will all happen in good time," he assured me.

"My father expects me to apologize to Lord Desmond and then accept his marriage proposal," I blurted.

He made no move as he continued to hold my hands. His gaze never wavered from mine. "Does he, then?"

"Yes, and I don't want to do either of those things. So, you see, you *must* help me. The only way my father will release this ridiculous idea of me marrying Lord Desmond is if he knows I'm promised to another."

"Promised?" he asked slowly.

Realizing what I said, I tried to rectify my mistake. "I-I mean only that if we were to be seen together, if you were to visit me..." My words trailed off.

"I see." He released my hands and stood, turning away from me.

I couldn't help but feel as though I'd blundered. I rose, too.

"Apologies, Mr. Lockhart. I should not have goaded you into the bargain. Perhaps I should go."

I started for the door. He caught my arm, turning me to face him.

"No," he said. "It's my fault, you see. I should not have agreed to the bargain when I know full well I cannot give you the information you want about the death of the previous Royal Sorcerer."

"Why not?" I didn't intend for it to sound like a demand, but it came out that way.

"Because I simply do not have access to that kind of information."

He looked forlorn when he said it. Guilt washed over me. I relaxed my tense muscles.

"Yes, of course, that makes sense. You wouldn't, would you? It was foolish of me to think otherwise."

I slipped my arm out of his grasp and took a step backward as the crystal came to life once again. It gave an almost sorrowful little buzz, as though it, too, understood the predicament I was in and that it was going to be very difficult to avoid it.

"But, perhaps..." A mischievous gleam came into his eyes. One corner of his mouth lifted. "We do not need a bargain for me to court you."

My heart thumped a wild beat. The crystal gave a short, little buzz of question. "What do you mean?"

Aiden took a tentative step toward me, taking my hand in his once again. "I mean perhaps, if you'll permit it, our courtship need not be a sham."

Again, my heart did a wild thunderous beat. So loud, in fact, blood whooshed through my head. The crystal responded, too. His brows drew together in question as he looked at me. Had he heard the buzzing just as Sophia had? My warning had clearly gone unheeded.

"You mean...you wish to court me *for real*?"

"I do, my lady." He brought my hand to his lips and placed a gentle kiss there. I stifled a gasp. "Do you permit me?"

"Yes, Mr. Lockhart, I permit you."

He brightened. "Good, but first you must stop calling me Mr. Lockhart. Let me hear you say my name."

I flushed hot to the roots of my hair. "As you wish, Aiden."

His name felt foreign on my tongue. Foreign and delightful. He seemed pleased with hearing it. Almost as pleased as I was saying it.

"And," I added, "you must call me Violet."

"I should like that. Now, shall we commence with our lesson?"

With his free hand, he waved to the piano. I nodded as he led me to the bench. I took my seat and began my next lesson.

CHAPTER ELEVEN

An hour later, I left him and the piano. Aiden promised to dine with us at our royal apartment later that evening. It left me with a giddy feeling in the pit of my stomach.

Sophia waited for me in the hallway as if to escort me to my singing lesson, but I had another engagement. It was time for me to head to the north lawn to meet Eliza, Jacob, and Kalen for a game of Bowls and a picnic. My stomach growled with a ferocious hunger. I realized then I hadn't eaten all day.

"I'm not going to my afternoon lessons, Sophia." I never broke stride as I headed through the castle.

"Are you certain? What shall I tell your father?"

"Tell him whatever you like, but I'm going to play Bowls."

With that, I grasped my skirts in my hands weaving through the mingling courtiers and nobles and leaving Sophia behind. Excitement skittered through me at the thought of doing something as rebellious as skipping my afternoon lessons. I was so distracted by the thought I never saw Lord Desmond coming. Only when he grabbed my arm and spun me to face him did I realize he was there. He shoved me toward one of the alcoves as my breath hitched.

"Unhand me." I tried to sound brave, but I wasn't sure it came off that way.

"Should I?" His gaze searched my face, then raked over me.

At that moment, I was glad I chose a high neck gown with long sleeves that covered every inch of skin. He pressed a thick leg against mine, his face inches away. His breath smelled of alcohol and his eyes were bloodshot as though he hadn't slept.

"I intend to marry you, Lady Violet." His hot breath fanned over my cheek as I turned my head.

"I have no intention of marrying you *or* apologizing to you." My heart pounded hard and fast. Somehow, I managed to look him in the eye as I said it.

"I'll go to the king if I have to," he said.

"And what? Demand my hand in marriage?" I jerked my arm out of his grasp, but he still pressed me against the wall. "He'll never agree to it."

"Other marriages have been arranged by the king for lesser nobles." He gave me a toothy grin. "Your father has already agreed."

Fury pounded through me. Unnerved, I pressed both palms flat against his chest and shoved. He was so taken aback I was able to wiggle free of his grasp. Clutching my gown in my fists, I took off through the crowd, running blindly through the castle in the hopes of losing Lord Desmond.

I burst through the doors to the garden and found my way to the north lawn, my heart still beating a wicked beat, my legs burning. When I was sure he didn't follow, I slowed to a stop to catch my breath and regain my composure.

Glancing down at where the crystal resided, I glared at it. "And where were *you* when I needed you? You fickle thing."

It remained silent.

Perhaps my chastising earlier made it go dormant. I didn't know what to do about that at the moment, but I would think about that later when I was back in my room. When I had the spell books to look through. When I had a moment to think in silence.

In the distance, I saw Kalen and Eliza waving madly to get my attention. Jacob stood by looking sullen as though annoyed he was made to participate. They had set up their picnic and were waiting for my arrival. I took another cleansing breath and headed their way, glad to have an afternoon distraction.

"Hi!" Eliza didn't hide her joy when she saw me. "We're glad you made it. Aren't we?" She elbowed her silent brother who merely nodded.

"We are," Kalen said. He glanced around. "Did your maid come?"

"Sophia? Oh, no."

"She could have joined us for the picnic if she wanted."

Eliza took care to sit on the blanket spread out on the lawn. She tucked her satin skirts under her and opened the basket. Jacob plopped down next to his sister and stretched out on his back, his hands under his head staring up at the sky. Kalen motioned to the other side of the blanket with a warm smile.

I mimicked Eliza and sank to my knees, then tucked them to the side, trying hard to forget the encounter with Lord Desmond. Kalen sat beside me, crossing his long legs in front of him.

"I wasn't sure if she was invited," I said, feeling awkward.

Eliza picked up a loaf of bread wrapped in a blue and white striped cloth. Then she pulled out a covered plate and placed it next to the bread on the blanket. When she saw her brother lounging, she poked him in the shoulder with her elbow.

"Sit up, you oaf, and have some manners in front of our guest."

He grumbled and frowned as he pulled himself up to a sitting position. He found a blade of grass and picked it, tearing it into small pieces. Eliza flashed me a faint grin, looking abashed. She resumed unloading the basket. Once everything was out, she handed us all white plates, then uncovered the dishes one at a time.

There were apples cut into wedges next to clusters of purple grapes still on the vine. Another plate hosted sliced yellow and white cheeses. The last plate was piled with cold sliced meat. She broke the bread into pieces and shared it all around.

"So!" she said as she filled her plate. "How do you like it here, Violet?"

"I've only been here two days." I picked a grape and popped it into my mouth. "I'm not sure I have an opinion yet."

She laughed. Kalen chuckled. Jacob remained silent with his head down.

"How long have you been here?" I asked her.

She tore one of the thinly sliced pieces of meat in half. "My whole life. Well, *our* whole lives." She cut a glance to her brother. "My father is the Lord Chancellor."

Shock rolled through me as I stared at her. "I had no idea."

Kalen piled his plate with cheese and apples and grapes. "It's because she doesn't like to brag."

I picked up a grape, holding it between my thumb and forefinger. If Eliza had been in the court her whole life, and her father was Lord Chancellor, then perhaps she knew what happened to the previous Royal Sorcerer.

"Then you must have known the previous Royal Sorcerer."

"I did. He was positively *dreadful*," she said, rolling her eyes.

"Oh?" I tried to sound as nonchalant as possible.

"He was a crotchety old man. Never had a kind word for anyone, not even my father. Always scowling or frowning. Always stomping around the castle as though he owned the place." She shook her head. "Good riddance, I say."

"That's not very kind of you, Eliza," Kalen scolded.

I cut him a glance. He was busy breaking pieces of cheese in half.

She sighed, as though her feelings couldn't be helped. "I know it's not. He was just so unpleasant."

There were so many things I wanted to say to that, so many more questions I wanted to ask when Jacob spoke.

"It's no wonder he's dead."

Eliza gasped. Kalen halted with cheese halfway to his mouth. I stared, mouth agape, at the boy who I assumed was painfully shy.

"Jacob." Eliza said his name on a low, heated breath.

He dropped his head, staring down at his plate. Eliza plastered on a sheepish grin as she looked back at me. It seemed I had an opening to ask my question.

"Was he ill?"

Eliza glanced around the north lawn, searching for anyone who might overhear. She leaned forward. Kalen and I both leaned toward her as well. She dropped her voice to a near whisper.

"I heard he took ill suddenly and was dead within hours."

She straightened, turning her attention back to her plate.

A hot prickling sensation went through me. Aiden had said the same. If he took ill and was dead hours later, then it had to be some type of poison. If someone went to the trouble to poison him, then why? And did that mean my own father was in danger from this assassin?

"But let's not talk about such dreary things!"

Her bubbly personality was infectious and it was hard not to agree with her. She reached into the basket and pulled out a carafe with a cork in the top, then four small wooden tumblers. She uncorked it and poured a pale liquid into each glass, handing one to all of us. I gave it a tentative sniff. It was sweet smelling.

"What is this?"

"Mead." She giggled. "From my father's personal stash."

I held the cup, staring down at the drink with apprehension. "Should we be drinking it?"

"Oh, yes!" She downed hers in one gulp.

Her brother did the same, then handed her his empty cup. She stashed it in the basket. Kalen held his, not drinking. I finally gave him a glance. He held his cup toward mine.

"Shall we, Violet?"

Our cups thumped in a toast. I took a sip. It tasted as sweet as it smelled. Kalen frowned, looking as though he didn't care for it at all. His gaze focused on something behind Eliza.

"What's that over there?" He pointed.

She turned. "Where?"

When she did, he dumped his cup in the grass next to him. I stifled a giggle as she turned back.

"I don't see anything."

"Ah, must have been my imagination." He shot me a grin as he placed the cup in the basket. "Shall we play Bowls?"

"Yes. Jacob and I have to be back to our apartment before the evening meal."

Though we hardly touched the food, Eliza packed it all up in a hurry. When she wasn't watching, I did as Kalen and poured out the mead. I handed her my empty cup and, as I watched her, I thought of everything she said about the previous Royal Sorcerer, if it was true he was murdered. Or perhaps it was idle courtly gossip. Either way, the whole thing made me uneasy.

I had to admit, playing Bowls with the three of them was more fun than I expected. The idea of the game was setting up six pins several feet away and then rolling a heavy ball toward them to knock down as many as possible. Kalen and I played against Eliza and Jacob. I was pleased to see my skill at tossing the ball down the lawn was impeccable and we ended up winning.

It did not escape my notice the crystal was silent throughout the entire game.

As I made my way through the castle back to our apartment, I spied Lord Desmond in the great hall speaking with a group of men. I didn't wish to have another run-in with him, so I ducked into the nearest room, pushing open the door and slipping inside.

When I turned to face the room, I realized I was in the royal library. Bookshelves lined every wall of the cavernous room. In one corner, an oversized fireplace took up the space, its hearth dark and cold. Leather chairs were on either side of it. The floors were covered in richly colored rugs, thick underfoot. One side hosted a large window with a small conversation area that included a loveseat and sofa in dark red velvet. Toward the back of the room, an oversized oak desk with a few books left there.

I had never seen so many books in one place before. The shelves soared upward to the high ceiling with rows and rows of books. A sliding ladder on one side. An iron spiral staircase on the other leading to the third level. Intrigued, I started up the staircase. As I perused volumes of the history of Rovaria, the door below me opened.

My heart thudded hard as I whirled to peer down at two men entering the library. One was the king. Another was a man I didn't know.

Oh, this wasn't good at all.

I dropped to the ground behind the balustrade, peering through the wrought iron and hoping they didn't see me or hear the swish of my skirts as I huddled on the ground. The crystal beneath my gown was, thankfully, silent.

The king moved behind the desk where he bent to open one of the drawers. He pulled out a decanter and two glasses. He poured amber liquid into two glasses and handed one to the other man.

"Are you sure your source can be trusted?" King Jeffrey asked.

"There are no doubts, your majesty. I had it from more than one of my spies," the man replied.

The king sipped his drink. "Then what is your recommendation?"

"We must hasten the timetable," he said, holding his cup in his large hand making it seem small. "We cannot afford to lose any time. Ashea grows stronger by the day."

Ashea. I pressed a hand over my mouth to keep from making a sound. Kalen was from Ashea. He said his brother returned home a month ago. Would he, too, be called home?

"What of the young prince?" the king asked.

"Perhaps if he remains our guest, Ashea will not be so quick to attack."

The young prince *must* be Kalen. He never mentioned it in the few times we talked. Not even Eliza, the Lord Chancellor's daughter, mentioned it which made me wonder if she knew his true identity. It sounded as though they intended to keep him in Rovaria. As a hostage? A bargaining chip? Either way, I wondered if Kalen was aware of their plans.

"Do you believe our new Royal Sorcerer will be ready in time?"

My eyes grew wide and round as I peered down at them. Ready for what, I wondered?

"We must discuss with him the urgency of the situation, your majesty. Simon must understand how important it is to be ready. We don't have much time," the man said.

"I will speak with him this afternoon," King Jeffrey said. "It would be best, Osmund, if you joined us. As Lord Chancellor, it will help to express to him the magnitude of the situation."

Lord Chancellor. Eliza's and Jacob's father. I pressed my hand harder on my mouth to keep silent.

"Yes, of course, sire. Anything I can do." He finally took a sip of his drink, then pulled away the glass to peer into the liquid. "A good vintage. One of yours?"

"Of course." A broad smile broke out on the king's face. "Aged nearly one hundred years."

"It's no wonder you keep it hidden." Osmund replied and chuckled.

They both drained their cups. The king returned the decanter back into the hidden part of the shelf.

"Come, let's speak to Simon. I believe he's in his spell room and it would be a good time to see him." The king waved him toward the door.

The door opened and closed behind them, but I remained where I was with my heart pounding a wicked beat. I waited until the count to ten before I moved from my crouched position. Once I sat on my knees, I counted to ten once again. I didn't want to take any chances they were still nearby.

Finally, I peeled myself off the floor and hurried down the spiral staircase. Moments later, I was out of library and walking as fast as possible back to our apartment.

CHAPTER TWELVE

My stomach churned acid. When I returned to the apartment, I burst through the door and closed it with a snap, leaning against it while I tried to regulate my breathing and slow my heart. I pressed a hand against my roiling stomach and closed my eyes, taking several deep breaths.

Papa wasn't here. I knew this, of course, because he was in his spell room and the king and the Lord Chancellor were visiting him now to discuss Ashea with him. That it grows stronger every day.

What did it all mean?

I moved from the door and sat in one of the chairs by the hearth. The crystal gave a tentative half-hearted buzz, as though testing me.

I pulled it from beneath my gown and held it in my hand, looking down at it. There was a faint glow within it, the tiny stars dancing around each other. It gave me another *buzz buzz.*

"Thank you for remaining silent," I whispered to it. "It wouldn't do for me to be discovered in the library with the king and the chancellor."

It responded with another little buzz and a flicker, as though it understood everything I said.

Which was ridiculous.

Wasn't it?

I turned it over in my hand, inspecting the jagged edge. I ran my finger down it, feeling the bumps.

"Where is your other half?" I asked it.

Its response was a little flash. I didn't know what that meant. I thought of the spell books and the scroll hiding in the bottom of my wardrobe. Clutching the crystal in my hand, I jumped to my feet and hurried to my room.

A quick peek into Sophia's room showed it empty. Good.

While everyone was out, it was my chance to take a peek at the books and the scroll I'd pilfered from Papa's spellcasting room.

I placed the crystal on the bed while rummaging through the wardrobe and retrieved the books and the scroll. I placed the books side by side next to the crystal, then peered at the titles once again. *Professor Quentin's Book of Magic* and *The Art of Spellcasting*.

And then there was the scroll.

It had been creased a little from me holding it under my arm when I took it from the spellcasting room as well as traveling in the deep recesses of the trunk buried under my gowns and petticoats. The red ribbon trailed out from it with what appeared to be a gold coin at the end.

Picking up the scroll, I looked for the seam to unroll it, but it wasn't there. As though it had some sort of magical spell to keep it closed. I examined the gold coin and discovered it wasn't a coin at all. It was a gold medallion with some type of heraldry on it that had been almost worn smooth. Faint outlines showed the edges of what was once a roaring lion.

I ran the pad of my thumb over the smooth side of the medallion. A flash of light appeared and then the scroll popped open. The edge appeared, becoming visible.

On the bed, the crystal came alive by emitting a bright, happy glow. The stars inside swirled and danced. I glanced from it back to the scroll. I unrolled it slowly, holding it up, but the parchment appeared to be blank.

Then, gradually, words began to appear across the top. Only one line I read out loud.

"Hear me, oh mystical forces that dwell."

When I stopped, the second line appeared. My heard thudded as excitement skittered through me.

It was a spell.

And the scroll wanted me to read it. I started to utter the next line aloud when the door to the apartment banged closed.

"Violet?" Papa called.

Hot fear shot through me. Why hadn't I had the forethought to close my bedroom door? I snatched the crystal from the bed and put it around my neck, tucking it under my gown.

"You must stop," I said, my voice a roughened whisper. *"Please."*

The glow faded to nothing.

Now for the scroll. It seemed reasonable to me that if I opened the scroll by running my finger over the medallion, the action would close it.

As I touched the medallion, it jerked from my hand and rolled up tight. Closed.

I snatched the books off the bed as Papa's footsteps neared. My heart in my throat, I shoved them under the bed and turned as he appeared in my doorway.

"Hello, Papa!" I said, breathless and a little too cheerful.

His brows drew together in suspicion as he scanned the room. "Are you well? Your face is flushed."

"I'm fine."

I walked to him, hooked my arm in his and led him away from my room.

"How was your day?" I asked, more chipper than I had a right to be.

"My day?" He sounded confused, as though he didn't understand why I asked.

I knew, though, he had been visited by the king and the chancellor and I suspected it wasn't good news. He looked haggard. His clothes were rumpled. His fingertips were stained with ink. I led him to the oversized chair by the hearth, his limp more pronounced due to his fatigue.

"You look tired, Papa. Have a seat. I'll fetch you some wine."

"Wine, daughter." He gave me an odd look, then wiped a hand over his face as he leaned into the cushions, exhaustion lining his face.

I scurried to the small dining area. The highboard had a silver tray with a pewter carafe and glasses. I poured him a cup of wine.

"I assumed the servants left us this carafe of wine." I carried it to him and handed it over.

He took it, though he peered down at it in confusion. "What time is it?"

"Nearly dinnertime and—" I paused and gasped a little.

I'd forgotten Aiden was to call on me for dinner.

"And?" One thick, dark brow rose in question as he pinned me with his gaze.

I twisted my hands together. "Well, Papa, you see..."

"Violet, what have you done?"

Annoyance flickered through me at the very idea he thought I'd done something and I needed to confess. I frowned. "I haven't done anything, Papa."

"Did you see Lord Desmond today?"

Oh, this again. I didn't want to tell him the earl had cornered me in the great hall on my way to the picnic. That he had threatened to go to the king if I didn't agree to marry him. Instead, I deflected.

"I haven't yet. Papa, there is something I wish to tell you. Something important."

"Where's Sophia?" He sounded distracted as he glanced around the apartment looking for her.

"I don't know. Papa, please—"

Before I was able to tell him about Aiden, a knock sounded on the door. I dashed for the door and flung it open, preparing to wave him off but it was only the servants with our dinner. Relieved, I stepped aside and allowed them entrance.

They bustled about, setting the table with covered dishes of steaming food that smelled delectable. From the highboard, they took out plates and set the table, then replenished the wine carafe. They'd even brought a silver tea service, leaving it next to the carafe.

"Ah, dinner." Papa rose from the chair, placing his wine aside never having taken a sip.

As he made his way to the table and the servants departed, Sophia arrived. She waited until they all filed out of the room, then closed the door behind them. Papa sat at the end of the table while Sophia uncovered the dishes.

Roasted pheasant was sliced into thick pieces on one platter. Another hosted cooked vegetables in a thick sauce. There was a basket of bread, a wheel of cheese, fruit and tiny lemon cakes for dessert.

"Papa, there's something I really must tell you."

He handed his plate to Sophia. She added slices of meat and vegetables.

"Well? What is it?" His voice was rough, demanding.

"You recall meeting my piano teacher, Aiden Lockhart?"

Sophia cut me a glance, her eyes wide and her brows raised, but she said nothing. Papa took the plate from her, oblivious to her reaction. He tucked his napkin into the top of his tunic and picked up his fork and knife.

"Yes? What about him?"

"Well—"

Just then a knock on the door. Papa looked up, his face full of question followed by annoyance by having his evening meal interrupted.

"I'll get that." I bustled to the door before either of them could say a word.

At the door, I cracked it open and peered out. There stood Aiden in his finery looking dashing with a warm, happy smile on his face. I pushed the door open wider, but put a hand on his chest.

"I haven't been able to tell my father you were coming," I said, my voice a low whisper.

"Oh? Should I go, then?"

"No!" I grabbed his hand and dragged him inside, closing the door behind him. "Please, don't. He'll be pleased. He just doesn't know it yet."

"If you're sure..." His words trailed off as I led him to our dining area. "Papa, Aiden has come to call. He'd like to join us for dinner."

Papa stared at me in shocked silence. Sophia refused to move as she remained rooted in place at the edge of the table. Finally, Papa removed his napkin and rose. He came around the table. My heart leapt into my throat, worried he was going to toss the poor man out. Instead, he extended his hand in greeting.

"We're pleased you could join us. Please, sit." He waved to the table. "Sophia, please make another place setting for Mr. Lockhart."

She nodded and set about getting out another plate and more utensils.

Aiden shook his hand with a grin. "Thank you for allowing me to join you."

Papa returned to his place at the head of the table, tucking his napkin into his tunic once more. Aiden gave me a surprised look at his manners. I merely shrugged. He sat at the side of the table. I took the place opposite him. Papa was to my left. Once she was finished, Sophia headed off to her room. I knew she would have her meal later after we'd finished. Still, a little guilt slashed through me knowing she wasn't allowed to join us.

"What brings you to dine with us?" Papa asked. He sliced into a piece of meat and stuck it in his mouth.

Aiden helped himself to slices of pheasant. "With your permission, my lord, I should like to court your daughter."

This wasn't planned. I gaped at him from across the table. Papa stopped eating to stare at him with an expression I couldn't read.

"You wish to court her?" he repeated.

"I do, indeed." He cut me a glance.

I tried to convey with my eyes the question of *what are you doing*, but appeared to have failed.

"I appreciate the sentiment," Papa said, "but my daughter is already promised to another."

I gasped. "Papa!"

"Oh, I see," Aiden said.

"I'm not," I said quickly. "I'm promised to no one."

"Violet..." He said my name in a warning tone.

"No, Papa. I do not wish to marry Lord Desmond, nor will I. I thought I made my intentions clear."

He cut a glance to Aiden, then back to me as he cleared his throat. "And I thought, daughter, I made it clear to you that you were to accept his marriage proposal."

Fury rose hot and wild inside me. The crystal around my neck flared to life with a quick, succinct buzzing.

"I *will not*," I responded.

Aiden slid his chair back and got to his feet. "Perhaps this wasn't a good time. I should go."

"No!" I shot to my feet, giving him an imploring look to stay. Then I turned to my father. "Papa, you are being unreasonable and stubborn about Lord Desmond. He is an old, vile man and I do not wish to marry him."

I rounded the table to stand beside Aiden. I hooked my arm in his. He shifted on his feet, uncomfortable, as Papa gave us both a look of disdain.

"Violet, I've had a very long, tiresome day. I would appreciate it if you would escort Mr. Lockhart the door."

My heart rammed hard and fast. The crystal buzzed in concert with it. Aiden gave me an odd look. There was no doubt in my head he heard the crystal's incessant buzzing as well, just as Sophia had. I flushed, my cheeks hot.

Aiden patted my hand. "It's all right, Violet," he said, his voice low.

I straightened and took a deep, cleansing breath. "I will escort Mr. Lockhart to the door, Papa, as you wish. However, there will be no more discussion of Lord Desmond."

His lips thinned in a straight line. I, of course, understood very well how much I pushed his patience, but at that moment, I didn't care. I pulled Aiden along with me around the dining table and toward the door, taking long, slow steps.

"I'm sorry," he whispered.

I gave him a sidelong glance. "My father is...unreasonable."

At the door, I opened it for Aiden. He stepped into the hallway and grasped my hand. "Please tell me tomorrow how things fare with your father."

I sighed. "Not well, I'm afraid."

I bid him goodnight and watched as he turned from our door and walked away.

CHAPTER THIRTEEN

I closed the door to our apartment, my stomach giving a wild spiral of fright. I didn't want to go back and face my father, but I knew I had to. I knew if I didn't, I would be in even more trouble than I already was.

I didn't understand why he was so insistent I marry this disgusting creature. I had no interest. I didn't trust him.

Reluctantly, I returned to the dining area. Papa was still eating, his plate nearly cleared.

"Sit down, Violet."

I lifted my chin, looking down my nose at him in defiance. "No. I've lost my appetite."

His gaze flickered up to mine. His terrible, unhappy gaze. He pointed to my chair. "Sit. And do not disobey me again."

With terror slinking through me, I sank into the chair, staring down at the plate of food going cold.

"Listen to me, now. I want only what is best for you. Marriage to Lord Desmond is a smart match. He has lands and title. He will take care of you long after I'm gone."

"Long after he's gone, too," I snapped, giving him my best look full of ire. "He's an *old man*, Papa."

His glare silenced me. I returned my gaze to my cold plate.

"He may be an old man, as you say, but you will be a countess. You will run his estate. You will be well cared for by him. These are the things for which I've been grooming you. Do you not want these things?"

I tried to ignore the malcontent brewing under the surface. The crystal continued to emit a low hum. Did he not know about Lord Desmond's financial situation? Or perhaps he didn't care.

"No. You know I don't." With as much courage as I was able to muster, I met his gaze. "I do not wish to be a countess. I do not wish to run someone else's estate. I do not wish to bear children for the sake of an heir."

His jaw clenched, the muscles flexing along the edge. "You cannot and will not be a sorceress, Violet."

"Why not?" I realized I sounded like a petulant child. "Why can I not pursue the one thing I want most?"

He tugged his napkin from his neck and threw it on his empty plate. "Because I forbid it. You know this. And I do not wish to discuss it again."

And with that, he rose from the table and stalked away. Moments later, his bedroom door slammed.

I remained staring down at the plate of untouched food.

Why didn't he want me to be a sorceress? Why didn't he want me to use or have magic? There was some reason. Some buried reason he was unwilling to share with me. I sensed it.

The crystal had not stopped humming, low and soft, since Aiden left.

What was there to do? With Papa in his room, it would be unwise to slip out to find Aiden and apologize. I certainly didn't want to run into Lord Desmond, either.

I pushed from the table and stalked into my room, closing the door with a snap. I stood there a long moment in the shadowy darkness, my back pressed against the door. My hands shook from anger.

I knelt and fished the books and the scroll out from under the bed. I slipped the crystal off my neck and placed it on the bed. It still emitted a low hum.

Now that I learned how to open the scroll, I was more interested in that than the books. I swiped my thumb over the medallion. The parchment opened.

The first line was still there, waiting.

I repeated the first line. The second line appeared, crawling across the page with the invocation. I read each line as it appeared.

Hear me, oh mystical forces that dwell,□
Grant me the power, within me to swell.□
I seek the might, to bend reality's thread,□
With this invocation, my destiny is fed.

With every word spoken, enchantments unfold,□
Mysteries unveiled, secrets untold.□
Let the realms converge, mortal and divine,□
An almighty sorceress, for all of time.

In the depths of my being, emotions reside,□
Through this spell, allow them to guide.□
With heart's fervor, my power shall soar,□
The might of my feelings, forevermore.

By the magic's embrace, let my will be done,□
With boundless power, as bright as the sun.□
By the utterance of this sacred decree,□
I am now all-powerful, my soul is set free.

I am the master of mystical domains,□
In this realm and beyond, my reign sustains.

So mote it be.

When I finished the spell, the crystal lit up, illuminating the entire room in a pale pink glow. The stars inside danced in a wild undulating dance, swirling around each other as though they were trying to merge but were unable.

As I continued to hold the scroll, a drawing appeared next to the incantation. A drawing of what the crystal looked like whole. I gasped.

Something had split it in half. Something had almost destroyed it. But what? How?

And where was the other half?

I reached for the crystal. As soon as I held it, a punch of power pulsated through my hand, up my arm, and then through my entire body. I sucked in a sharp breath, my back bending backward as I tingled with the odd sensation. My hands shook. An odd vibration skittered through me, making me jittery. As though I stood on the edge of a precipice about to tumble off.

The light in the crystal faded and went silent.

The scroll in my hand rolled up and closed, as if it had merely waited for someone to speak the words aloud.

I stared down at the crystal in my other hand, wondering how and where Papa acquired it. There was no way to ask him, either. He would be angry with me for stealing it from his spellcasting room and I didn't want to incur more of his wrath.

What was I to do now?

The only thing I knew to do. I slipped the crystal back over my head and tucked it under my dress. Then I hid the spell books and the scroll once again in the back of my wardrobe, covering them with the shawl. I toed off my shoes and perched on the edge of the bed, trying to decide if I should sleep or not.

But I wasn't sleepy.

In fact, my eyes were wide open.

I cracked open my bedroom door and peered out. There was no movement or sounds. I shoved open the door wide and stepped into the hallway in my stocking feet. Sophia's door was closed. Papa's door was still closed. Silence.

Slipping through the apartment, I noticed the dinner dishes had been cleared. The food was gone, much to my dismay as my stomach rumbled.

On the highboard, there was a basket of bread covered with a linen cloth. I broke off a piece and nibbled it as I made my way through the apartment.

No candles were lit. Even the hearth was devoid of a fire since the weather had warmed.

The balcony beckoned. Perhaps I needed some fresh air to calm my ragged nerves. I pushed aside the gossamer curtain and opened the door. A cool evening breeze fluttered past me.

I stepped into the night, leaving the door open behind me. Overhead, stars twinkled, reminding me of the swirling stars inside the crystal. Below, our view was of the castle grounds. Dark rounded shapes indicated low bushes around the area. In the distance, the crashing waves were faint but ever-present. I had forgotten how close we were to the Fallrood Sea.

Voices filtered from below. One sounded angry. I scanned the area, looking for the speakers but they were concealed within the shadows. Then, a figure stumbled across the lawn, as if drunk. I gripped the stone handrail and peered down, trying to make out who it was. It appeared to be a man. Another figure came into view, this one with stable footing. It was a woman.

She grasped him by the arm to help him remain standing.

"You've gone and made a fool of yourself," the woman said, her tone chastising. "You've been in the cups and the cards again, haven't you?"

"Unhand me, woman." He jerked his arm free. It sounded like Lord Desmond. "And what do you care about my drinking or my gambling?"

"How stubborn you are," she said, her voice gruff with anger. "How much did you lose this time?"

So, he was a gambler. It could be the reason he was in financial trouble with his estates. Perhaps he gambled away his money, using his land and title as collateral for his debts and that's why he was in dire straits, why he was looking to my father to marry me so he could get his hands on the forty thousand gold. But how much could forty thousand gold really help if he was deep in debt?

He straightened, as though her words had sobered him. "Lady Bridgette, that is none of your concern."

I was interested to know who the mysterious Lady Bridgette was. In the shadowy darkness, I was unable to see her features or even the color of her dress.

"You're correct. It isn't. Especially now since you've called off our wedding. I know you're panting after Simon's daughter."

My eyes widened at her mention of me. She *knew* about me. More importantly, she knew Lord Desmond was trying to woo me.

"If you think she's your escape out of your troubles, my lord, I would think again."

Cold spikes of shock skittered up my arms, raising gooseflesh and making the hairs on the back of my neck stand on end.

In the darkness, Lord Desmond staggered toward her. She reared back, but he caught her by her upper arms and dragged her closer.

"Make no mistake. I will have her. I am close to convincing her father to go to the king and make the marriage arrangements. And when she's married to me and under my control, I will do what I did to the *other* Royal Sorcerer."

She shoved him away. "You're despicable and nothing but a drunken fool."

Then she hurried away with a swish of skirts. But Lord Desmond followed her, calling her name. Their voices faded into the distance. But

I was left with a lot of questions and a deep, disturbing fear pounding through me.

CHAPTER FOURTEEN

I laid in bed on top of the covers, full clothed, staring at the ceiling with my heart racing. My skin still seemed to vibrate with whatever happened to me when I read the spell. The crystal was humming away in concert to my heart. I replayed the conversation from Lord Desmond and Lady Bridgette over and over in my head.

What did he mean when he said he would do what he did to the other Royal Sorcerer? Suspicion lanced through me.

It was only when a sharp knock on my bedroom door came that I was startled out of my thoughts. I sat bolt upright on the edge of the bed, my hair a mess and my clothes rumpled.

"Yes?" I called.

The door cracked open. Papa stuck his head inside.

"Ah, you're awake. Good." He pushed the door open wider and stepped into the room just across the threshold. He seemed not to notice I still wore the same gown as last night and for that, I was grateful. "Violet, I believe I owe you and your friend, Aiden, an apology."

"You...do?" I was so taken aback by this sudden reversal I wasn't sure what to say.

"I behaved poorly last night. I can only blame my rudeness on a trying day with the king and the Lord Chancellor."

He raked a hand over his face. I noticed once again his fatigue and the lines creasing the edges of his eyes, the dark circles under his eyes. As though he hadn't slept a wink all night. He heaved a sigh.

"How can I make things right?" he asked.

I stared at him, shocked. My mind raced as I tried to come up with an answer. "I suppose I could ask Aiden for dinner this evening. If you'd like."

A weak smile came across his face as he nodded. "Yes, that would be nice. Do find him and invite him along. I will make sure Sophia speaks with the servants to arrange another place for him this evening."

"Thank you, Papa."

He stepped over to the bed and gave me a quick kiss on the top of the head. "Have a good day in class."

And then he was gone. I gaped after him, staring at the space he vacated wondering why the sudden change of heart. I was glad, though. Glad to ask Aiden back for another evening meal. There was a small part of me that worried he wouldn't accept, but now wasn't the time to think about that.

A moment later, Sophia was at my door. She took in my appearance with a frown.

"You slept in your clothes," she said. "Why didn't you ring for me?"

"Well, you were sleeping and the evening was awkward and I couldn't sleep anyway..." My words trailed off as I lifted my hands in surrender and gave her a shrug.

She gave an exasperated sigh. "Let's get you dressed and ready for the day, then."

As she unbuttoned the back of my gown, I began to unravel the long plaits around my head, pulling them free. I ran my fingers through my long dark hair, massaging my scalp with a contented sigh.

Once I was down to my shift, the crystal was visible beneath the thin white material. It emitted a pale pink glow. Not enough to light up the room, but definitely enough to be visible under the material. Sophia stared at it in wonder.

"What is that?" she asked.

"Do you want to see it?" I asked.

She nodded.

I pulled it out from under the shift and, leaving the crystal still around my neck, held it out to her. She stepped closer and leaned down to examine it, the light from the crystal illuminated her face in a dusky glow.

"There are stars inside it," she said, her voice full of wonder.

"Yes," I agreed.

"What do they do?" Her gaze lifted to mine, question in her eyes.

"I don't know."

Though the stars spun madly after I said the spell, now they merely moved languorously.

"It's really beautiful." She had a blissful smile on her face as she gazed at it.

I wasn't sure what to say to that. Instead, I said, "I better get ready for class."

"Yes, of course!"

She helped me dress in a gown of pale blue satin with elbow-length sleeves ending in white ruffles. As usual, I tucked the crystal into the bodice of my shift. She combed my hair and plaited it into one long braid down the back. When I was ready, we headed out to the first class. But

I wasn't in the mood for history or reading *The First King* again. At the doorway to that class, I paused and turned to her.

"I'll see you after," I said.

She nodded and headed back to the apartment. I waited until she was well out of sight before I scurried away from the door. I needed to see Aiden to make my apologies about last night and invite him, once again, to dine with us. My gut clenched at the idea of him refusing because he was so humiliated the night before. Even the crystal had something to hum about in concert with my feelings.

As I hurried across the great hall, there I saw Lord Desmond. He pinpointed me with his bloodshot eyes. He unfolded his lanky body from the chair he was sitting in and lumbered toward me. I wondered if he was still a little drunk from the night before. There were bags under his eyes and it was clear to me he was sleep deprived.

I tried to steer away from him, but his long gait ate up the space between us and he was at my side in an instant. His hand clamped on my elbow, his fingers digging into the flesh there, as he steered me away from the crowded room.

"A word, my lady?" His rancid breath wafted over me.

I tried not to gag. "Release me." I said it in my best authoritative tone.

"I think not." His face turned dark, shadowy, as he led me away.

We ended up in the library, where I had overhead the king and the Lord Chancellor only the day before. He gave me a shove into the room, closing the door with a snap behind him. I backed toward the window, my heart in my throat and the crystal gave a more defined hum than it ever had.

"What do you want?" I asked, backing away from him and eyeing the door. It was the only way out.

"I'm giving you one more chance," he said, "to agree to marry me."

"Never."

Fear pounded through me as he advanced. I had to keep my wits about me. I moved sideways to position myself in front of the windows thinking there was a way to fling open the sash to call for help.

"I tried to be a gentleman," he said, still advancing. "But you are a stubborn girl."

I was backed against the wall near the windows, my hands behind me on the ledge. The window, though, was deeper than I anticipated and I was unable to reach the lock.

"Even more stubborn than my first wife, gods rest her soul," he sneered.

The window ledge dug into my lower back. "You killed her, didn't you?" It was a guess.

Judging by the look of surprise he quickly masked, though, my guess was correct. "You know nothing."

He lunged for me, his hands reaching for my throat. I put my hands up to block his attack. His long fingers wrapped around my wrists. He jerked me toward him, his rancid breath on my face and his body heat radiating over me. I sucked in a sharp breath as he gathered both my wrists in one of his powerful hands. He was strong and easily overpowered me.

He shoved me against the window, his free hand trying to pull up my skirts. I cried out, struggling against him. He paused his violation long enough to backhand me.

"Keep quiet or this will go very badly for you."

His hand returned, yanking up my skirt and then fumbling underneath. The crystal beneath my gown had gone into a frenzied hum, pounding against my skin in concert with the wild beat of my heart. I had to *do* something instead of letting him try to do unsavory, unwanted things. I wiggled a foot free and, using as much force as possible, I stomped down on the top of his foot.

He yelled, his hand on my wrists going slack enough for me to tear free. I shoved him backward as he tried to recover and stumbled away from him. He spun back toward me, though, his fingers grasping the edge of my sleeve, and jerked. A rip sounded in the stale air as the shoulder seam split. He managed to regain control and grabbed me from behind, his arms wrapping around my upper body.

He pushed me forward, shoving me toward the sofa.

"Fine, then," he breathed. "We'll do this the hard way."

A strange sensation came over me, then. I was suddenly light-headed. The crystal started to glow beneath my gown, pulsing faster and faster. The hum grew louder and louder. I sucked in a breath through my nose, my hands fisting at my side.

He shoved me forward, face first over the back of the sofa. His hips ground into the back of me. One hand went over my mouth.

"Keep quiet and this will be over soon enough."

No, no, no, my brain shouted.

I needed help. I bit down hard on his palm, the metallic tang of blood filling my mouth. He grunted, cursed, and gave me a shove as he pulled his hand away. The bite mark was clear in his palm as he held his wrist. His terrifying gaze landed on me.

"You will pay for that."

Now that I was free, I spun away from him, searching for a weapon. Any weapon. My hand landed on the nearby vase and I snatched it up, spinning back toward him and flinging it at his head.

The porcelain connected with the side of his head, smashing it to bits. Broken shards rained down around him. It was then I noticed the bright pulsing under my gown. Lord Desmond charged again.

A loud hum exploded from the crystal. Light flared. A bright beam streaked from my chest, hitting him. He reared back, his eyes rolling into the back of his head. He stumbled backward, landing on the ground with a thud. Lord Desmond's eyes were wide, unseeing. His skin turned pale. His lips were blue and a charred hole in his tunic. There was the metallic twinge of magic in the air.

I took a step away from him, gasping, my eyes wide as I stared down at him. He wasn't moving.

The crystal had gone silent and dark.

"What did you do?" I whispered.

There was no reply. I took a tentative step toward him, looking for signs of breathing. There were none.

"Oh, gods..."

Kneeling, I placed two fingers against his neck. There was no pulse.

Lord Desmond was dead.

CHAPTER FIFTEEN

I burst out of the library making sure to close the door behind me. Panic stricken, I hurried through the castle to Aiden's music room. I didn't know where else to go. I didn't even know what to do. I didn't know if he would or could help me, but he was the only one I trusted.

I killed him. *Killed him.*

No, correction, the crystal killed him. Somehow, it sensed I was in danger and it protected me from him. I didn't *want* him dead. I wanted him to leave me alone.

He all but confessed to murdering his first wife. If he killed her, then what was to stop him from killing the previous Royal Sorcerer? If he did, then he would likely know the king would want my father to come to court as the replacement. And if he knew that, then he knew I would come with him.

But why attack me? Unless his plan was to ruin my reputation so no other man would have me, thus forcing the king to draw up the marriage contract between the two of us.

I shuddered with revulsion at the thought.

At Aiden's music room, I burst through the door unannounced. The boy at the keyboard stopped playing, his head snapping up and his eyes bright with surprise. Aiden stared at me from behind him, his expression perplexed at first and then replaced with concern.

"Violet?"

"I-I need to speak to you. Urgently."

Aiden gave a nod without any questions, then patted the boy on the shoulder. "William, you may be excused. Good work today."

William gathered up his music on the piano and scurried past me without so much as a wayward glance. I shut the door behind him and then lost all strength. My knees gave out and I tumbled to the ground in a heap.

"Violet!"

Aiden was at my side in an instant, scooping me off the floor and helping me to my feet. He led me to the oversized chair and sat me down. Then he poured a cup of steaming tea, dropped in one cube of sugar and a dollop of cream, and handed it to me. The scent of bergamot wafted to me as I took the cup and inhaled the aroma.

"What's happened? You look a fright."

I stared down into the reddish-brown liquid, looking for courage. Oddly, the crystal remained dormant.

"Your gown is torn." He stood over me, peering down at me with something akin to alarm. "Who did this to you?"

"Lord Desmond," I whispered.

He stood a long moment, then pulled the other chair closer and perched on the edge. He removed the cup I held and placed it aside, then took my hands in his. There was something comforting about the way he held my hands. The way the pad of his thumb stroked the smooth skin on the back of my hand.

"Your hands are cold. Violet, what happened?"

I stared down at our intertwined fingers, marveling at how warm his were. How soft. How perfectly trimmed the nails were.

"I was coming here to talk to you about last night. To apologize. Papa...he wanted me to invite you to dinner again because he felt bad about last night." I lifted my gaze to meet his and saw the worry in his depths. "But Lord Desmond caught me on the way. He...he pulled me into the library."

I halted, swallowing hard as it came back to me in a rush. The way he grabbed me, pushed me against the window. The way his hand fumbled with my skirt.

"He attacked you." It wasn't a question.

But I nodded anyway as a sob cracked my throat.

He shot to his feet. "We must go to the king at once. His behavior cannot go unpunished—"

I stood, rushing to him and grabbing him by the arm. "No! We cannot go to the king."

His brows knit in confusion. "Why not? Violet, this is serious—"

"He's dead," I blurted.

Aiden stilled, his face going completely impassive as he looked at me. Understanding dawned as he realized the truth of it. Dread skipped through me and for a moment, I thought he would be angry. He would pull away. He would shun me. He would fear me. He did none of those things.

Instead, he wrapped me in his arms and held me, holding me tight as though he would never let go. I inhaled the scent of him, the faint smell of sandalwood and leather and wondered why a piano teacher would smell of these things.

"It was self-defense," he said into my hair and then kissed my temple.

While he was correct that it *was*, in fact, self-defense, he didn't understand it wasn't *me* who did the killing. I wrapped my arms around his waist and buried my face in his chest wondering if I should tell him the rest of the truth. Would he understand?

"Is he still in the library?" he asked.

"Yes. I..." I paused, pulled away and looked up at him. "I smashed a vase against his head."

"I've seen the vase in the library. I'm sure it won't be missed."

"But that didn't kill him," I said, ignoring his quip.

One eyebrow raised. "What did?"

I stepped out of his arms and turned away, gazing down at the location of the now silent crystal. My heart pounded as I pulled it out from under my gown.

"There is something I want to show you." I peeked at him over my shoulder. "Can I trust you?"

"I think, under the circumstances, you know you can." He almost sounded offended.

I slipped the crystal off my neck and held it in my palm, closing my fingers around it and turned back to him.

"It's a small thing, really, but I think it's attuned to me."

"What is?" His gaze flickered from my face to my enclosed hand.

I opened my fingers one by one and stretched it out to show him. He stepped closer, peering down at the crystal that had gone dark and silent since the attack on Lord Desmond.

"What is it?"

"Magic." The words came out a roughened whisper. "It understands my emotions. When he attacked me, it started to hum and pulse with a vibrant light. When he tried to grab me, a bright light flashed." I paused, swallowed hard. "And then he was dead."

"You killed him with magic," Aiden said, the words slow and deliberate as he met my gaze. "It's against the law to kill another using magic."

He was right, of course. I knew the laws of the land better than anyone. Papa lived by them. And yet, he, too, had killed with magic when we were attacked by the bandits on the road here. Did he feel as I did now? With guilt swarming through him? Fear of the consequences? No, likely he didn't since he came riding out of the forest driving the carriage looking exhilarated.

And here I was, wielding a terrifying power I didn't understand. Now, there was a dead man. Dead by my hand.

Terror and despair shuddered through me. Hot tears sprang to my eyes as I stood there, wondering if he judged me. If he would take me to the king for punishment. Because surely punishment for the murder of one of the nobles would be death.

He closed my fingers around the crystal, holding his hand over mine for a long, quiet moment. Our eyes met. There was a deep understanding and compassion in his. No judgement.

"I will see to his body in the library," he said. "Tell no one else what you told me."

Shock rolled through me as I stared at him.

"Promise me," he said, squeezing my hand.

"I promise."

"Remain here. I will be back as soon as I can."

He released me and headed for the door.

I paced the small confines of the music room until my feet ached. After Aiden left, I tried to sit and drink a cup of tea but it had gone cold. I'd long since given up sitting and trying to remain calm and still. I had too much pent-up nervous energy. Too much fear and worry clawing its way through me.

I wanted to peek outside the room, but I dared not.

Instead, I paced and paced and paced. Strangely, the crystal had not hummed or buzzed. It was as though it had gone dormant.

Long shadows cast across the floor from the one window, indicating it was nearing sundown. It had been hours since Aiden left. No one had come. Not even the servants. Not even another student. I expected I would see at least one other student at the door and I would have to make excuses for Aiden.

At last, the door opened. I halted, my shoes scuffing on the wood floor as I spun to see who entered, my heart pounding a mad tattoo in my throat.

It was Aiden. Fatigue lined his face. His shoulders slumped as he closed the door behind him and leaned against it, his unreadable gaze landing on me. I twisted my hands together trying hard to be patient and wait for him to speak first. Worry gnawed my gut.

"Lord Desmond's body has been removed from the library," he said, his voice flat.

I swallowed hard waiting for him to continue. He took two steps toward me, then halted within arm's reach.

"Your father and the Lord Chancellor were already there when I arrived," he continued.

My stomach churned acid. "Do they know it was me?"

He shook his head. "No. They don't suspect. But they know there was an altercation in the library."

"The broken vase," I said.

"Your father inspected his body. He saw a bite mark in his palm. You bit him?"

I flushed hot. "Yes." The word came out on a rush of a whisper.

He gave me a grin of approval. "Good girl." Then he composed himself to continue. "He also saw the distinct signs on the charred place in his chest. He knows he was killed with magic," Aiden said.

My heart skipped a beat as the blood rushed from my head, leaving tiny black pinpricks in my vision. My knees wobbled. Aiden hurried toward me, wrapping an arm around my shoulders to steady me.

"Violet, tell me truthfully. Does your father know about that crystal?" His gaze glinted with concern and question.

I shook my head. "Only Sophia knows and she swore she wouldn't tell him."

He ran his hand over his chin, the skin of his palm bristling against the smoothness of his face.

"There is something I wish to tell you. Something that is not widely known and I ask you to keep it to yourself. Tell no one. Not Sophia. Not your father," he said.

It sounded dire. I nodded, biting the edge of my lower lip. He tucked my arm in the crook of his elbow. Together, we walked to the pair of oversized chairs where he motioned for me to sit. He sat across from me, as we did earlier in the day when I burst in with the terrible news I'd killed Lord Desmond.

"I am no piano teacher," he said.

I gaped. "Then...what or who are you?"

He started to answer, then paused and pressed his lips together in a thin line. "Before I answer, tell me what you know of the kingdom of Ashea."

"Ashea?" I repeated, wondering why he asked. Prince Kalen was in my history class. We'd played Bowls and laughed together.

"Their political allegiances, if you will," he added.

My knowledge of politics was limited. I cared not for the subject, but tried to answer as best I could. "It is a desert land inhabited mostly by nomadic tribes on the southern end of the continent. The king..." I paused, trying to recall his name. "King Dameon?"

He nodded, encouraging me to continue.

"King Dameon rules from his desert palace in the capital of Zuwaanee," I said. "The royal family is well known for spending their wealth on whatever they wish. We have a trade agreement with them for spices. Saffron, ginger, turmeric, and certain textiles. The silks and satin I enjoy."

"Yes, good. And tell me, what do you know about the highlands to the west?"

"Is this geography as well as a lesson in politics?" I asked, confused by his questions.

He gave a half-hearted smile. "Tell me what you know."

"Dal Breifna is a mountainous region in the western highlands and is a wild country inhabited by an ancient, reclusive people known as the Dalmonii," I said. "We have no trade agreement with them and haven't in a thousand years. They were once ruled by a High King, but no one has had contact with them in several centuries."

All those lessons drilled into me over the years had, at last, paid off.

"They are not so reclusive," Aiden said. "They are planning an invasion of Rovaria with the help of the kingdom of Ashea."

I blinked, dumbfounded. "How do you know this?"

"I am a spy for King Jeffrey," he said, matter-of-fact.

I sucked in a sharp breath. I was at a loss for words as I sat across from him. My nails dug into the cushion of the chair arm as a cold tingling sensation took up residence in the middle of my chest. An immediate question sprang to mind.

"Why would they invade Rovaria?" I asked.

"Ashea wants more lush land and a water source. They are finding it more difficult to find fresh water due to their severe drought. Dal Breifna is interested in expanding their borders to a more habitable area. And you are correct—they were ruled by a High King. However, no one has been able to find out if they are still ruled by a High King and if so, *who* that High King is."

"But...what does this have to do with Lord Desmond?"

"Lord Desmond, the vile earl that he was, was the messenger between the two factions. He was here to gather information about the king's forces, to see how strong of an army Rovaria has and to find a weakness. He was passing secrets to each of the two countries, who also have spies in our court."

I thought again of Kalen and wondered if he was one of those spies. None of this made sense. I pressed cold fingertips to my forehead.

"He was also a drunk and a gambler," Aiden went on. "He used his lands as collateral on the numerous gambling debts he owed. When they came to collect, he was unable to pay because he made deals with both Ashea and Dal Breifna. He was sliding them information in return for payment. And yet, he squandered those payments away on dice and cards and drink."

"And his insistence that I marry him?" I asked.

"He needed a wife to produce an heir to his estates to keep it out of the hands of the crown. King Jeffrey intended to reclaim his lands to the west of the capital to settle his gambling debts. Until he ended up dead," Aiden said.

I leaned back into the cushions of the chair, my head spinning with all the information. "I believe he attacked me because he wanted to ruin my reputation and, therefore, force me to marry him."

Aiden nodded. "Yes, I believe that was likely his motivation." He scooted forward, perching on the edge of the cushion. "Violet, when you asked me to find out about the death of the previous Royal Sorcerer, I wondered if you had some information you were afraid to share with me. Do you know something?"

I shook my head. "No, not at the time I asked you. But I overheard Lord Desmond speaking to Lady Bridgette last night. They were outside, under my balcony. He said when I was married to him and under his control, he would do what he did to the other Royal Sorcerer. Aiden..." I paused, leaning forward and dropping my voice, "did he kill the man?"

His face turned grim as he clenched his jaw, the muscles flexing there. Finally, he gave a stiff nod. "Yes and I believe he intended to kill your father next."

My gut clenched at the thought. Lord Desmond was willing to do whatever it took to get what he wanted. Me, Blackthorne, a war. I despised him all the more.

"There is one more thing I need to tell you," he said. He reached for my hands, taking them in his and giving a gentle squeeze. "I have to leave."

"Leave? Where are you going?"

"The king is sending me to find answers. There are rumors coming from Whitefell there is activity near the borders."

Whitefell was a small village in the west close to where the borders of Dal Breifna, Ashea, and Rovaria all met.

"What sort of activity?"

"Lord Desmond started something he can no longer finish. However, there are others who are willing to complete the task. Others who wish to see war. There are many who dislike King Jeffrey and his politics. Many who want to see his ruin and the downfall of the kingdom."

I didn't understand politics, nor did I care for them. I much preferred my blissful ignorance of royal machinations. Now, though, it was taking Aiden away from me when we had only just begun to understand each other. Him with his secrets and me with mine.

"But Whitefell is over a day's ride," I said.

"It is," he said with a nod. "But I must go and send word back to the king, especially if there's trouble brewing. I'll return as soon as I'm able."

Thinking of Aiden going to Whitefell left me bereft in a sea of loneliness. He was my only ally. With him out of the castle, what would I do should someone discover the truth about Lord Desmond's death?

I shoved that thought aside. There was no sense in worrying over something that hadn't happened yet.

He gave me a sly smile. "Will you miss me?"

"Yes," I answered at once, though I hardly knew him. "I don't know what I'd do without you after today."

He smiled as though pleased to hear it. He tucked my hand in the crook of his arm. "Let's get you home. I have only an hour to pack before I leave."

Only an hour and then he would be gone. My heart ached at the thought.

CHAPTER SIXTEEN

Aiden walked me back to my family apartment. I was still trying to grasp he was a spy for the king, that Lord Desmond was trying to start a war between Rovaria, Ashea, and Dal Breifna. But the two factions had lost their liaison, which made me wonder what would happen next. Would they still try to invade Rovaria? Or would they stand down now that they no longer had their spy?

I had no answers, of course, and neither did Aiden.

At our apartment door, he kissed my fingers. "Get some rest. I will see you soon."

"I hope so."

"And Violet..." He gave my hand one last squeeze. "I'm glad you came to me. I'm glad you trust me."

He released me and left me standing there. I watched him walk away, disappearing around a corner before I finally pushed open the apartment door and entered.

Papa was seated in the chair by the hearth. His elbow was propped up on the arm rest, his head in his hand. He looked up when I entered. I saw the dark shadows under his eyes and the deep lines of exhaustion in his face. I hurried over to him.

"Are you well, Papa?"

He heaved a sigh and leaned back in the chair, his head against the cushioned high back. "It's been a long, terrible day."

I took the seat opposite him, clasping my shaking hands in my lap and waited. His gaze lifted to mine.

"Did something happen?" I asked, trying to keep my voice as neutral as possible.

"Lord Desmond was found dead in the royal library this morning." He sounded tired when he said it.

I gasped and did my best to sound surprised. "Dead?"

"The Lord Chancellor suspects he was murdered."

"Was he?" I asked, my voice weak.

"It perplexes me, really," he said, as though he didn't hear my question. "It appeared he was killed by a blow to the chest with magic. But I know of no other magic user in the court aside from me. I was in my office when it happened meeting with the king."

"You think someone killed him with magic?" I clutched one hand into a fist, my nails digging into the palm.

"Yes. It won't be too difficult to find this person of ill repute. If there is another magic user here in court, then they will reveal themselves in time."

I thought of the crystal around my neck, how it had remained silent since that morning when a punch of magic hit Lord Desmond in the chest. I kept my face neutral, trying to remain as passive as possible. I disliked the earl, but I never wanted him dead.

"So, my daughter, it appears you will not have to marry him after all."

What an odd thing to say.

I had no reply as he rose and limped from the living area. Halfway to the dining salon, he paused and turned back.

"Oh, if you invited Aiden, I do hope you called him off. I'm afraid I'm not up to having visitors. I'll be having dinner in my room."

"He's not coming," I said, my voice hollow and thin.

Papa nodded and continued to his room, the door closing abruptly behind him.

All of this was so strange. He hadn't even noticed the tear in my sleeve as Aiden had almost the moment I arrived to speak to him. Papa seemed very distracted and out of sorts and I doubted it was merely because of the death of Lord Desmond. There was something else going on. Something he wasn't telling me. Perhaps something he was unable to tell me.

His work with the king must be taxing. Since we arrived and since he started working with him, he had grown more and more fatigued. Looking older than he did when we arrived. Whatever he was doing, it drained him of all energy.

Sophia bustled in as I sat there ruminating on everything that had happened that day.

"My lady, there has been some dreadful news," she said.

"I've heard," I said, not wishing to think about it another minute. "Papa told me."

She remained where she was, worry lining her features. "They say he was murdered. By someone with *magic*. That it was someone who was hired to kill him!"

My head snapped in her direction. "Where did you hear that?"

She flushed hot as she shifted from one foot to the other. "From the others..."

"The other servants?" I got to my feet and smoothed my sweating palms down my skirt. "It sounds like idle gossip to me."

She plucked a nonexistence thread from her sleeves and lowered her head. "Apologies, my lady. You're right. I shouldn't listen to the gossip."

I heaved a sigh as I moved to stand next to her, taking her arm in mine. "You know, it's hard not to listen to. And who knows, there could be some truth to it."

We walked through the dining salon. My stomach rumbled and it was then I realized I hadn't eaten all day.

"Oh, my lady, your sleeve is ripped. How did that happen?"

I cursed myself for not thinking to put her on the other side of me. Not that it mattered. She would have seen it before too long anyway.

"I was clumsy. I tripped. My sleeve caught on something as I fell and it ripped. It's nothing a needle and thread can't fix." I made it sound as though it wasn't anything to be worried about.

"Shall I help you change out of your dress?" she asked. "I can mend it for you tonight."

"I can manage. I have a bit of a headache. I'd like to lay down for a bit."

"Very well, my lady. Would you also like your dinner in your room?"

I hadn't considered that but since Papa was locked away for the night, I may as well be, too. I nodded. "Yes, please."

I released her and went on to my room, closing the door.

Truthfully, I wanted to burn the dress I wore because it would forever remind me of this horrible day and Lord Desmond's death. I wanted to stop thinking about him and everything. Everything, that was, except Aiden.

I sat on the side of my bed and toed off my shoes, then leaned back. My head throbbed at the temples. Exhaustion pounded through me from head to toe.

A moment later, a soft knock sounded on my door. Sophia poked her head in with a tray of covered dishes and a tea service. She placed the tray on the nearby dressing table and gave me a sideways glance.

"Are you certain you don't want help with your gown?" She eyed it, clearly concerned over the rip in the shoulder.

It did make sense for her to help me. Especially since I was unable to reach the laces on the back of the dress. I relented and nodded.

Moments later, I pulled on my dressing gown over my nightgown. I unplaited my hair and brushed out the wavy length. The crystal remained around my neck.

Sophia took my gown to mend and left me to eat and rest. She'd brought me slices of roasted chicken, bread, a variety of cheeses, sliced apples, and grapes. I didn't realize how ravenous I was until I had gobbled it all up, leaving nothing but crumbs behind. I poured a cup of tea and held the warm liquid between my hands as I perched on the bed staring at the wardrobe where the spell books and the scroll were hidden.

What was I going to do now?

I took a sip of tea, then put aside the cup on the nearby nightstand. On impulse, I went to the wardrobe and retrieved the scroll, running my thumb over the medallion. When it opened, I unrolled it.

The spell was still there as well as the drawing of the crystal. I examined it closely. It was an elongated shape, coming to a point on the bottom and a point on the top with smooth sides. Even the drawing showed the tiny stars inside. I wondered where to find the other half of the crystal and what had happened to split it in half.

Sitting on the floor by the wardrobe, I reached inside and pulled out one of the books. It was *Professor Quentin's Book of Magic*.

The title was embossed in gold across the front of the green leather-bound book. The pages were yellowed with age and smelled musty. I put aside the scroll and flipped through it, pausing every so often on a page here and there. There were spells written in a language I didn't understand. There were spells written in the common tongue. There were crude drawings of herbs and plants.

And then there was a drawing that made me stop cold.

It was a drawing of the crystal intact. Like the one in the scroll. Beneath the drawing in a scraggly handwriting were the words *Pendant of Sheylara.*

Next to the drawing, was a description in the same handwriting.

The pendant was mined from a cavern in the ancient world. The rare gemstone is halcionite and can no longer be found anywhere on the continent.

No one is quite sure how old it is, but the general assessment is that it is older than the time of the First King. It was made from a larger gemstone for his queen, Sheylara, by a powerful sorcerer. He pulled the very stars from the sky to imbue it with unspeakable powers. The pendant, it is said, destroyed the queen and nearly destroyed the kingdom.

I examined the crystal in my hand. If the gemstone was older than the time before the First King, then it must be several thousand years old. I swiped my thumb over the smooth surface on one side, the jagged on the other.

Now that I knew what to call it, what it was, I wondered if speaking the words of the spell was now a mistake. If it had unspeakable powers and destroyed the queen, then how could it not destroy me, too?

The text didn't explain how the pendant worked, only that it had power.

I closed the book and hid it once again in the bottom of the wardrobe along with the scroll. I padded back to the bed, still holding the pendant in one hand. The ribbon I used as a makeshift necklace was beginning to fray. I needed to find something more sturdy to use.

Fatigue hit me hard as I sank into the bed, still clutching the pendant. After the events of the day, I wasn't sure if I'd be able to sleep. But moments later, my eyes drifted closed and I was out.

CHAPTER SEVENTEEN

The next morning, I awoke with a start. I was curled on top of the bed covers with the pendant still clutched in my hand. I slipped it over my head, letting it hang in front of my nightgown.

I thought about the passage I found in the book about the pendant. I thought about how a powerful sorcerer gave it the power from the very stars overhead and wondered if that were true or merely a legend. Who was this sorcerer? Was he the king's royal sorcerer? Or someone else?

I really didn't need to have answers to these questions, but my curiosity was piqued.

Sophia hadn't awakened me, which made me wonder why. I slid off the edge of the bed and opened the door.

Her door was closed. Papa's door was open. I ventured into the hallway and glanced around, but the apartment appeared to be deserted. I wandered into the dining salon. The table was spotless. The highboard was empty.

The door to the apartment opened and Sophia entered. I started to hide the pendant, then stopped myself when I remembered she was already aware of it. She startled when she saw me with a little gasp. She carried a basket that emitted a wonderful smell of cinnamon.

"Good morning, my lady."

She placed the basket on the table and tossed off the linen covering. Nestled inside were slices of cinnamon raisin bread. She offered me a piece. I snatched up a slice and delighted to discover it was still warm.

"Been to the kitchens?" I asked.

"Yes." She flushed.

I tipped my head to the side as I peered at her. "What about being in the kitchen has you blushing?"

She tugged a piece of bread from the basket, then slid into one of the chairs. I sat opposite her. She had a dreamy look on her face, a small smile playing on her lips. One I had never seen before.

"You met someone," I said.

She nodded. "He's the baker's son. He also bakes." She motioned to the bread.

"It's delicious." I took another bite, savoring the spicy sweetness as the bread melted in my mouth.

"You don't mind?" she asked, looking at me through her lashes.

"Why would I mind?"

"Well, because...I don't want him to be a distraction."

I snorted. "A distraction? After what happened yesterday, I think we could all use one of those."

A faint smile flickered over her face, then was quickly replaced by a more somber look. "Your classes were canceled today because of what happened."

"Ah, I wondered why you didn't wake me."

"You looked exhausted yesterday. I thought I would let you sleep," she said.

I was touched. The truth was, I wasn't really exhausted until I climbed into the bed with the newfound knowledge of the pendant.

I didn't know what to say so instead I broke off another piece of bread and ate it.

"Where is Papa?" I asked finally.

"I heard him leave before dawn." She finished her bread and brushed the crumbs from her hands. "Shall I help you dress?"

I nodded, though I wasn't sure what I was going to do with my day. I certainly didn't want to stay in the apartment with nothing to do. I thought of Aiden and wondered if he was in Whitefell by now.

After Sophia helped me dress in my favorite blue satin gown, I headed out of the apartment to look for Kalen or Eliza. I found neither one of them.

Disappointment flooding me, I wandered through the great hall looking for them. There were a few groups of nobles clustered together. As I glanced around at the unfamiliar faces, a few cast sidelong glances at me. Discomfort flickered through me. And guilt. It was hard not to ignore the guilt.

In my haste to disappear from the great hall, I exited into a hallway and immediately got lost in the twisting and turning. I ended up at the end of a long hallway lined with torches. It led to a curving stone staircase. I paused at the foot of it and glanced up, trying to decide if I should follow it.

As I contemplated it, the pendant came alive with a short burst of a hum. As if it urged me to go on.

Placing one hand on the stone wall to keep my balance, I took the narrow steps one at a time and climbed up, up, up. A narrow slit in the stone gave me a view of the eastern lawn. I realized then I was climbing one of the towers in the east end of the castle. Likely forbidden, but now that I was halfway up, I didn't want to turn back. The staircase was narrow, the only light coming from the slits every few feet in the stone. At the top, there was a small landing and a door.

The arched door had heavy iron hinges. The handle was an iron ring.

The pendant hummed again. This time a little louder.

I glanced down to see a faint glow under my gown.

Did it want me to go inside?

I lifted the circular handle and gave the door a shove. It groaned and creaked as it opened a crack. It was heavier than I anticipated. I pushed it harder until it opened all the way.

Standing in the doorway, I peered inside the shadowy room, which was curved like the tower. Arched windows with pale stained glass lined one wall, letting the faint morning light filter inside. The other two curved walls hosted bookshelves from floor to ceiling full of books caked in dust. An old wooden desk sat in the middle with papers strewn about and a book left open, as if the owner had left with the intention of returning and yet had not. A tall vial with a cork in the top was next to the book. In the vial, shiny pearlescent beads. Cobwebs hung from the corners. Dust motes danced in the slash of colorful light coming from the windows.

I took a tentative step. The pendant glowed a bright pink under my gown. I pulled it out and held it aloft. The stars inside danced with reckless abandon. As though it was happy to be in this room.

Another tentative step and I glanced up. The ceiling was painted a dark blue with the constellations in copper. By the way the light reflected off them, they appeared to glow. As I peered up, I made out the Goddess of Life, the outline of the Southern Horn, the Sword of the First King.

The pendant continued to hum a happy little tune as it flickered to life beneath my bodice. I slipped it off from around my neck. Inside, the stars swayed in a gleeful little dance and the light pulsed in concert with the movements.

I smiled, running my thumb over the smooth crystal.

"It's almost as if you're happy," I whispered.

Upon hearing my words, it paused its dancing and then blinked. Once. Twice.

I sucked in a sharp breath as understanding dawned. My brows drew together. "You understand me, don't you?"

Blink. Blink.

"Two blinks for yes?" I asked.

Blink. Blink.

Awestruck, I gaped down at the tiny thing in my hand and marveled at it. Gooseflesh rose on the back of my neck. My heart picked up at a quicker pace. It...*understood* me.

"This is unbelievable." My voice was quiet in the expanse of the room.

Blink.

"One blink for no." I giggled. "I understand. It's not unbelievable to you because you understand me."

Blink. Blink.

I grinned. "Well, I wish you could tell me why I was drawn to this place." I waved my hand around the old room.

I moved around the end of the desk, peering down at the thick layer of dust along the top. The open book appeared to have writing in it. The ink had faded from years exposed to the elements. I blew across the pages, stirring up a cloud of dust and then wishing I hadn't. I sneezed.

Removing the dust didn't help. The ink was still faded. The words were hard to make out.

I bent closer to the book. Only a few words stood out to me.

Starry expanse. Timeless dream. Stars pure light.

"The words are faded," I said. "I cannot read them."

Blink. Blink.

I peered down at the pendant in my palm. "You want me to read them?"

Blink. Blink.

"How can I when the ink is faded?"

Blink. Blink.

This time a more urgent *blink, blink.*

"All right. I'll try."

There was no chair, so I bent closer to the book. The handwriting was that of a careful hand, of someone who wrote precise letters. Someone who was well educated, perhaps. Someone who wanted to make sure these words were not lost.

And yet, the words were faded on the paper to nothing more than a pale yellowish color. The pendant continued to blink over and over. I held it down to the page, as if the pink glow would illuminate the words for clarity.

The first line became clear.

"In the realm where magic weaves..."

Blink. Blink.

I glanced around the desk, looking for...something. I didn't know what. A magnifying glass, perhaps. I spied the drawer on the front of the desk in the center. I tried to pull it open, but it wouldn't budge. I placed the pendant beside the book to use both hands. Grasping the handle with both hands, I gave a mighty yank.

The drawer only came open a bit, but not enough to see inside of it.

Another yank. This time, I pulled so hard, the desk wobbled a bit toppling the vial with the pearlescent beads. The cork flew off and skittered across the open book. The beads scattered across the pages. When the morning light hit the beads, they lit up with a bright glow and then appeared to seep into the page.

I gasped, trying to wipe them away but it was no use. The beads were absorbed into the pages.

Next to the book, the pendant flashed and hummed with excitement. I peered down at the open book before me and saw, with surprise and shock, the words were much clearer on the page. As if the beads had illuminated the ink.

And so, I began to read aloud.

In the realm where magic weaves, □
By ancient words and mystic deeds, □
under the starry expanse above,□
I call upon the power of love.

From galaxies far and nebulas bright, □
Infuse this pendant with the light
and gather stardust's cosmic gleam,□
with the essence of a timeless dream.

In the velvet vastness of the cosmic sea,□
I cast my call with a heartfelt plea,□
To gather magic from realms afar,□
And bind it tightly to this pendant's star.

Pink as the dawn's first blushing light,□
Infuse this gem with powers bright,□
This pendant now holds astral fire,□
A conduit of magic that never tires.

This pendant holds magic's might,□
Empowered by the stars' pure light.
As I will it, so mote it be,□
In starlit grace, forever free.

I paused, holding my breath and waiting. When I spoke the words in the scroll, an intense power went through me. However, speaking these words appeared to make nothing happen.

The pendant went quiet. The light inside it faded. The humming stopped.

I picked it up. "It's a spell?"

Blink. Blink.

I dragged my lower lip through my teeth, recalling the passage I read in the book about the pendant. I closed my eyes, envisioning the page. The words played through my mind.

It was made for his queen, Sheylara, by a powerful sorcerer.

I sucked in a sharp breath as I looked up at the ceiling, thinking of the next sentence as dawning came. I stood in the very room of that sorcerer who created the pendant. It had to be. There was no other explanation. He must have loved the constellations and knew how to harness their starry power. What a gift he had.

"*He pulled the very stars from the sky to imbue it with unspeakable powers,*" I recited.

An excited *blink, blink.*

"This is the spell that made you?" I asked, feeling awkward with the phrasing. But it seemed the only sensible thing to ask.

Another excited *blink, blink.* And inside the pendant, the stars twirled.

"And that's why nothing happened. Because the spell has already been cast."

Blink. Blink.

Incredible. I righted the vial, placed the cork back on top as it was before it toppled over. I took a step back from the desk but something in the drawer caught my eye. I paused, peered down at it and saw something glittering there in the dusty, shadowy depths.

I pulled out a fine silver chain with tiny links and a small clasp. As soon as I did, the pendant lit up again.

"A chain for you?"

Blink. Blink.

Grinning, I removed the tattered ribbon and stuck it in my pocket. I slipped the end of the silver chain through the hole in the pendant and clasped it. Then slipped it back over my head. The length was perfect.

"That seems right now."

The pendant agreed.

"But you have to go back into hiding now."

Blink.

"Just for a little while," I amended. "No one can know about you. I worry what would happen if they found you."

A long pause, then *blink, blink.*

"Good. We best be going."

I tucked the pendant under my gown once more, then hurried out of the dusty room, closing the door behind me.

CHAPTER EIGHTEEN

I hurried down the winding steps, my hand trailing the stone wall to keep my balance. Dust caked my skirt and hands, but I didn't mind. There was a buoyancy in my walk as I trotted down the stone staircase, smiling with my discovery.

Not only was the pendant able to communicate with me, but I also uncovered the original spell that had created it.

At the end of the staircase, I headed back down the long hallway with the torches lining the wall. The only way to go was to the left and then I had a choice to make. Left or right? I wasn't sure which way would lead me back to the great hall because I was lost earlier.

I chose right, hoping it would lead me back. Instead, I ended up in another long hallway lined with more torches. But at the end of this hall, a door stood open. Light slashed into the hall from the room. Faint voices filtered out.

I should have turned back but didn't. I walked onward. As I approached the open door, I recognized the voice of the king. I paused, pressing my back against the cold, stone wall as I inched closer.

"You think we should send the boy home, then?" the king said.

"Yes, your majesty. Even if Prince Kalen was sent here as a guest, things could take a turn for the worse should Ashea go through with their plans."

I recognized the voice of the Lord Chancellor. This was the second time I managed to eavesdrop on one of their conversations.

"What do your spies tell you, Osmund?" the king asked.

I pressed a hand against my mouth to remain silent.

"News of Lord Desmond's death traveled to King Dameon. He knows he's lost his informant, but I do believe he will retaliate," he said.

There was a clink of glass.

"And Dal Breifna? What of them?"

"I haven't been able to determine if their leader is intent on moving forward. In fact, I haven't been able to determine *who* their leader is," the Lord Chancellor said. "The Dalmonii are a reclusive sort. The last mention of their High King was over a hundred years ago. I rather doubt he still lives."

"The last High King's seat was in Innahill and I intend to find out if it's still there. I sent one of my best to Whitefell yesterday," the king said, his voice firm.

Aiden. He was talking about Aiden.

"Whitefell is not a strategic outpost. Why there?"

"Because there are forces gathering near the border. If he can breach the woods, then he can find out if the High King is still in Innahill."

It sounded dangerous and suddenly I worried for Aiden's safety. The pendant buzzed with a ferocious vibration.

"'Tis a wild country, sire. The Wandering Wood holds many secrets. The highlands are treacherous—"

"It matters not," the king said, cutting him off. "If there is a threat there, we need to know sooner rather than later."

"Yes, of course, sire."

I inched away from the door, the pendant still buzzing. As if it understood what they were talking about. When I was far enough away, I picked up my skirts and hurried away hoping my footsteps didn't give away my presence. I had heard enough and I didn't want to get caught eavesdropping on the king and the Lord Chancellor. At the end of the hallway, I turned the other way, but I was still hopelessly lost. Another turn, another twist and finally I made my way back to the great hall.

There were courtiers and nobles roaming and lounging in the area. A woman caught my eye. Mostly because she wouldn't stop staring at me with her sharp, assessing gaze. I tried to ignore her as I made my way across the room with my heart in my throat.

But she wasn't going to allow me to get away. She unfolded her elegant body from the chair she sat in and headed directly for me with a swish of satin and silk skirts. Her scarlet gown hugged her round curves, pushing her ample bosom upward giving the world a peek at her cleavage. Her dark brown hair was piled high on her head in elaborate curls and pinned with a large peacock feather that curved over her updo.

When I failed to slow, she hurried and fell in step beside me.

"You must be the sorcerer's daughter. Violet, is it?" Her voice sounded familiar but I couldn't place it.

"What if I am?" I asked, defiant.

She placed a hand on my arm. "A moment, please."

I halted, gazing up into her deep brown eyes. "Who are you?"

"I'm Lady Bridgette."

She was the one Lord Desmond spoke to the night before I...well, the night before he died. The one who told him he was a drunken fool. The one who was supposed to marry him but he had called off their wedding.

I didn't know what to say to her, if anything, so I said nothing.

"I wanted to meet you," she said.

My brows drew together. "Why?"

"Because I wanted to see for myself what you have that I don't." Her gaze raked over me.

At the moment, I felt exposed. Beneath my gown, the pendant hummed a warning.

"You have youth and beauty, I see," she said and then dropped her arm. "I suppose that's why he wanted you rather than me."

A twinge of sadness crossed her face. And for a moment, a bit of guilt went through me. Guilt for killing Lord Desmond. Guilt for standing in between him and Lady Bridgette, though why I had no idea. I didn't even know she existed until that night when they stood on the lawn under my balcony and argued.

"And truthfully..." She paused, took a step closer to me and lowered her voice. "He was nothing but a drunk. You deserve better."

"Well," I said, finally finding my voice. "I don't think that matters so much now since he's dead."

I hadn't intended for my words to be callus and cold, but the moment they escaped my mouth she took a step back, shock rolling over her face before she managed to control it.

"I-I'm sorry," I managed. "I didn't mean for it to sound—"

"Exactly as it did," she interrupted, and then emitted a deep sigh. "I do not think there will be many who will mourn his loss save for those he owed money."

"Why are you telling me this?" I wanted to know.

She gave me a sad smile. "Perhaps because I wanted you to know you should be grateful you didn't marry him. And perhaps I merely wanted to have an up-close look at you to satisfy my curiosity."

I lifted a brow. "Your curiosity about me?" The pendant hummed against my skin, but a different sound this time. Something that sounded more like interest.

She tipped her head to one side, looking me over. I prayed she didn't hear the pendant's humming. "Yes. He was determined to marry you because he had his eye on Blackthorne. He no doubt had planned a way to get it. It's good you escaped marriage to him, my dear."

I knew he wanted Blackthorne. Papa had promised it to him when we married, but even Lord Desmond understood the estate would pass to my firstborn son. Unless he intended to do away with me, first. Then it would pass to my husband, but only if my father was deceased.

When the thought struck me, an icy prick of horror stabbed me. He was determined to marry me—no matter how he had to do it. Ruining my reputation was an excellent way for him to force me. If he killed the previous Royal Sorcerer, then he surely had plans to kill Papa, allowing me to inherit the estates. And then...

I shut off the thought. The guilt I had for killing Lord Desmond dissipated quickly.

She patted me on the shoulder and then walked away, a sinking feeling in the pit of my stomach. Her words didn't ease my conscious. Not one bit. And I wasn't entirely sure why she wanted to speak to me and tell me those things. I already had an understanding Lord Desmond was a despicable person. Having her confirm it gave me no comfort.

All it did was make me glad he was dead. That and glad Blackthorne was no longer within his reach.

I needed to find solace and returning to our apartment wasn't it. I made my way through the great hall and out into the castle gardens where Aiden and I had met that first night after banquet. In the daylight, things looked much different.

Spring was definitely in the air. Dark storm clouds gathered in the western sky. Despite the warming temperatures, there was still a chill on the breeze. One that was difficult to ignore. I found my way into the rose gardens, the sweet scent nearly overwhelming yet invigorating.

I paused in the middle of the walkway and glanced around to see if anyone was about. The gardens were strangely empty this time of day, which was fine by me. I pulled out the pendant, holding the slight weight of it in my hand and wondering, again, where the other half was.

I also wondered if I would be able to perform that levitation spell I'd tried so hard to do prior to leaving Blackthorne. I spied a rock in one of the flower beds. Closing my eyes and holding out my hand, I imagined lifting the rock and placing it in my open palm.

In my other palm, the pendant sensed magic and emitted a low hum. I whispered the words to the levitation spell. The pendant hummed louder. Cracking open one eye, I saw the rock rising higher and higher into the air, then traveling toward my open palm and dropping down into it.

I gasped.

I had done it.

I'd managed to make the levitation spell work.

"So, you *can* do magic!"

Kalen's voice surprised me. The rock fell from my palm as I jumped and spun around to face him. He walked up the pathway with a grin on his face as he approached.

"Well, I never said I couldn't," I said, remembering the first day we met.

As I looked at him then, I realized he didn't appear to be a prince of Ashea. With his easy smile and his casual gait, he seemed like any other person our age.

"You didn't but I wanted to give you a hard time anyway. Why didn't you show us that day?"

Then his gaze caught sight of the pendant resting in my other hand. I was so stunned by his sudden appearance I hadn't thought to hide it.

"Ooo, what's that?" He leaned down to get a closer look at it. "I've never seen anything like that before. Are there stars inside it?"

"Yes," I said. "It's a pendant." Not a very detailed explanation. By the disappointed look on his face, it was clear he wanted something more.

"A *magic* pendant?" he asked.

"I'm not sure." I closed my hand around it and then stuck it back under my dress. "I'm really not supposed to have it. I hope you won't tell anyone."

"Tell anyone what?" Eliza called.

I suppressed an inward groan. She and her brother hurried down the path. Kalen spun to face them with a bright look on his face.

"Does she have a secret?" Eliza asked, her gaze glinting with amusement and interest.

Kalen cut me an apologetic glance. "I saw Violet levitate a rock. She didn't want anyone else to see."

"Oh, you can levitate a rock?" Eliza clapped her hands together with excitement. "Show us some magic."

Jacob remained mute at her side, but he eyed me with interest.

"I'm really not very good at it," I said. "I was...practicing." I cursed myself for attempting a spell in the open gardens. "My father doesn't like me to perform magic."

"Why not?" Eliza propped her hands on her hips as if the thought of a sorcerer's daughter not doing magic was shocking.

"He has other aspirations for me," I said, floundering for a response.

"Show us something, please," Eliza begged.

Feeling pressured, I glanced around looking for another rock to levitate. I decided the one I dropped would work well enough. Closing my eyes and holding out my hand again, I whispered the words. The pendant under my gown hummed again, as though helping. When I heard a little gasp, I opened my eyes to see the rock rose into the air and then landed in my palm.

Eliza clapped. Jacob's eyes were wide as he stared at me. Then he pointed at my throat.

Or what I thought was my throat. I glanced down to see the pendant glowing under the material of my gown.

"What's that?" Eliza asked. "There's something glowing under your dress."

I managed a smile. "It's nothing. Just a trinket."

"It's more than a trinket, I think," she pressed and stepped closer.

"Show her, Violet," Kalen urged.

"I really shouldn't..." My weak voice trailed off.

"Kalen's seen it?" She glanced from him to me and back to him. Then she stuck out her bottom lip in a spectacular pout.

"Quite by accident," he admitted.

Eliza's gaze landed back on me as she continued to pout. I understood that probably worked on her father and that's how she got her way. At least the pendant had stopped glowing and humming.

"It's just a necklace I found," I said. "Sometimes it glows."

She inched closer. "Can I see it? *Please*? Jacob wants to see it, too. Don't you, Jacob?"

He nodded as he moved to stand next to his sister. Kalen was on the other side of her. They surrounded me in a semi-circle, hiding me from others who may be wandering the gardens.

"If you promise not to tell anyone I have it," I said, "I'll show you."

"We promise," she said with an emphatic nod.

I wasn't worried so much about Jacob since he was mostly mute. It was Eliza I didn't fully trust. Or Kalen. He was, after all, a Prince of Ashea.

I pulled the pendant out from under the neckline of my gown. With the long chain, it was able to rest in the palm of my hand. Both Jacob and Eliza bent to get a closer look at it.

"Oh, it's lovely. There are stars inside it!" she exclaimed. "It looks like half is missing."

"It is," I affirmed.

She lifted her gaze back to mine, her eyes narrowing in thought. She tapped a finger against her chin as she took a few steps, stopped, turned and came back to stand in front of me.

"I believe I've seen something like this before," she said.

My brows lifted in shock. "You have? Where?"

"In my father's office," she said. "Yes, I believe it was just like this. Perhaps it's the other half?"

Excitement skipped through me. If the other half was here in the castle, then perhaps that's why the pendant was so active. Perhaps *it* knew the other half was here and that's why it led me to the old sorcerer's chamber. It suspected the other half would be there. But instead, there was nothing more than the chain and the spell that had created the pendant.

She hooked her arm in mine then, mischief lighting her eyes. "Let's go find it."

I tugged my arm out of hers. "Oh, no. I couldn't. I can't." I quickly tucked it back under my dress.

"If it's a magical pendant, and it's missing its other half, shouldn't you have it to put it back together? To make it fully powerful, I mean," she reasoned.

"No," I said quickly. "I shouldn't even have it at all."

"My father is meeting with the king and the High Council. Your father should be meeting with them, too. I know neither of them will be in their office. We should go look," she insisted.

"No," I said, shaking my head. "What if we're caught?"

"We won't be." She grinned, hooking her arm in mine again. "What do you think, Kalen? Should we see if the other half is in my father's office?"

He shifted from one foot to the other, discomfort flickering over his face. "I don't know…"

Frustrated, she turned to her brother. "Jacob? What do you think?"

He gave an emphatic shake of his head.

"Oh, you are no fun. None of you!"

She released my arm and turned away, stalking back up the walkway. Jacob gave me a shrug and fell in step behind her. But as she hurried away, I watched my only chance at getting the other half of the pendant leaving. And, despite my misgivings, I found myself calling out to her to wait.

Eliza halted in the middle of the path and turned back, question on her face.

"Are you sure this is a good idea?" Kalen asked.

"No," I said. "But neither was taking the pendant in the first place."

I took a deep breath. I was going to find the other half.

CHAPTER NINETEEN

I was a ball of nervous energy as we walked back into the castle and through the great hall. I tried very hard to keep my nerves under control, but even the pendant around my neck and tucked into my dress sensed something for it started emitting hums in short, static bursts. Thankfully, it did not glow again.

The office of the Lord Chancellor was just behind the great throne room and, as it turned out, right next door to Papa's spellcasting room. As we approached the Lord Chancellor's office, Papa was coming out of his office closing the door behind him. When he saw us, he halted, his eyes wide with question.

"What's this?" he asked. His gaze alighted on each of us and halted on me.

"I'm taking them to see my father's office," Eliza said, as if nothing was amiss.

She flashed a broad smile. If she was startled by his sudden appearance, she didn't show it. I admired the way she walked up to the Lord Chancellor's office door and pushed it open as if it was something she did every day. As if she wasn't trespassing with theft of the other half of the pendant on her mind.

"He's not in there," Papa called.

"It's ok." Eliza gave him a wave. "We'll only be a minute. My father won't mind."

But Papa continued to stand in the hallway and look after us. My gut churned with the sudden worry that he knew we were up to no good. I flashed him a smile as I followed Eliza, Jacob, and Kalen into the office, leaving the door open behind us.

"See? This is where my father helps the king make all the important decisions," Eliza said, her voice loud enough for anyone loitering in the hall to hear.

I took a step back into the doorway, leaning back to see if Papa was still there but he had moved on. I blew out a shaking breath, thankful he had decided we were up to nothing but a tour.

"Is he gone?" she whispered.

"Yes." I stepped back into the room.

Eliza moved behind the massive desk, her gaze roving over the top of it. "I was sure I saw it here one day."

I took in the rest of the room. A massive bookshelf was on one side. Behind the desk, a credenza with a large decanter holding an amber liquid and several crystal glasses. Quills and inkpots were scattered across the top of it along with several sheets of parchment. The desk itself was spotless.

Eliza pulled open drawer after drawer, but to no avail. When she closed the last drawer, she frowned, looking down at the desk with displeasure.

"It's not here," she said.

I didn't want to admit I was crestfallen that the other half of the pendant was still missing. It was hard to accept it wasn't here. Even the pendant under my gown hummed forlornly.

"It's all right, Eliza," I said. "It was worth a try anyway."

She rounded the desk and joined us in the center of the room, glancing around at the high ceilings as though looking for hidden compartments.

"Perhaps he moved it," Kalen suggested. "Or gave it to someone else."

Eliza's eyes went wide. "Yes, of course. He wouldn't keep a *magical* object, would he? He would give it to your father. Right, Violet?"

There was a mischievous glint in her eyes. My stomach clenched into a tight knot. I knew exactly where she was headed. "We're not going in my father's office."

"Just a peek won't hurt."

She hurried past me and out the door. I cut a glance at Kalen who gave me an apologetic grin. We hurried out after Eliza. Jacob took his time leaving the Lord Chancellor's office and took up a spot in the hallway, leaning against the wall. As though he wanted no part of her snooping.

Neither did I.

Eliza was at my father's office door, turning the handle with a creak.

"I don't think we should be doing this," I said, my voice wavering.

By now, she had the door cracked open and stuck her head inside. She paused there a long moment, then turned to face me. Her eyes were wide.

"The place is a disaster. Is your father disorganized?"

"I suppose he could be," I said, thinking back to the night I stole the pendant.

His spellcasting room back home wasn't exactly tidy. I recalled the desk was scattered with items. Parchments. Scrolls. Books. Quills and inkpots. Even the bookshelves were crammed with books. The cubby with the scrolls stuffed full.

"I don't think we'll find anything in there without going inside." She opened the door wider and stepped inside the doorway.

My heart rammed hard against my chest as I followed. The pendant reacted with a quick succession of excited buzzing, as if urging me on. But deep down, standing in Papa's office without his knowledge was wrong and I understood that deep within my bones.

"Let's see what's here." She headed for the desk.

"No!" I said on a gasp. I reached for her, grabbing her hand before she could take another step. She spun back to face me. "Please, don't."

"You don't want to find it?" she asked and gave me her pout.

"Not today. I-I don't think we should be in here. My father would be unhappy."

"Leave it, Eliza." Kalen stepped next to me, motioning for her to come out of the room. "We don't want Violet to get into trouble."

She frowned. Her shoulders slumped as if defeated. She muttered agreement and then stepped around me to the door. The pendant, however, continued to give off an excited buzz. I ignored it as I stepped out the door. She closed it behind me. My heart slowed, but my hands still shook from the very idea she was willing to rummage through his things.

I wasn't even allowed to do that at Blackthorne.

"You spoiled all my fun, Kalen," she said with her pout.

"And you're trouble, Eliza." He said it with a smile.

Jacob, however, remained mute leaning against the wall. His eyes watching us and taking everything in. I wondered why he didn't talk much. Was it a childhood trauma? Or was it simply he didn't like to talk?

"Well, what shall we do with the rest of the day?" Eliza hooked her arm into Kalen's, then, and started back up the hallway.

I followed behind them. To my surprise, Jacob fell in step beside me. He gave me a sideways glance and a tiny smile as if he understood my plight with my father's office. Then it was clear to me. He was silent because his sister was so domineering and overbearing.

"Perhaps we should play a game of Bowls," Kalen suggested.

"Yes! Let's! What do you say, Violet?"

I didn't exactly have anything else to do. "Yes, let's." Then I gave Jacob a glance. "What do you think, Jacob?"

Surprise etched his face when I asked him. He wasn't sure what to do. Eliza gave us both a shocked glance over her shoulder as she and Kalen continued to walk.

"He'll play," she said.

"I'd like for him to answer," I said, giving him a secret wink.

His cheeks flushed hot and bright as he peered down at his feet. And then he said, ever so softly, "I'd like to if you'll be my partner, Violet."

Eliza gasped. "But *I'm* always your partner."

I gave him a genuine smile. "I'd like that."

We both shared a grin enjoying the fact we both shocked Eliza to the marrow of her bones.

"Traitor," she muttered.

"Ah, now, you'll like being my partner," Kalen said, giving her a little nudge. "It'll be fun."

"I suppose. But Jacob and I are always partners."

"Not today," I said brightly.

Kalen snickered. Even Jacob gave a little half-hearted laugh. By the time we exited the castle and headed to the north lawn, though, the weather turned. The storm clouds I saw earlier were now directly over us. Thunder rumbled across the sky followed by a flash of lightning.

"I guess that means no Bowls," Eliza said with a frown.

Truthfully, I was relieved. I wasn't much interested in playing any lawn games. As we stood there in the late afternoon, it started to sprinkle.

Back inside, we decided to go our separate ways. Kalen returned to his apartment. Eliza dragged her brother off to some other activity in the library. And I was left alone again wondering what to do with my time.

Inspiration struck and I headed through the castle to Mr. Martin's classroom, hoping to find him there. The door was ajar, allowing me to peek inside. He sat behind the desk, making notes on a paper with his head bowed and quill scratching along the parchment. I gave a quiet knock on the door.

His head popped up. When he saw me, he gave me a quizzical look then waved me inside.

"Hello, Violet. Please come in. I'm afraid I don't quite know what to do with myself since classes have been canceled the remainder of the week."

"The rest of the week?" I asked. I hadn't heard that.

"Yes. By the king's command. What can I do for you?"

"I have a question about the poem, *The First King*. I was wondering ..." I twisted my hands together, hoping the pendant remained quiet.

"Yes?" he asked, his bushy brows raised.

"Well, I was wondering why the poem didn't mention his queen?"

"Ah, a wonderful question, indeed." Gone was the stern teacher. His face lit up at the mention of the queen. A broad smile broke out on his face. He motioned to one of the student's chairs in front of his desk. "Will you sit?"

I took the seat nearest the desk. "The poem doesn't mention it."

"You are correct. It doesn't. Do you know why?"

I shook my head.

"Because he did not take a wife until he had conquered this land." He sat back in his chair, looking well pleased with his answer.

"What can you tell me about his queen, then?" I asked.

"I'm afraid not much." He leaned forward, lacing his fingers together and placing them on top of the desk. "There are not many mentions of her in the history books."

"But we know he had a son, because he betrayed his father and took over as king."

"Ah, yes. He did. Some say it was because he and his father were always at odds. His son grew to be strong and mighty. He planned his coup for years, they say. Having secret meetings and building his own army so that he could take over when the time came," he said.

"But why would he want to overthrow his father?" I asked.

"Hard to say," he said, running a hand over his smooth chin. "There are different accounts. Some that say his mother—the queen, of course—had something to do with it. Others say the son thought his father was too old to continue to sit the throne and that Rovaria needed a stronger, younger king to lead them into a new era. War was brewing, you see. War with Dal Breifna."

This was news to me. I didn't know much about the second era with the Second King because most of the legends and poems and songs were written about the First King. He was a celebrated hero.

"You don't know anything about the first queen?" I tried to get more information about her. All I knew about her was her name—Sheylara—and that the pendant was named after her and made for her.

He took a deep breath, expelled it. "This is only a myth," he began, "and so I don't know if there is any truth to it. Some believe the First Queen came from Dal Breifna. She was a princess, daughter of the

Dalmonii High King. That was why Dal Breifna wanted to war with Rovaria. They wanted their princess back."

"But she didn't want to go back?" I asked.

"The First King stole her from her kingdom, offered her riches and jewels if she would stay. He had a pendant made specially for her by the royal jeweler and presented it to her as a wedding gift," Mr. Martin replied. "So, she stayed and she produced a son for him. And she loved him, so the myth says."

But what if she didn't love him? What if she had the sorcerer turn the pendant into one of magic? One she intended to use as a weapon? And what if she was the one who usurped her husband, not their son?

"Did Dal Breifna go to war with Rovaria?" I asked.

In all my studies, I hadn't heard this part of the history of Rovaria, though I should have. It would have been a turning point for the First King.

"Indeed, they did. They arrived by the cover of night through the Wandering Woods. They burned villages. For every day the High King's demands went unanswered for the return of his daughter, another village would burn. The First King refused to allow these atrocities to continue. He rode out to the battlefield with his army of nearly five thousand strong to face the High King of Dal Breifna.

"But the First King refused the High King's demands. And so, they fought in the shadow of the Wandering Woods until the High King had no choice but to retreat back to his highlands."

When he lapsed into silence, I wondered what happened next. The High King retreated and then what? The First King returned to his castle and his queen with the triumph over her father?

"I've never read this story," I said.

"It's not in any history book," he said. "At least, none that I've found."

"How did you find it then?"

"The royal librarian of the time recorded it, illuminating it with intricate drawings and painting the pictures with vibrant colors. The book, though, was badly damaged in a fire of the royal library that destroyed nearly all the books." He paused, opened the desk drawer and brought out a tome wrapped in cloth. He placed it on the desk and removed the covering with a gentle hand. "I found this in an abandoned monastery a few years ago hidden away."

The leatherbound book looked as though it had been charred. Some of the edges of the pages were singed and black. There was a corner missing. The binding looked as though it would crumble at any moment when opened. Carefully, Mr. Martin opened the cover. It cracked with its advanced age.

I rose to my full height and leaned over the desk to get a better look. A musty scent wafted up from the page yellowed with age. In a careful, fluid hand were the words *The Battle for the Queen*. I stared at it for a long moment in wonder.

"I should return it to the royal library, I suppose," he said, his words thoughtful. "But I didn't have the heart to do it."

"No one knows you have it," I guessed.

He shook his head. "No. Not even the current royal librarian. It is a piece of Rovarian history no one wants to acknowledge. Even a few pages are missing from the back of the book." He closed it and then, very slowly, turned the book over and opened the back cover. There were clearly pages that had been torn out. Their jagged pieces stuck out from the spine.

"Why would someone rip out pages?" I asked.

"Likely there was some history written there that someone did not want others to know."

My immediate thought was the queen. Why would she, though? Unless she had something to hide.

Mr. Martin closed the book and wrapped it back in the cloth, returning it to the drawer.

"What happened to the queen?"

"She's lost to the pages of history after the war with Dal Breifna. One can only assume she lived a long life."

Something told me different. The pendant gave a tiny buzz underneath my gown but didn't light up. And I wondered if it had heard the story and understood what Mr. Martin told me.

"Thank you for telling me," I said. "And for sharing the book."

"You seem very interested in the queen. Why is that?" he asked.

I thought of the book hidden in my wardrobe and the information it held about the pendant. I resisted the urge to reach up and touch it. I gave him a small smile.

"It occurred to me that while we study the epic poem of *The First King*, there is nothing written about his queen. Only that his son overthrew him for the throne and became the Second King."

He smiled. "Perhaps I will find a way to add her to our discussions in class."

"Thank you for your time, Mr. Martin," I said.

"I'm glad you stopped by." He rose from the desk and walked me to the door. "Classes will resume next week, I believe. I'll see you then?"

I nodded. "Yes, of course."

I bid him farewell and headed back into the hallway as he closed the door behind me. I paused there, thinking about everything he'd told me and the singed book he showed me. There was a missing piece of information, though. About the son overthrowing his father for his throne. Where was the queen at that time?

I vowed to find out, even though I had no idea how.

CHAPTER TWENTY

Since it was getting late in the day, I headed back to our apartment. Upon entering, I halted in surprise to see almost every surface covered in gowns. Some of them were mine. A couple I didn't recognize. Sophia emerged from the bed chamber with another armload and let them fall in a heap on one of the chairs.

"Sophia, what are you doing?"

She spun around to face me with wide eyes, surprised to see me there. Then she giggled, pressing a hand against her chest.

"You scared me!"

I moved deeper into the living area, eyeing all the gowns. One that caught my eye was a deep blue with silver threads woven throughout. I lifted it from the chair and held it up.

"Isn't that magnificent?" she said on a breath.

"Where did this come from? Why are there gowns scattered all over the place?"

"You haven't heard?" she asked.

I shook my head.

"The king has announced a grand ball!" She clapped her hands as though it was the best news she'd heard all day.

"A ball?"

"Yes. It's in two nights! I thought we should see what you had to wear." She waved her hand across the mound of silk, satin, velvet, and taffeta. "As I was pulling them out to look at them, there was a knock on the door."

"But this isn't mine." I peered down at the blue gown in my hands. I hadn't seen it before, so I knew it didn't belong to me.

"Yes, I'm getting to that. This one arrived for you. And this one." She pointed to a delicate ball gown in seafoam green silk nestled in a large box with the lid askew.

I moved to stand next to her, looking down at the gown in the box. "Where did they come from?"

"One of the king's messengers brought them. There was no note for that one." She pointed to the green one in the box. "Or for that one. It didn't even come in a box." The way she said it made it sound as though it was scandalous.

I fingered the delicate pale green silk. "It's lovely."

"Oh, it is. I was hoping you would take it out. I long to see it." She gave a wistful sigh.

I handed her the blue gown. She took it, draping it over one arm as I pushed the lid off. The green silk gown looked like a dream of layers inside that box. There were dainty rosettes sewed to the front of it. I lifted it up, pulling it away from the box and then holding it up to my shoulders so the length of it would fall to the floor. The skirt was intricate layers that fell in what appeared to be waves. Swishing the skirt, I watched as they moved back and forth in a dreamy languid undulation of material.

Both of us sighed in admiration, then exchanged a grin and giggled.

"It's the loveliest gown I've ever seen," she said, sounding wistful.

I glanced back at the box and saw a small note folded in half with a red wax seal. I reached down and picked it up.

Sophia's eyes went wide. "There *was* a note. Who is it from?"

Shrugging, I handed her the gown and then popped the nondescript seal and unfolded the letter to reveal a perfect penmanship. I read it aloud.

Please accept this gift for the grand ball and save a dance for me.

It wasn't signed.

"Is it from Aiden?" she asked, her eyes wide with wonder.

"I can't think of anyone else who would send it," I said. "But why? Why would he send me a ballgown?"

"Because he likes you?" she suggested with a grin.

"But we hardly know each other."

And yet, he covered for me with Lord Desmond and even helped dispose of the body. He never told the king or Papa it was me who had killed him with magic. We parted with no promises between us. It was hard to believe that was only yesterday.

Still, I was baffled by the gift.

"Which one will you pick?" Sophia asked, glancing between the blue and the green gowns.

Reaching out, I ran my fingers down the soft silk of the green gown.

"I'd pick that one, too," she said on a rough whisper.

We grinned at each other.

"It's very lovely," I said and she nodded agreement. "All right. Green it is. We better get these put away before Papa comes home."

I helped her pick up the mounds of gowns and return them to my room where the wardrobe stood open. The stolen spell books were still nestled in the bottom under the discarded shawl. Not that I didn't expect them to be, but it was still a relief to know they were there and still hidden.

As we hung up the last gown, the door to the apartment opened and closed with a slight bang. Both of us hurried out to see Papa lumbering to one of the chairs by the dormant hearth. He fell into it, his head in his hand as he slumped over looking exhausted.

"Sophia, will you please ring for dinner? And some tea."

"Yes, of course." She scurried out of the room and hurried to do as I asked.

With a tentative step, I approached Papa and perched on the chair opposite him, waiting to see if he would acknowledge me. He didn't. And so, I sat in silence as I waited, leaning back into the cushions of the chair. Finally, he heaved a great sigh and lifted his head, his bleary eyes meeting mine.

He hadn't looked so haggard earlier that day when I saw him in the hallway at the Lord Chancelor's office. Had the meeting of the High Council been that stressful?

A weak smile played on his lips. "Ah, Violet. I didn't hear you come in."

"It's all right, Papa," I said. "You look exhausted. Are you well?"

"The king is most demanding," he said. "As is the High Council. Some of the things they are asking me to do..." He paused, his words trailing off. He shook his head, rubbing his forehead between his thumb and forefinger.

I thought of the Lord Chancellor sitting on the High Council, making demands of my father. Of Eliza and how she wanted to snoop through Papa's office without nary a qualm. And I could only think of one question to ask him.

"What are they asking you to do?"

Contemplation crossed his face as he looked at me, clearly trying to decide if he should answer or not. Before he decided, Sophia returned with a tea cart, wheeling it into the small living area. He glanced her way, relief evident on his tired face. Sophia paused long enough to pour a cup of tea and hand it to him. She knew he liked it without cream or sugar. The steam rose up from the tawny liquid as he held the cup close to his face, closing his eyes, and enjoying the warmth and the scent. She then handed me a cup.

"Thank you, Sophia," I said.

"The servants will arrive shortly with dinner." She dipped a curtsy, then scurried off to the dining salon to prepare the table.

I took a sip of tea and waited to see if Papa would answer my question. He continued to hold his tea cup with a look on his face I was unable to read.

"Violet," he said, my name slow and with purpose on his lips. "I want you to make me a promise."

"A promise?"

"If things become unsettled here in the capital, I want you to take Sophia and return to Blackthorne."

He sounded so serious, so tired, so worried that my insides jangled with the first hint of fear. Even the pendant gave a silent hum of concern.

"What do you mean, unsettled? Is something happening?"

I had an inkling of an idea, of course, since my conversation with Aiden. He'd told me about Lord Desmond being the spy for both Ashea and Dal Breifna, that they both wanted to invade Rovaria for different reasons, but invade nonetheless. That he was off to Whitefell to find out what was happening on the border.

"I cannot tell you more than that." He set aside his tea cup, then, and reached for me. I placed one hand in his. He squeezed my fingers tight. "If things become dangerous for you here, I want you to go. Promise me."

My gut clenched. I squeezed his hand back. "I promise, Papa."

He seemed satisfied with my answer and released my hand, picking up his cup once more. He sipped his tea and we fell into silence for a long moment.

Then I said, "The king is having a grand ball."

This seemed to make his shoulders slump. "Yes, I know. I tried to talk him out of it. But he seems to think it would be a good distraction, especially after the death of Lord Desmond."

I swallowed hard, a lump forming at the base of my throat as guilt swept through me once again. The pendant sensed it and gave a short burst of a hum. Papa shot me a sideways glance of question as if he, too, heard it. I prayed the pendant would be silent. Then, he gave me a forced smile.

"Though I suppose he's right. It *will* be a good distraction. Are you looking forward to it?" he asked.

The image of the seafoam silk dress came to mind as well as a feeling of warmth and delight cascading through me. The thought of Aiden sending it to me, anonymously, and asking for a dance made the butterflies in my stomach erupt.

"Yes, I suppose I am."

"Good."

He finished his tea and set aside his cup just as a knock on the door sounded. Sophia hurried to answer it and let in the servants with our dinner. They made quick work of setting it up and then scurried out quickly, none of them making eye contact with any of us.

Papa got to his feet, unfolding his tall, tired body with slow movements. "Shall we?"

I nodded and carried my cup with me as we made our way to the dining salon. I had a feeling, though, something terrible was brewing.

That night, I was unable to sleep. I laid in my bed staring at the ceiling with the pendant heavy against my chest. Since I retired, it had been humming almost nonstop. When I removed it and stuck it under my pillow, it hummed louder and started to glow. It had been nothing but a nuisance. Now, I held it clasped in my hand, trying to make it stop.

It wouldn't.

My body vibrated with a sort of nervous energy I had not felt before. As if some deep-seated urgency murmured under my skin. An inherent demand thrummed there, desperate for me to get out of bed.

I opened my palm and stared down at the pendant emitting pale pink light and watching the stars swirl inside as if in a maelstrom of its own making. It continued to emit a low-level hum.

"What is it? Why won't you stop?"

Naturally, it was unable to answer. I heaved a sigh and flung off the bedclothes, placing my bare feet on the cold floor. It seemed happy with this movement and gave me two blinks for a yes.

"You want me up, I see. Whatever for? It's the middle of the night."

It blinked twice again.

I slipped the pendant over my neck, then reached for my dressing gown and pulled it on. The humming increased and the flashing turned to an excited response.

"All right, then. Let's see if I can figure out what you're up to," I said to the pendant.

I opened my bed chamber door a crack. Outside my room, it was dark and silent. Papa's door was closed as was Sophia's. They were both likely sleeping.

Pulling the door open all the way, I stepped into the hallway between our rooms and paused. The cool draft in the apartment made me shiver and gooseflesh rise on my legs and arms. The pendant, it seemed, liked this progress. I crept through the apartment, past the dining salon and into the living area. When I approached the balcony door, it blinked once for *no*.

Turning, I started for the apartment doors and halted.

Blink. Blink.

A yes, then. It wanted me to leave the apartment.

"I shouldn't," I whispered. "What if Papa woke and found me gone? He'd be mad with worry."

Blink. Blink.

This time a more urgent *yes*.

"At least let me light a candle."

I crept toward the door, taking slow steps in my bare feet and pausing at the entry table. I found a candle in the drawer and lit it.

Once the candle was lit, I turned to look behind me to see if anyone had awoken. No sounds or movement. Taking a deep breath, I pulled open the door and slipped out into the hall, pulling the door closed behind me with a soft snick.

But which way did the pendant want me to go? Back to the sorcerer's room I found? Or somewhere else?

Creeping through the hallway in my nightgown seemed odd. I glanced down at the pendant. It blinked twice again for yes.

I started though the hallway, heading to the great hall. There was no one about except for a few guards who appeared to be snoozing at their posts. Some help they were if something happened. I slipped past them unnoticed. When I headed for the hallway behind the great hall, the pendant blinked once. No.

"No?" I whispered.

One blink.

"Then where?"

Holding the candle aloft, I glanced around the silent room at the empty tables and chairs. Not a soul stirred. Shadows flickered over the walls, giving them an ominous glow.

Earlier that day, Eliza had taken us to her father's office, which was next to Papa's. Perhaps that was where the pendant wanted me to go? I headed in that direction. It gave me two encouraging blinks.

My heart throbbed a wicked beat as I slipped through the hallways, undetected. Unnoticed. And before too long, I stood before Papa's office door. It blinked twice in a frantic, encouraging beat.

"You are going to get me into trouble for this," I said to the pendant.

It blinked once. No.

"Yes, you are."

Even as I said it, I reached for the door handle and tried to twist it. Locked.

"It's locked. Now what?" I asked, as if the pendant had an answer.

It appeared to understand me, though. It began to glow brighter and brighter and brighter until a spark slashed out from it and hit the keyhole. There was an audible click and then the door popped open a crack.

I stifled a gasp.

"You...you did that."

Blink. Blink.

I wasn't sure what worried me most. The fact that it understood me or the fact that it just did magic to unlock Papa's door for me. I pressed my hand against the aged wood and gave a slight push, opening it far enough for me to enter and then pushed it closed behind me.

The room was dark save for the moonlight slashing through the one gothic window on the far side of the wall. The night was clear, but the bright moon blocked out all the stars around it. Holding the candle in my shivering hand, I moved deeper into the room as my eyes adjusted to the darkness.

His office was disorderly with scroll, books, parchments, inkwells and quills scattered on top of the desk. I moved closer to the desk and peered down at one of the parchments on the top. His handwriting was shaky, messy and not like his normal self at all. I leaned closer. A drop of wax dripped and landed directly on the parchment in front of me. I swore under my breath and straightened the candle immediately but the damage had been done. He would know someone had been in his office.

But the words written on the parchment turned my blood cold.

Spell of Unmaking

He had written a spell stanza after the title but it was too dark for me to read his scrawl. The pendant, though, glowed brightly emitting pink light into the room. I was able to see the written words more clearly but some of the handwriting was different—not Papa's at all. Someone else's yet the final two stanzas were written in his hand.

By the fire's blaze and spirits' might,□
I stand before the dark of night,

With courage strong and facing our foe,□
Their strength shall not deal a final deathblow.

Let this protect my honored liege
From a wild and hostile siege

Now, with this verse of ancient speech,□
The universe begins to breach,

By words, the threads of fate unwind,□
Unmake the enemy, leave naught behind.

I stared at the words, my heart in my throat, and suddenly everything was clear. The king and the High Council asked Papa to create a spell to defeat Ashea and Dal Breifna. Papa's words rang back to me.

Some of the things they are asking me to do...

They wanted him to use magic to defeat them. Something he would find to be against the very fiber of his morals. He told me, even from a very young age, magic was to be revered, honored, and never to use it with high emotions.

I thought of the bandit he'd killed on the road. But that was in self-defense. Did that make it so different from the Spell of Unmaking, which was more like genocide? Did he have any qualms about destroying an entire race of peoples? Didn't he realize he was on the verge of using dark magic?

Perhaps he did and that was why he appeared to have aged tenfold since our arrival. Because he was forced to write a spell that would destroy King Jeffrey's enemies.

A shiver of fear went through me.

The pendant continued to glow. The stars inside danced and swirled as if restless.

Not knowing what I was looking for or why I was here, I needed to get out as quickly as possible. Seeing the Spell of Unmaking utterly terrified me and I understood so much about why Papa looked exhausted these last few days.

Things were becoming more and more clear. He was brought here after the death of the previous Royal Sorcerer no doubt to complete the work he began.

I turned to flee the room, to go back to our apartment, to my bed chamber where I would climb in bed and try to forget I ever saw such a horrible spell.

But as I turned to the door, the pendant began making a frantic pulse, lighting up the room in flicking light. The closer I got to the door, the more frantic it became.

Something was in this room that it wanted me to see or find.

I spun back to the desk, holding the pendant now in my palm.

"What? What is it you want me to see? To know?" I demanded. "I cannot understand you."

And then something caught my attention. A book on the shelf nearby was outlined in a pale pink glow. My heart rammed hard in my chest as I peered at the shelf, wondering how a book could be outlined in the same pink glow as my pendant.

I moved closer to the shelf, my eyes fixed on the glowing book. As I walked to the bookshelf, I blew out the candle, then placed it on the floor at my feet. I pulled the book off the shelf but realized with some dismay it wasn't the book glowing.

It was coming from a tiny crack behind the book.

A secret compartment?

I lifted the pendant higher to illuminate the empty space on the shelf. There was, indeed, what appeared to be a tiny slit in the back of the shelf. It went up and across, but other books obstructed it. I moved them off the shelf in a frenzy and moments later, there was a glowing outline of what appeared to be a small door.

"Is this it?" I whispered.

Blink. Blink.

With shaking fingers, I felt the back of the shelf trying to find a way to open it. There was a small latch on one side in the shape of a circle. I slipped my finger inside it and gave a weak yank. It came open.

Pink light flooded the room, blinding me. It took several moments for my eyes to adjust. The pendant in my hand was just as bright as the one in the nook. I released a shuddering breath as I reached inside.

My fingers landed on a cool piece of crystal. Crystal that resembled that of the pendant in my other hand. I wrapped my hand around it, shielding the light as I pulled it from the nook. When I opened my hand, I stared down at a jagged piece of crystal.

A jagged piece of crystal that matched the other side of the broken pendant.

"Oh, gods," I whispered. "*This* is what you wanted me to find. The other half. You sensed it was here earlier today, didn't you?"

Blink. Blink.

I stood rooted in place as I looked from the pendant to the missing piece and back again. Unsure what would happen when I placed the pieces back together, I thought it would be wise to close the secret compartment and return the books to the shelf. I slipped the second piece of the crystal into my dressing gown pocket, and then put everything back the way it was.

"You have to stop glowing now," I said. "I can't have you doing that when I return to my room."

It dimmed to nothing but a faint flow, but the one in my pocket was still bright, illuminating the fabric of my dressing gown.

"And the other one, too," I said.

A long pause and then it dimmed, too.

I snatched up the candle at my feet but had no way to light it. I would have to find my way back to my room in the dark.

CHAPTER TWENTY-ONE

The storm blew through that afternoon with gale force winds, leaving behind chilly evening air. So chilly, in fact, gooseflesh skipped up my bare legs under my nightgown and down my arms. At least, I liked to think it was the drafty castle that made me feel that way and not the fact I held both halves of the pendant.

I slipped by the guards unnoticed, thank the gods, and made it back to the door of our apartment without detection. A few more steps and I would be back in my bed chamber. Giving the door a gentle push, it creaked open as I stepped inside. And froze, straining my ears for any sound that might alert someone to my presence.

Darkness and silence.

Blowing out a breath, I closed and latched the door, then hurried to my bed chamber. Once I was safely ensconced inside, I snuggled under the bed covers still in my dressing gown. The chill had taken up residence in my bones. I burrowed deep under the quilt, pulling it to my chin.

For a long moment, I laid there trembling under the covers staring at the ceiling. I took a deep breath, then another to still my rapidly beating heart.

There was some urgent need pressing into me to put the pieces together. It was the same urgent need that drove me out of my bed, through the castle, and to Papa's office.

The pendant around my neck gave me an emphatic buzz.

I shivered with both trepidation and anticipation. As much as I wanted to put the two halves together, it terrified me. What would happen to the pendant then? It already sensed my emotions and was able to somewhat communicate with me. If both halves were finally put back together, then what?

There was only one way to find out.

I reached into the pocket of my dressing gown and pulled out the other half. The moment I did, the pendant in my hand pulsed a bright pink glow. The second half, the one I'd stolen from my father's office, also pulsed in concert with the pendant. I took a moment to examine it. Like the pendant, it, too, had a swarm of stars inside it dancing and swirling and gyrating. As though it sensed its other half and wanted nothing more than to join its sibling.

Every muscle within me quivered. My stomach fluttered. Even my breathing was erratic. My palms had broken into a hot-cold sweat.

Laying on my back wasn't the way to do this. I dropped both crystals into my lap and then fluffed the pillows behind me, then scooted to a sitting position. The crystals were both glowing. I took the pendant in one hand and the piece of the crystal in the other. Glancing between the two of them, I lined up the jagged pieces on both sides. Taking a deep breath, I slowly pushed them together.

There was an audible *snap* as though they had been waiting for years to come together. As soon as the pieces were joined, it hissed. The two pieces fused together, resembling the picture on the spell scroll. The glow from the now solid pendant was so bright, I had to squint against the light. Which made my anxiety increase. The last thing I needed was for Papa or Sophia to come bursting in here wondering what was going on.

The light burned bright and then slowed to a faint pulse. Inside, the stars from each half swirled and danced. There was an obvious seam where the two pieces had come together.

Then, suddenly, it flashed a brilliant white light. Something delightful cascaded over me, sending warm tingles through me from head to toe. I gripped the pendant in my hand, leaning heavily into the pillows and then I was blissfully and finally asleep.

A wild knocking on my door pulled me out of a deep, dreamless sleep. I pried my eyes open as Sophia burst into the room, excitement lining her face. I realized I still had the pendant in my hand and quickly shoved it under the covers, holding it at my side.

"My lady!" she gasped. "You're still asleep?"

I yawned, not bothering to cover my mouth in a most unladylike fashion. "What time is it?"

"It's afternoon." She sounded exasperated as she put her hands on her hips.

I sat bolt upright. "Afternoon?"

In my exhaustion from roaming the castle halls at night, I overslept. I dragged my fingers through my tangled locks. Sophia remained rooted in place at my bedside staring at me, her eyes wide and round as she looked me over.

"What happened to your hand?" she asked. "And why are you sleeping in your dressing gown?"

I glanced down to see my hand appeared to sparkle. I released the pendant in my hand under the covers to shove up the sleeve of my dressing gown. My arms also sparkled. As though a brilliant sheen had been painted along my arm. Shoving the quilt aside, I hurried to the bathing chamber to peer at myself in the mirror.

The sheen of light was on my face, down my neck, on my upper chest. All of my skin everywhere.

"By the gods," Sophia said on a low breath. "You look as though you're glowing."

I spun to face her, a frantic desperation pumping through me. My heart throbbed a mad tattoo in my throat. How would I ever explain this to Papa? I couldn't even explain it to Sophia.

"I-I don't know what happened to me."

She looked me over with a critical eye. "What did you do, Violet?"

Her tone sounded accusatory which did nothing but irritate me. "Don't take that tone with me. I am the *queen*."

The moment the words escaped me, I gasped and covered my mouth with my hands, stumbling backward against the washbasin. Sophia's brows drew together in question, her eyes still wide trying to understand me.

"What did you say?" she said on a shocked, rough whisper.

"Nothing. I said *nothing*. Sophia..." I stepped toward her, reached for her hands, and grasped them in mine. "You have to help me. No one can see me like this. Especially not Papa."

She frowned as she looked me over. "How do you...what do you want me to do?"

"Find makeup or something that we can paint over my skin to hide..." I released her, glancing down at my hands, moving them back and forth under the light and watching as my skin glittered with what appeared to be—

Oh, gods.

Stars. There were stars imbedded in my skin and, much to my horror, my skin appeared to be a pale pink.

The pendant.

The pendant did this to me.

But how? Why?

Dizziness swept through me. My knees went weak. Sophia hurried to me, pulling me to her slight frame to keep me on my feet.

"My lady!"

She walked me to the bed. My stomach churned acid as I perched on the edge. She scurried back into the bathing chamber and returned with a damp rag. She pressed it against my forehead.

"Gods, you're burning up. Perhaps you shouldn't go to the grand ball."

I caught her hand in mine and held it. "No. I have to go. I mean, I *want* to go. I'm going."

She gave me an odd look as though I'd lost my head. Perhaps I had. My chest tightened, the pain of it lancing through me. I took the cool rag from her and swiped it over my face, but it did nothing to assuage the panic pounding through me.

"I'm fine." I tried to convince her as much as myself.

"Well, then, I better see what I can find to cover your skin."

"Yes." I nodded agreement.

She left me sitting on the edge of the bed. I heard the apartment door bang closed as she departed. I sat ramrod straight on the bed, straining my ears to listen for any movement or sound. Then I rose and stepped to my open doorway and peered out. Papa's bedroom door was wide open. I tiptoed to it and peered inside.

It was perhaps the first time I looked inside his bed chamber. The bedclothes were rumpled in the center of the bed as though he had tossed and turned and finally gave up and rose. The wardrobe stood open a crack. Several pairs of his shoes were tossed haphazardly on the floor. The chair opposite the bed held a mound of clothes. Tunics, pants, overcoats, a cloak.

I stepped back into my room, turning to the bed. There, in the center of it, the pendant emitted its faint pink light, making a small glowing circle under the material. With my heart pounding, I stepped to the bed and flung back the blankets.

The pendant rested on the mattress, pulsing its pink light and the stars swirling inside in a happy dance. I wanted to reach for it, but I was terrified. Terrified of what it would continue to do to me if I held it once again.

But the power...oh, the power it emitted called to me. Without realizing what I was doing, my hand reached for it. My fingers wrapped around the chain. I lifted it up to my neck, slipped it over my head and felt the weight of it against my chest. A calming sensation went over me as my eyes fluttered closed.

A faint magical nudging had me wrap my hand around the crystal and then suddenly I was someone else. Somewhere else. I was trapped inside the pendant. Terror blasted through me with such violence I stumbled backward, tripping over my own feet.

And then all was calm again. Calm and cool and commanding. But I sensed an overbearing presence pressing against my subconscious.

Oh, Violet. There you are, my darling. I have waited so long for you.

The voice—a soothing, whisper-soft female voice—fluttered through my mind.

We were connected, the pendant and I, in a way I didn't understand.

"Who are you?" I whispered.

She chuckled a sort of evil laugh that echoed through my mind. *Who am I? Why, my sweet girl, you know who I am.*

I shook my head hard, trying to release my hold on the pendant but couldn't. She—whoever she was—held me in her thrall.

"I-I don't."

Ah, but you do. You simply don't remember yet. For fifteen long years, I have waited for you to return to me. Longer than that have I waited for someone like you. Someone with the power to help me.

A choking gasp lodged in my throat.

"Help you do what?" I asked.

There was no response, but the crushing presence was still lingering in the back of my mind. I didn't understand what that meant or why. I released the pendant. It thumped against my chest and continued to glow. The stars continued to swirl.

I paced the small confines of my bedchamber, my heart an erratic beat and my nerves on the edge of a knife. I sensed *her* inside my head, longing for freedom from the confines of her imprisonment.

To help me escape.

The words whispered through my mind in her voice.

To help her escape. From the pendant?

There is magic in you. Powerful, enchanting, masterful magic.

I shook my head. "That's not true. I have no magic. Papa—"

He wants you to think that. He wants you as far from him and his sorcery as possible. Because he knows if you discover your own magic deep within you, you will destroy him.

I pressed cold, shaking fingers against my lips. "I don't believe you."

It is the truth. You came close to destroying him once. To releasing me from my prison. But you don't remember.

"You lie!" My voice was a high-pitched shout.

Return to the sorcerer's tower. Look for his journal. Then you will understand.

I stifled a gasp. The sorcerer's tower was where I found the chain. Where there were stars painted on the ceiling. In desperation, I shoved off the dressing gown, flung off the nightgown and went to my wardrobe, looking for a garment I could dress in without help. I found a gown in pale yellow with long sleeves and a high neck. It would cover most of my sparkling skin and would have to do. With frenzied movements, my hands shaking the entire time, I quickly pulled it on and slipped my feet into leather slippers. In the bathing chamber, I ran a comb through my unruly hair and then tied it back at the nape with a ribbon.

I needed to get out of the apartment before Sophia returned, so I had to hurry. I dashed for the door and slipped out.

With my heart in my throat, I hurried to the sorcerer's tower, hoping for answers.

CHAPTER TWENTY-TWO

No one paid me any mind as I hurried through the grand hall, passing courtiers and nobles. Kalen caught sight of me and gave a wave, but I ignored him, pretending I never saw him as I hurried into the hallway behind the grand hall.

I paused, sucking in deep breaths as I glanced left and then right. I heard Kalen calling my name. With a gasp, I took off down the right hallway, hoping it was the way to the sorcerer's tower. When I was sure I was far enough away from him, I paused and pulled the pendant out from under my gown. I held it in my hand, peering down at it.

"I think you led me there before. Now I need your help to get there again."

It flashed twice.

Go to the end of the hallway. Turn left. Follow it to the bottom of the stairs.

Her voice drifted through my mind. I followed her instructions and found myself at the bottom of the curving stairs. I took them up and up and up, my legs burning from exertion until I was at the top staring at the door.

I pushed it open and stepped inside. Dusty footprints were along the floor. Mine from the first time I came here. The air felt different. As though it were heavy, almost oppressive. Not at all like it was before. I closed the door, scanning the room looking for something that looked like a journal. At the desk, I tugged hard on the drawer to pull it open. As before, it took several tries before it came open.

Nothing except dust was inside. I leaned down to look into the back of the drawer and saw the edge of what appeared to be a book. Reaching into the back of the drawer, my fingers brushed over a leather book. I pulled it out and held it, gazing down at the plain brown cover cracked with age.

Placing it on top of the spell book, I gently opened the cover. It crinkled with its age. The pages were yellowed with faded ink, yet still readable. The first page simply had the word *Journal* scrawled across it in a careful, perfect hand.

I glanced down at the pendant around my neck. It was strangely quiet. No blinking, no glowing, no stars swirling.

I turned the page. The second one was an account of a journey northward through the Shattered Desert. The Shattered Desert was part of Ashea, in the northern end of the kingdom.

The description continued with details of how the sand dunes shifted colors in the fading light of day. From a pale brown and to a shimmering pink. The author wrote that he—at least I assumed he—paused to take a vial of the fine sands that looked to be shaped like tiny stars. When the sun dipped below the horizon, he made camp for the night with his makeshift tent.

When the sun is gone, the heat of the day is also gone and the cooling desert night is upon me. The hot, arid air quickly turns cold. Overhead, the stars appear to be nothing more than small twinkling diamonds in a sea of inky black. Almost as though a mirror of the dunes below me. As I write this, I shiver in the chilly desert breeze. There are faint sounds of unseen animals nearby. Sounds I have never heard before. I began my trek from the port city of Kharan. I have only come across two settlements, neither of which could offer me a mount. And so, I continue on foot northward through the Shattered Desert toward fresher, greener land. It cannot come soon enough.

I glanced around the room, hoping to spy the vial with the tiny grains of sand shaped like stars. Alas, it was not to be found on a cursory glance.

I flipped past several more pages of traveling until at last I came to one titled *The King in the North*.

I paused here and read the next few paragraphs to discover that the King in the North the author referred to was actually the First King.

The King in the North arrived by the light of the full moon on a wicked sea. From where, no one knows. He seemed to have walked out of the surf of the Fallrood Sea with the tide and his army at this back to invade and claim the kingdom as his own. He proclaimed himself the First King of Rovaria and then turned his eye westward to the wild country.

More boring description. Pages and pages of a battle with the country to the west—Dal Breifna. But as I read, I recalled what Mr. Martin said about the First Queen.

She was a princess, daughter of the Dalmonii High King. That is why Dal Breifna wanted to war with Rovaria. They wanted their princess back.

As I read, though, there was no mention of the Dalmonii princess. At some point in the text, the author referred to himself as the Royal Sorcerer and Lord Chancellor to the First King.

Another page and I froze, staring down at the name I recognized. *Sheylara, the First Queen.*

I recalled the words from Professor Quentin's book about the pendant being made for the queen by a powerful sorcerer. I suspected the author of this journal *was* that sorcerer. The next passage confirmed that.

The king sent his men across the continent to fight for his cause and to show his might. To conquer the lands as the one true king. To make those in the outer reaches of the country bend the knee to him. But the desert kingdom refused to bend and, since there was nothing for the taking there, the king allowed them their independence, content to let them be in their arid lands.

One knight returned with a large gemstone he mined from a cavern on the eastern continent, but he was so delirious with thirst and hunger and fatigue, he could not recall where he found it or even how he had managed to return to the capital.

The king was enamored with the gemstone as was the queen. He bid me make a pendant for her to show his love for her and so, I did. I commissioned it from the royal jeweler, then finished it with a touch of magic.

The queen has eyes that remind me of starlight on a moonless night. Her beauty is unrivaled by any other in the kingdom. My love for her burns bright and hot, like a candle flame in the dead of night. Illuminating a perfect circle and chasing away the shadows.

Aye, that's the truth of it. I love her. And yet, she does not love me. And so, I made the pendant for her and poured all my love and hate, envy and possessiveness into the pendant. For when she wears it, it will make her feel all these things and more. If I cannot have her, neither shall the king.

A cold sensation skittered up my arms as I stared at the words. The first sorcerer, the Lord Chancellor, the man the First King trusted, enchanted the pendant for the queen *because she did not love him back.*

"Did it destroy you?" I asked, gazing down at the pendant.

It responded with one blink. No.

"Then it controlled you?"

Blink, blink.

Ah, so the pendant controlled her. It hummed a little vibration I didn't understand. The light pulsed, as if trying to give me a signal.

"There's more, isn't there?"

Blink, blink.

But what? The pendant controlled her. If it controlled her, then the magic inside it must be very powerful. I looked back at the book and read aloud, "*If I cannot have her, neither shall the king.*"

Blink, blink.

I sucked in a sharp breath.

"If it controlled you, and it didn't destroy you, then...are *you* the First Queen?"

Blink, blink.

Oh, gods.

My heart nearly stopped as I stared down at the pendant, the stars swirling around and around. I had so many questions. First and foremost, how did the pendant become the First Queen, Sheylara? Or, perhaps the better question was how did the First Queen become trapped *inside* the pendant?

I turned my attention back to the journal and flipped to the next page but it was blank. All the subsequent pages were blank. There was only one reason I could think of that the author would stop writing in the journal. My stomach churned acid as I glanced down at the pendant, remembering the woman's voice slipping through my mind, telling me I would help her.

I shivered.

The journal, however, did not answer the question of how it—she—knew I was powerful. Powerful, enchanting, masterful magic she said.

"Are you trapped inside the pendant?" I asked, looking down at the object.

Very clever of you. Yes, I am.

"The sorcerer did it to you, didn't he?"

Because I did not love him back, she said. *He cursed the pendant so that when I put it on, I would feel all the emotions he had while cursing it. And when I refused him, the spell he created also cursed me. I have lived inside this crystal since that day.*

And, after a thousand years of being trapped, she wanted to be free again.

"You know who I am," I said, the realization finally hitting me.

Blink, blink.

"How?" I demanded. "How do you know who I am? How do you know I'm powerful?"

I will show you. Grasp the pendant in your hand and close your eyes.

I hesitated. A sense of fright bloomed through me as I peered down at the faintly glowing pendant. She must have sensed my reluctance, for her voice filtered through my mind again.

If you wish to know the truth, do it.

I lifted my hand, wrapped my fingers around the pendant and closed my eyes. It warmed and hummed and glowed. The light from it seeped between my fingers.

A vision exploded into my head of my father, when he much younger. He was in a garden surrounded by white and yellow flowers sitting on a blanket spread on the soft grass. There was a woman with him and a child. The woman I had never seen before. The child looked to be about two years old dressed in a pale pink gown with a matching ribbon in her dark hair. She sat on the blanket next to the woman playing with a rag doll. The woman kissed the girl on the forehead and then smiled up at Papa, who knelt next to them both.

"I have a gift for you, love," he said.

"A gift?" Her green eyes—eyes that were much like my own—lit with joy.

I understood, then. This was my mother and the child was me. My breath hitched. A strangled sob escaped.

Keep watching, my darling, Sheylara said.

Papa reached into his pocket and pulled out a blue velvet bag. He handed it to her. She took out a blue pendant on a silver chain. It glinted in the afternoon light as she gasped surprise and slipped it around her neck.

"Oh, Simon, it's beautiful."

"Do you like it, my love?"

"I love it." She lifted up on her knees to kiss him on the cheek.

He grinned and it was the only time I had seen Papa look so happy, so serene, so at peace. He reached into his other pocket. "I have one for Violet, too."

He held a pink velvet bag in his outstretched hand. My mother took it, opened it, and pulled out a pink pendant on a silver chain. I pressed a cold hand over my mouth when I realized it was the pendant I now held.

My father had the pendant when I was a child? How did he acquire it?

"She's a bit young for something so grand, isn't she?"

"It's the perfect gift for her," Papa said.

He took it from my mother and slipped it around my neck. Me, being the child I was, dropped the doll and took it in my small hands, holding it.

"Where did you get it?" she asked.

"From a merchant in the Port of Dunfail."

Neither one of them saw as I picked up the pendant and held it, putting it in my mouth to taste it. I pulled it back, a frown on my face, then held it up to the sunlight. It shimmered and hummed in my hands and something glinted inside it—the stars, I guessed. I emitted a small sound, not exactly a word, and then the pendant lit up, bright and hot.

"Simon?" my mother asked.

He tried to reach for it, to take it back, but I wouldn't release it.

"Violet, let me have it."

It was as though I was unable to release it. My mother tried to pry it from my hands but I managed to get to my feet and teeter away.

"Simon, do something." There was a hint of panic in her voice.

Papa reached for me again, but I stumbled back away from him on my stubby little legs. As though something controlled me. The pendant glowed brighter and brighter, pulsing a wicked beat as the stars inside swirled and swirled and swirled. I said a word from the child version of me, a word I didn't know and then suddenly a flash of light shot out from the pendant. The force of it knocked me off my feet. I landed on my back, hitting the back of my head on the ground, and started to wail.

Papa shouted something incoherent. I rolled to my side, still crying, and pushed back up to my feet. My mother was on the ground, her eyes open but not seeing. A charred place in the center of her chest. I had released the pendant. It was broken in two, the pieces on the ground next to me.

Papa cradled her in his arms, holding her lifeless body against his chest and sobbing. His leg was bent at an odd angle, blood seeping through his pants around a charred spot.

In the present, I released the pendant and stumbled backward, silent tears rolling down my cheeks, sobs clogged in my throat.

"You killed her!"

No, you did, my darling.

I shook my head hard. "No, no, no. I didn't mean to do it. I was a child!"

You did. I told you there was a power inside you. Even at the age of two, you understood it. You sensed it. You used it. Your father understood it, too. That was why he cursed you, why he stripped you of your magic. Why he was determined to keep you from using magic.

A sob hitched in my throat. The tears wouldn't stop.

"Why did you do it?" I still refused to believe I was the one who had killed her.

You have untapped, raw magic, my darling. I need it—you—to escape this prison. I tried to escape that day, but I failed. I will not fail again.

I believed her.

I jerked the pendant off my neck, squeezing it in my hand to silence it. To silence her. I was nothing but a conduit for her escape, a way to get what she wanted most.

And yet, my father had lied to me all my life. He had never told me the truth of what happened to my mother. I needed answers. The pendant continued to glow and hum. I stuck it in my pocket.

Ignoring it, I burst out of the sorcerer's room, leaving it behind to find my father.

CHAPTER TWENTY-THREE

I ran down the curved stairs, my shoes slipping. With my heart ramming hard in my chest, I managed to stay on my feet but the fear of tumbling down the remaining stone steps was very real. I paused there long enough to calm myself enough to continue.

At the bottom, I turned down the hallway, my vision blurred with the truth of it all. I had one destination in mind—Papa's sorcery room. He would be there this time of day. He would be working.

I stumbled through the great hall, into the fray of nobles, shoving past them without looking, without seeing. I thought I heard my name from a familiar voice but I refused to stop to see who it was. Kalen or Sophia. It mattered not.

When I arrived at his office, I burst into the room without knocking. He sat at his messy desk, writing something as the king stood beside him, peering over his shoulder. Startled, his head snapped up. Even the king gave me a wide-eyed look.

"Violet?" Slowly Papa came to his feet, question and concern on his face.

I pulled the pendant out of my pocket, clutching the glowing thing in my fist. The creases of my fingers were lit up in pink light. The silver chain dangled from my palm in a haphazard way.

"Why have you never told me the truth?" I demanded, my voice ragged with tears.

King Jeffrey gaped at me and then glanced at Papa. "Simon?"

"Apologies, your majesty." He came around the desk, toward me, as if to console me.

I put up my other hand to stop him. "Don't come any closer, you liar."

"Violet!" My name was a reprimand, his tone laced with anger and his face pinched with fury and embarrassment. "What is the meaning of this? What's happened to you? What do you have in your hand?"

Holding out my hand, I unfolded my fingers one by one so he could see. So, he would know the truth of what I had. His angry glare went from my face to the pendant in my palm. His eyes went wide and round and then his face paled as he stumbled back a step or two, bumping against the edge of the desk. He pressed a hand against his heart.

"Where did you get that?" he asked, his words a roughened whisper.

Silence descended between us as I remained mute. We stared each other down in a sort of enraged fury. The king, however, had the good sense to move toward the door, skirting around me as though I had the plague.

"I, ah, will see myself out."

The door clicked closed behind him. I continued to stand there, holding the pendant, staring at my father as tears streamed down my face.

"You *lied* to me," I said at last.

"Where did you get that, Violet? I demand to know—"

"You demand *nothing* of me," I snapped. "And you know very well where I found it. Half was in your spellcasting room at home. I found the other half here hidden in this very room."

"That's impossible," he scoffed. "You..." He paused, then corrected himself. "It was destroyed."

"By me when I killed my mother," I said.

He pressed his lips together in a thin line as he swallowed hard. Guilt swept over his features for a brief moment before he controlled his expression. He looked away, unable to meet my gaze and it was all I needed to confirm the horrible, deadly truth.

"It's true, isn't it?" I demanded.

"Yes," he said, the word ice.

I clenched my fist around the pendant again and held it down by my side. "You don't deny it, then. That I killed Mama."

"That *atrocity* killed your mother, Violet. Not you."

"Yet you punished me anyway," I said, the heat of my words spilling out. "You stripped me of my magic. You cursed me to live a life without it. And *you never told me the truth*."

He held his hands up as if in surrender. "I did what I thought was best for you. Your magic is—"

"You mean *was*," I interrupted.

"No, it's still there. It's a riotous, unruly force deep inside you I have never seen before. Nor had your mother. She, too, had magic. She, too, was powerful. But not like you, Violet. Even when you were little, you exhibited magic the likes I had never seen before."

I remained silent, waiting for him to continue, to tell me what he meant by that. He raked a hand through his dark hair, fluffing the top of it into an unruly mess.

"We lived in a small cottage near the Port of Dunfail. On the wharf, there were fortune tellers, scribes who would write you a poem for a few coppers, and merchants who sold their wares. Your mother loved to visit the colorful booths and watch the ships come into port. She liked listening to them sing their sea shanties as they made anchor and dropped their sails. There were many merchants who came from the other continents to peddle their wares."

He paused and began to pace the confines of the office in front of his desk.

"One day while we visited, there was a fortune teller. An old woman who had a curved back and was hunched over. Her hands were long, slender, and gnarled. She had a hook nose, missing, yellow teeth, eyes black as the night, and wore a faded red cloak over her threadbare clothes. I remember her distinctly because of the way she spoke to us—*her*," he corrected.

"My mother?" I asked.

He nodded. "She said, 'Come closer, dearie, and let me tell your fortune.'" He stopped pacing long enough to shudder, as though the memory held something sinister. "I urged her not to but she was drawn to her. She carried you on her hip. You couldn't have been more than a year old at the time.

"Her black eyes flickered from you to her, a wicked smile on her face. I urged her to come away, but she shrugged me off. She wanted to hear what the old woman had to say.

"She said, 'I see great power deep inside the babe. Great, wild, un-tamed power. Be warned, dearie, she will be your undoing.' Your mother was at once unsettled. She hurried away from the booth. I will never forget the look on her face. She was terrified. The old woman called after her, demanding payment or she would curse her. I tossed her several gold coins. She seemed satisfied with that."

He paused again, leaning against the edge of his desk. Fatigue lined his face. He seemed older than he was only days ago. Likely the stress of writing the Spell of Unmaking for the king. And here I was adding to his troubles, but I deserved an answer. I deserved the truth.

"What does this have to do with the pendant?" I asked.

"It was the same day I bought it. That—" he nodded to it clutched in my hand, "and one for your mother. After she spoke to the fortune teller, she lost interest in the wharf, but I still had business there. She sat at a sidewalk café while I took care of it. On my return to her, I saw the merchant selling the crystals. That one, in particular, caught my eye."

"Why did you give me this pendant?" I shook it at him in my fist.

"I didn't know what it was. I thought it was a mere trinket. I didn't realize it was enchanted. Or that it had the ability to destroy. Not until that day. When your mother died, I was bereft in a sea of mourning. I feared the pendant had done something to you, and so I did the only thing I thought was right.

"I picked up the pieces and hid them away until I could properly dispose of them. I sent one of the servants with one half. I told her to cast it into the sea."

But she didn't. Somehow, the pendant found its way back to Bell-brooke, back to where it was created.

"Then I got word my father died and so I packed us up and moved to Blackthorne to inherit the estate. And, truly, I wanted to leave the port behind."

I understood why he left that house near the port. He didn't want any memories of the place where my mother died. Where I had killed her.

"And you kept the other half," I guessed.

"Only because I worried it had done something dreadful to you. I thought the other half was gone forever. I hid away the half I kept."

"But it was in your spellcasting room, on your desk. I saw it there."

He stared at me long and hard and I realized I confessed to my crime.

"So, you took it," he said, anger glinting in his eyes. "You were specifically told not to enter that room."

I deflected by changing the subject. "You cursed me. You removed my magic."

He shook his head. "I did no such thing. I merely suppressed it." He took a step toward me but I backed away. "Violet, please. Give me the pendant. It's too dangerous."

I pressed my fist against my chest and backed away. "No. It's mine."

"Violet—"

"I will not!"

Good, my darling. Keep the pendant close. You are more powerful than he is and he fears that about you.

I ignored her voice in my head and said to my father, "It belonged to me once. I intend to keep it."

To prove it to him, I placed the pendant over my head, letting it hang around my neck. It glowed. The stars swirled. There was a magical sense to it—to me—that gave me a sort of comfort I'd never felt before. And I liked it.

Worry lines creased his face. "Please, Violet."

"You will cease writing the Spell of Unmaking," I said then.

But it didn't sound like my voice. It sounded like *hers* and there was nothing I could do to stop it. My knowledge was her knowledge. She understood he intended to wipe out her people.

His eyes widened. "How do you know about that?"

"I know many things. I know you are planning to use it against King Jeffrey's enemies when he goes to war. I know you intend to destroy them with magic, which we both know wielding dark magic is forbidden."

Guilt swept over his features before he managed to control it. He understood what was asked of him and yet he continued to write the Spell of Unmaking. He continued to go along with King Jeffrey's evil plans to destroy the Dalmonii and the Asheans.

"How could you?" I asked.

He clenched his jaw so tight, the muscles flexed along the edge. Then his eyes narrowed with suspicion. "Who are you really? You are not my daughter."

It was an attempt to deflect my question, to not answer because he knew I was right.

"Oh, I am. I am very much your daughter. But I have the power of the pendant within me now. You cannot stop it. You cannot control it." I knew she was controlling me. She was making me say these things. I was unable to stop her as her force grew deep inside me, as she pushed away the real me and took over. "The Dalmonii will come and when they do, I will be ready."

With that, I spun on my heel and left his office.

"Violet, wait—"

As soon as the door closed behind me, she released me from her spell. I sagged against the door, as though the breath was knocked out of me, my heart pounding an erratic beat. My stomach clenched into a tight knot.

What had I done? Had I ruined my relationship with my father? All because of *her*.

The truth will set you free, my darling, she whispered in my mind.

"Shut up!" I pressed my hands against the side of my head as it throbbed.

I ran from his office.

CHAPTER TWENTY-FOUR

Blinded by my anger, I ran through the great hall, ignoring everything and everyone. I didn't know where I was going or what to do in light of the new information I had about my mother, the pendant, and my father. Part of me wanted to rip off the pendant and cast it into the sea. The other urged me to keep it. What worried me the most was sensing the queen's presence pressing into my mind. As though she and I had merged upon the reunion of the two halves of the pendant. I didn't want to lose myself.

The truth with set you free.

Her words burned through me. I still had unanswered questions. Did her son really overthrow his father for the throne? Did the First Queen know that happened? Or was she trapped inside the pendant by then?

I exited the castle into the afternoon air that was crisp and bright. I saw the stable and immediately headed there, thinking of Peppermint. Perhaps a ride would help calm my nerves.

Entering the stable with the familiar scent of straw, leather, and animal instantly calmed me. As though he sensed my presence, Peppermint stuck his head out his stall and snorted a greeting. I grinned as I approached him and placed my forehead against his patting the side of his nose.

"I've missed you, too," I whispered.

He nuzzled my neck.

"I should have visited you sooner, but I've been busy."

Truthfully, I hadn't thought of my dear horse since we arrived. Everything had happened so fast. The last few days were a blur. Even now, the pendant gave off a hum and emitted a faint glow.

Movement in the stable caught my attention and I lifted my head. One of the stable hands, a boy not much younger than me, approached with a faint smile on his dirty face.

"Pardon me, my lady. Would you like me to saddle your horse for you?" he asked.

I glanced down at the gown I wore. It wasn't fit for riding, but at the moment, it didn't seem to matter. I nodded and stepped back away from the stall. He saddled Peppermint in swift order and, as I stood there waiting, it occurred to me I could ride away from there. No one would miss me or even realize I was gone.

When he was ready to go, I climbed into the saddle and galloped out of the stable.

I was free.

The stable was on the south side of the castle, I realized, as I rode away with a frenzy gripping the reins in my hands. There appeared to be a trail leading away from the castle, winding its way down the hill toward the village. But then it turned sharply to the left. Ahead, there was a gate leading off the castle grounds and then I was headed toward the West King's Highway, which led to the port city of Breedon and the Fallrood Sea.

An idea formed.

Breedon would have ships in the port. I decided to book passage on one of those ships and leave the continent. Where I'd go, I did not know. Anywhere away from here. Perhaps Haven Island. The only thing of worth I had was the pendant. I could use that to barter passage.

Not Breedon, she said in my mind.

I clutched the reins tighter and glanced down at the pendant that glowed with a fierce brightness. "Then where?"

Go west to Kasari.

"But that's in..." My heart skipped. "Dal Breifna."

Yes. Find the High King.

"The High King is there? King Jeffrey thought he was in Innahill."

King Jeffrey is a fool. The High King sits in Kasari.

My brows drew together. "But that's more than a two-day ride. And why would I find the High King?"

There is another way to travel there. The way of my people.

My nerves jangled as I pulled in the reins and came to a halt in the middle of the road. I stared down at the stars swirling and dancing.

"How?" I asked.

You have the power within you. I will show you.

The images burst through my mind with such a force, I put my head in my hands. While I understood what she wanted me to do, I didn't understand how to execute it.

"But how can I travel like that to a place I have never seen?"

I will help you, if you will allow me.

I hesitated, staring down at the pendant. Fear rattled through me.

Give me your permission, Violet, and I will take you to Kasari.

I took a deep breath, expelled it as I glanced around the deserted highway. I looked over my shoulder at the castle high on the hill. The castle full of lies and deceit and betrayal.

Finally, I nodded. "You have my permission."

The glowing of the pendant increased until it was a bright pink light blinding me. It was so bright, even the stars were not visible any longer.

An image of a world I had never seen before came into my mind. With lush green fields and a castle surrounded by trees and behind it, mountains with snow-tipped peaks rising into a pale blue sky.

A long pathway led from a small loch up to the castle. Five strong, round towers soared high into the sky surrounded by thick walls made of white marble. Simple windows were scattered around the tower walls in perfect symmetry, along with holes of various sizes for archers and artillery along the walls. Large statues of heroes and kings decorated the walkway up to the entrance, memories of glories of the past.

The presence of the First Queen filtered through my mind, urging me to move. In front of us, the world turned hazy and blurry, as though the very fabric of space had opened up. And there, on the other side, was that world that I'd seen in my vision. I took up the reins in my hands and nudged Peppermint into motion with my heel. He whinnied as he took off and leapt through the space in front of us.

And landed on a green, lush ground not far from that castle. Peppermint came to an abrupt halt. In front of me, the sun dipped toward the horizon, giving the marble walls an ethereal glow. Behind me, a cool breeze tousled my hair. I sensed the metallic twang of magic in the air and through my veins.

Go, now, she urged. *Go to the castle.*

"What do I do when I get there?" I asked.

I will help you.

I sensed her deep in my mind now, pushing to the forefront of my conscious as I nudged Peppermint toward the front of the castle.

Two guards stood outside the walls at the gate armed in full armor, as though they expected an attack at any moment. Each had a sword at their side. Glancing up at the walls, I spied several archers spaced evenly along the wall, their bows at the ready. Kasari was deep into the kingdom. They did not expect visitors here. The Dalmonii were known to be reclusive from the rest of the continent.

My gut clenched into a tight knot as I rode to the gate and halted. I eyed the two guards but was unable to see their eyes through their plated helms. And suddenly Sheylara was there.

"I come to see the High King," I said, though the voice was not my own. It was that of the First Queen. She shoved me aside and took over, leaving my own self in the background.

The guard on the left lifted his visor and stepped forward. His face was covered in a red beard. His eyes were a bright green as he peered at me.

"And you are?" His voice was deep and resonate with the hint of an accent I had never heard.

"I am Sheylara, daughter of Valeth Akin'dar. I have returned to my ancestral home."

His expression was unreadable as he peered at me, then gave a sideways glance to the other guard who made no move. His gaze returned to mine.

"Valeth Akin'dar has been dead for nearly a thousand years. You cannot be his daughter."

"I come from the kingdom of Rovaria," her voice said, strong and sure and undeterred, "freed at last from my long imprisonment. I ask to see the High King."

The first guard looked back again at the second. Some silent communication passed between them. The first guard turned back to me and waved me down off the horse.

"Come, then. We will stable your horse."

I dismounted and followed him through the gate while the second guard took Peppermint's reins and headed off to the stable. Here in the highlands, the wind whipped through me, cutting through the thin material of my gown. I held my head high as I followed the guard into the great hall.

Yet I was not myself. I was someone else. I was *her*. Strong, confident, resilient.

Possessed.

A trickle of fear went through me and for a moment, me—Violet—wanted to fight her and regain control. But then, wasn't this what I always wanted? Freedom? Autonomy? Power?

He pushed open the oversized oak door, the metal hinges groaning from age. Sheylara's memories surfaced. The castle had not changed.

The door banged closed, plunging us into shadowy darkness. A few candelabras lit the empty great hall. An oversized hearth on one end remained cold and dark. Overhead, there was a gallery with an oak handrail. Enormous oil paintings of every king and queen lined the walls. A curved staircase covered with a plush garnet rug covered the stairs and ended on the other end of the great hall.

"Wait here."

The guard left me standing there alone. I clutched my elbows and shivered, a sense of my true self coming through. But still the pendant around my neck glowed and pulsed, giving me courage. Still, Sheylara's mind intermingled with mine.

I will speak to the High King, she said.

"I'm afraid." My true voice came out a ragged whisper.

There is no need.

Long, quiet minutes ticked by until at last, footsteps echoed through the hall. The guard returned with a man I assumed was the High King behind him. He was tall, with a shock of red hair, a thick red beard with strands of gray. Crinkles were at the corners of his bright blue eyes. He wore a thick tunic, black pants, and a fur mantle cloak, a silver clasp in the shape of a triskelion at his throat. His black boots were well worn, scuffed and covered in dirt.

But the thing that surprised me the most was the delicate point of his ears. While this was a shock to me, it was not to Sheylara.

The guard nodded in my direction and came to a halt while the High King approached me slowly, scrutinizing me with his bright blazing gaze. I shifted from one foot to the other, about to speak, when suddenly the First Queen was there again in my mind, shoving aside my own thoughts.

"My guard tells me you claim to be the daughter of Valeth Akin'dar, but this cannot be true since he has been dead for nearly a century," the man spoke.

"Valeth was my father," Sheylara said. "I am the Stolen Princess, returning home after my imprisonment."

His eyes narrowed to slits as he stared at me. "The Stolen Princess?"

"What is your name, High King?" she asked, her voice soft yet demanding. "Are you not a descendant of Valeth Akin'dar? Only one from the line of the True High King can sit the throne of Dal Breifna."

Silence descended. He took several steps toward me, his fierce gaze fixed on me. And yet, I, Violet, did not flinch because it was Sheylara who resided inside me now. I understood that. It was as though I merely watched through my own eyes, but speaking with her voice and her thoughts.

"Valeth Akin'dar rode into battle against the one who called himself King of Rovaria. If you are who you say you are, tell me this king's name. And tell me who he truly was, for his true self was only known by a few."

A smile lifted the corners of my mouth. "His name was Marreth Ravamar. He came from the Fallrood Sea to claim the continent and to find his mother, who was human. His father was a sea elf, which made him a half-elf or, as we sometimes call them, a halfling."

Deep inside my mind, I gasped. This information was not in the epic poem, *The First King,* and only something his wife—his queen—would know.

His face was impassive as he continued to look at me, his eyes hard and glinting. Finally, he said, "I am Faelnar Akin'dar, a direct descendant of Valeth Akin'dar who was killed during the war with Marreth Ravamar. And, aye, you are correct. He was a half-elf. Of the sea and of the land. 'Tis why he wanted to claim the continent for himself."

"And he did not succeed," she said. Then she—I—gave a deep bow. "*Voralae elyndor, vaelisor valenar.*"

I am your servant, your majesty.

"Why are you here? And why do you not look like the Stolen Princess?" the High King demanded.

"Forgive me, your majesty. I have been trapped all these long years in a place of not my making." I held up the still glowing pendant. "The girl is my conduit. The only way I can communicate with you. Eventually, she will help free me. But now, there is something more pressing. You plan to attack the kingdom of Rovaria?"

"How do you know that?" His eyes once again narrowed to slits.

"I come from the castle in Bellbrooke. The girl is the royal sorcerer's daughter. We have both seen the Spell of Unmaking he plans to unleash upon you and the Asheans when you attack. He intends to destroy you both," I said.

Everything deep inside me wanted to stop her, wanted to tell her to be quiet. But the damage was already done. She told him what I knew. She understood all too well what Papa and King Jeffrey had planned once they attacked the kingdom. I betrayed them and my kingdom.

"You tell me this information freely. Information not even my spies have been able to gather."

"I do," I said with a nod. "It is the truth. I have seen it. Even now the royal sorcerer finishes the spell. Even now, the fool King Jeffrey waits for you to attack. He has spies along the Wandering Woods. He does not know where you are, but it is only a matter of time before he finds you. He thinks you are in Innahill."

He gave a snort of derision. "He thinks that because I gave him that information. I *want* him to think I'm in Innahill. It is the ancestral home of the High King but you, princess, would know we have long since left there. That castle lies in ruins. Our home is here in Kasari in the Five Towers. Here, we make plans to defeat Rovaria."

Of course, she knew that. Sheylara grew up in this castle here in Kasari. The High Kings ruled from Kasari for nearly two centuries.

"You will not defeat him if he unleashes the Spell of Unmaking," I said.

"Then you must tell me how I can defeat him."

Smiling, I said, "There is only one way."

Things began to happen. Things I couldn't control. It was as though I lived outside my body as I watched Sheylara take over everything about me. She had consumed me, shoved my true self to the back of my mind and taken over all that I was.

I allowed it. Mostly because she was powerful and confident and understood how to talk with the king and his men. King Faelnar took her—me—to his war council where they conferred for hours about when and where to attack. She used every bit of knowledge I had of the current state of the kingdom, which wasn't much. She also used her past knowledge. As things progressed well into the night, I understood what she wanted.

She wanted revenge.

Revenge on a kingdom that no longer existed. Revenge on a sorcerer who was long dead. Revenge for all the wrongs that were committed against her when she lived. When she tried to love a king who did not love her, who did not want her for anything more than a pawn in his great game.

It was true. He was a halfling. He was of the sea and of the earth. He never found his mother, as he so hoped. When he discovered she was long dead, it destroyed him and turned him mad. This was the story the High

King told. And yet Sheylara loved the First King for a time. For a time, they were happy, even though she was the Stolen Princess. They had a son. The son who would ultimately usurp the throne from his father while she was trapped inside the crystal by the sorcerer who loved her.

It was all such a strange tale. One I would not believe had I not seen through her eyes the truth of it all. Or read the sorcerer's journal. Or unleashed the power of the pendant once I connected the two halves.

When exhaustion came and I was no longer able to stand, the king had his servant show me to a chamber deep within the castle walls. We headed up the long staircase, passing by the gallery of oil paintings. One in particular caught my eye and I paused.

The girl looked about my age with long, flowing blonde hair cascading in luxurious waves to her waist and the brightest, greenest eyes I had ever seen, reminding me of my own. She had an angular face, with high cheekbones, a pointed chin, a long, narrow nose, and full, red lips. The tips of her ears came to delicate points. Below the painting was a nameplate reading *Princess Sheylara Akin'dar*.

"Ah, the princess," the servant said, as he paused next to me. "She was a beauty, wasn't she?"

I nodded.

"She was the High King's only child. He was devastated when she disappeared."

My gut clenched as a weak whimper shifted through my mind.

The servant continued on past the oil paintings and I hurried to catch up. We made our way down another hallway and ended at the first door on the right. He pushed it open, allowing me inside. It was a large room in one of the towers with a hearth blazing with a bright fire, a fur rug on the floor, an oversized four-poster bed covered in thick quilts. This castle was not equipped with running water as the one in Rovaria and so I only had a chamber pot and a wash basin.

But I thanked the servant anyway as I kicked off my shoes and sat on the edge of the feather mattress, gazing around the room and wondering what I had done. It seemed Sheylara had gone quiet in my head and I was alone once again with my thoughts.

Did my father miss me? Did he even know I was missing? And what of Sophia? Had she returned to our apartment to find me gone and wonder where I was?

I thought about Aiden. Where was he? Still in Whitefell? Had he returned to find me gone?

The ball was to be that evening and yet it seemed as if that was only a dream. My skin still shimmered. Here, though, the High King and his war council seemed unconcerned with that. They were more interested in using me and Sheylara to defeat King Jeffrey and his army.

Which meant he would defeat Papa, the royal sorcerer.

A part of me understood he *had* to defeat him, to keep him from using the Spell of Unmaking. But I worried that what the Dalmonii had planned would destroy more of Bellbrooke and its inhabitants than I was comfortable with.

A knock sounded on the thick door.

"Come in."

The door pushed open and a woman entered. She was older, with sprigs of graying hair sprouting out from under her white cap. She was plump but had the kindest face I'd ever seen with bright blue eyes. She wore a servant's gown in drab gray and carried a stack of what appeared to be clothes.

"His majesty asked me to bring you these," she said, a hint of an accent like his. "He said you arrived with nothing."

I nodded.

"Aye, then, let's get you changed. It's late and you'll be wanting to sleep, I imagine." Her smiled reached all the way to her eyes.

Her name was Nyana and she had served the High King her entire life. She told me this as she helped me out of the thin gown and into a nightgown. She turned down the bed. As she stoked the fire, I climbed between the softest sheets I'd ever felt. I nestled down under the blankets, pulling the quilt to my chin. She tucked me in, giving me a smile I wouldn't forget.

"Rest, now. In the morn, I'll come fetch you to break your fast."

And then blew out the candles at the bedside and was gone. Only the flickering fire lit the small chamber, casting long, dark shadows on the walls around me. I thought it might be impossible to sleep, but moments later I was lost into darkness.

CHAPTER TWENTY-FIVE

*B*ellbrooke Castle

Simon paced the confines of his royal apartment, the fear knotting in his gut. The girl, Sophia, sat in one of the chairs by the hearth, her eyes bright with fear and her face pale. She had returned to the apartment to find it empty and had no explanation for his daughter's whereabouts. No one had seen Violet since she stormed out of his office after confronting him. He was sick with worry for her, especially when he discovered she took her horse from the stable. One of the stable hands recalled saddling Peppermint for her. She rode out the south end of the stable and wasn't seen again.

But without knowing which way she went it was all but impossible to track her down.

Where in the gods was she?

The king, at least, had the good sense to cancel the ball that evening in light of recent events.

A knock sounded on the door, startling both of them. He glanced at Sophia, who sat ramrod straight in the chair, her back not touching the cushions. She stared at the door with apprehension and alarm. The knock sounded again.

"Well?" he said to her.

She jumped to her feet and hurried to the door, pulling it open and stepping aside. A servant entered.

"The Lord Chancellor and King Jeffrey request your presence immediately in the king's private chambers," the servant said. "I'm to escort you at once."

Hope there was news about Violet rose in his breast as he followed the servant out of the apartment and into the hallway. It seemed an eternal walk to the king's private chamber. When they arrived, a quick knock and then the servant pushed open the door and stepped aside.

Osmund and King Jeffrey waited for him as he approached. The king sat behind his large desk. Osmund was in one of the chairs, giving him a look he couldn't read. The Lord Chancellor's face was pale.

"Sit, please, Simon."

"Do you have news of my daughter?" he demanded, ignoring the king's suggestion.

Osmund motioned to the chair across from him. "You may want to sit down for this."

"Tell me the bloody news!" he roared.

Osmund, who held a piece of parchment, stretched it out to him. "We received this moments ago. A raven. From Dal Breifna."

"Dal Breifna?"

Simon snatched the paper from his hand and read the scrawling handwriting.

We have the sorcerer's daughter. If you want her returned unharmed, you will meet us at the Wandering Wood north of Millhall at the border of Rovaria and Dal Breifna when the sun is high in the sky on the morrow. I await your response.

It was unsigned. Simon read the letter over and over, then glanced up at the two of them.

"Who sent this?" he asked.

"We can only assume the High King. His raven is waiting for a return message," Osmund said.

Simon's gaze met the king's. "And what is your reply?"

"We cannot meet him that soon. Even if we left now, a company the size of ours cannot make that trek by noon tomorrow," Jeffrey said.

"Then I shall go myself. Give me parchment and—"

"Simon, it is fruitless. Millhall is more than a day's ride."

"That barbarian has my daughter." His voice was deep, rough, angry. "I will not sit here and wait for him to kill her so he can start a war."

"A war has already started," Osmund said. "The Asheans are coming."

"Because you refuse to let the boy return home. You think holding Prince Kalen as a hostage will keep the Ashean king at bay?" Simon shook his head. "You are a fool. You are both fools. I regret my actions. I regret allowing you both to coerce me into finishing the Spell of Unmaking."

"Simon, do not make an enemy of me," King Jeffrey said, the warning tone evident in his voice.

"Or what? You'll murder me as you did your previous Royal Sorcerer?" Simon clenched his hands into tight fists. "Who will you have take the fall for that since Lord Desmond is dead?"

King Jeffrey put his hands flat on the desk and pushed up from his chair slowly. "How dare you—"

"Do not pretend offense, your majesty," Simon interrupted, his patience growing thin. "I have long known the truth of it. You killed your own Royal Sorcerer and used our friendship because you thought you could control me as you could not control him. That's over now. I feared you. I no longer do. I'm going to get my daughter back."

He spun toward the door.

"How dare you turn your back on me. On our friendship. Have I not been generous with you? And your daughter? I allowed her to accompany you since you seemed reluctant to leave her behind where she belonged," the king said.

His words cut deep. Simon kept his back to the king as he closed his eyes, regret spreading through him. He regretted bringing her here, yes. He also regretted trying to force her to marry Lord Desmond, for she was right to despise the man. He was merely trying to do what he thought was best for her. It had all gone horribly wrong.

All of it had gone horribly wrong.

She'd run away because of him. His deceit. He should have told her the truth from the time she was a small child. He should have allowed her to learn magic and become the sorceress she always wanted to be.

So much regret.

He could change none of that now.

He turned back to face the king and the Lord Chancellor. "What will you have me do? Leave her to die at the hands of the High King?"

"Perhaps," Osmund said, his voice quiet and slow, "we offer an alternative to the High King."

"What do you mean?" the king asked.

"We agree to meet him, but we need more time. We take the entire company to meet him in two days instead of one. Put the calvary in front. The infantry can follow and arrive a day later."

"The High King makes no mention of arriving with his army," Simon pointed out.

"And yet he doesn't mention he will arrive *without* it, either," Osmund replied. He turned his gaze back to the king. "I will write the message and send it back, then we can begin our journey at once."

When the king said nothing, merely pressed his lips together in a stubborn thin line, the Lord Chancellor leaned forward.

"Sire, we both have daughters. I know what I would do if I were Simon. The question is, what would *you* do?"

Simon watched the expression on the king's face soften as he thought of his daughter, the crown princess who was the light of his life.

"I would go to war for her," he said at last, his voice soft. Then his gaze lifted and met Osmund's. "Very well. Reply to the High King. Tell him we will be there in two days but no sooner. Explain to him why. And then we will destroy him *and* his kingdom."

The king gave him a sharp look, determination in his eyes.

Though Simon was relieved the king had agreed, he understood he was to use the Spell of Unmaking to wipe the Dalmonii from the continent.

He also understood he was forbidden to use such dark magic.

He would find a way around that as they made their trek across the kingdom and he would find a way to save his daughter *and* the Dalmonii.

CHAPTER TWENTY-SIX

Sheylara lived in my skin now, which was an odd sensation peering out of one's own eyes and yet having no control over one's own actions. At least my thoughts were still intact, but I sensed it was only a matter of time before she controlled that as well.

We sat at the oversized scarred wooden table in the High King's council chamber with several of his generals, his chancellor, and his head treasurer. Wars were expensive, and yet the High King had been planning it for quite some time. The royal armory had been busy making swords and armor for the last several years as the High King remained silent and aloof in the Five Towers.

She shoved aside my consciousness and lounged in the high-backed chair with the fancy scrollwork of her country, one arm resting on the table, the other in my lap. The messenger had arrived with the reply from King Jeffrey. High King Faelnar unrolled it and read it with a grimace.

"The king begs for one more day to give them time to travel to the meeting point." He tossed the parchment on the table in disgust. "Already he breaks faith with me."

"And intends to bring his entire army," Sheylara's voice said. "It is why he seeks more time."

High King Faelnar ran a hand over his thick beard, his skin bristling against his callused palm. "He intends to attack."

"As do you, my king," his chancellor, Corfeis, said. "You merely hoped to take him by surprise."

Faelnar cut him a sharp glance, his bright blue eyes hard as ice.

"Is it not true?" Corfeis said, his tone unflappable. His face was expressionless as he peered at the king with his dark, brooding eyes.

Faelnar glanced away, clearly unhappy Corfeis said what all were thinking. Then he focused his grim gaze on me.

"And what do you think, princess?"

Sheylara shifted through my mind, coming to the forefront. There was something brewing deep in her thoughts, but it was difficult for me to read.

"We give him the extra day. One more day will not hurt. And we have the advantage of sifting to the location within minutes. He does not. He and his army will be fatigued while we will be well rested."

There was a long bit of silence. One of the generals shifted in his chair as he glanced from me to the High King, question in his gaze. Faelnar clenched his jaw, his lips flattening into a thin line.

"She makes a good point," Corfeis said. "No need to arrive any sooner."

"And if King Jeffrey does not come?" Faelnar asked.

"He will come," Sheylara said with conviction.

Faelnar's gaze narrowed as he looked at me. "I'm trusting you with this. You better be right."

I shifted in my seat but Sheylara was confident and had no qualms about giving the High King the information about King Jeffrey. She'd already briefed them about the size of his army. The Dalmonii far outnumbered his.

A shudder shifted through me as I thought of that. She intended to destroy them, though I could not discern how. It frightened me. Every moment she spoke as me was another moment my true self was lost. Another moment I had to claw my way back to myself. She was getting stronger.

"Trust me," Sheylara said.

"Sire, the hour grows late," Corfeis said. "Perhaps we reconvene in the morning."

"There is nothing more to talk about. All the plans are made. It is the best we can do," Faelnar said. "Now, we will rest and prepare for our departure. I trust you have that in hand, Corfeis?"

He gave a nod. "Of course, sire."

"Then we will meet on the east lawn outside the Five Towers at dawn tomorrow." The king rose from his seat at the table.

The rest of us followed and bowed to him. He made his way out of the council chamber, the door banging closed behind him. Once he was gone, the others returned to their seats as if to continue the meeting.

"You may go, princess," Corfeis said. "We have other business to discuss."

I paused there a long moment, my gaze landing on each and every face staring back at me. My gut—or rather Sheylara's—told me something was amiss. Were they conspiring behind the High King's back? And if so, to what end?

At last, I gave a deep curtsy and headed for the door. It was clear I wasn't wanted there. If they were planning a coup, I needed to find out and time was short.

The door clicked closed behind me. I stood there a long moment, listening but their voices were muffled. Sheylara was in my mind again, controlling me. My footsteps started down the long hallway away from the council chamber. Though she had lived in this castle hundreds of years ago, she still knew the layout. It hadn't changed much since her father ruled.

Turning left, I headed down another corridor and paused at a door. I glanced around but no one was about. Pushing it open, I entered the cold, dark chamber. There were no candles lit here. The furniture was covered with sheets. Cobwebs hung from the corners. The room looked as though it had not been occupied in a very long time.

I headed to the far wall where there was a bookcase. It, too, was covered in dust and cobwebs. I reached for the middle shelf, grasping it and giving it a mighty pull. It groaned on the hinges as it swung open, revealing a secret passageway. Glancing about, I noticed there was an unlit torch in the bracket.

Without even thinking, I snapped my fingers and whispered the word, "*Aeluminar.*"

Fire lit the torch, illuminating the passage. I pulled the bookcase closed behind me and grabbed the torch out of the bracket. Turning right, I headed through the passage, the fire bouncing off the stone walls making shadows dance around me.

But I was not afraid. *She* was deep inside me, giving me the courage. I paused at a wall with what appeared to be a secret door. Taking a deep breath, I pushed it open a crack. Thankfully, the hinges were silent as it swung open to reveal a tapestry and beyond, I heard the men's voices from the council chamber.

"I do not think we should trust this girl. Who is she really? Does her claim as the Stolen Princess ring true?" It was one of the generals speaking.

"She has knowledge only the Stolen Princess would have," Corfeis pointed out. "Knowledge of the identity of First King of Rovaria."

"But that does not mean she is who she says she is," said the general. "There are historical accounts she could have read and memorized."

"She does not look like one of us," another said. "She looks human." He said the word *human* as if a bad taste was in his mouth.

"My lord, she must be an imposter. The princess has been dead for centuries," the general said.

"I admit there is a part of me that wishes her claim to be true," Corfeis said, his voice tinged with sadness. "However, it is hard not to agree with you, Gorwin."

"Then we're all in agreement?" Gorwin whispered.

There was a long pause, then in unison they all said, "Aye."

"When we meet at dawn," Gorwin said, "I will arrest her and throw her in the dungeon to live out her remaining days, however long they may be."

The sound of chairs scraping along the stone floor sounded in the room, then footsteps to the door as the men exited.

I pulled the secret door closed, my heart ramming hard and fast in my chest.

Their plan will fail, Sheylara's voice said in my mind.

"How will we defeat them?" I asked.

Give yourself to me. Trust in me. And I will make it right.

My hands shook as I stood in the dank passageway, watching the torchlight flicker along the walls. Did I trust her? I wasn't sure. I wasn't sure what she intended to do or even if I would be able to become myself again if I fully gave myself to her.

You've always wanted this power, she said. *Now embrace it, Violet. Become who you were born to be.*

She, of course, understood better than anyone how I craved the power to become a great sorceress. Was this the way with her in my head, controlling me? It didn't seem right. But it did seem like the only way.

The pendant glowed and pulsed, lighting up the area around me. The stars danced and gyrated, tumbling around each other inside the pendant. It vibrated in my hand, as if urging me on. I took a deep breath.

"I give myself to you, Queen Sheylara."

The pendant exploded with light all around me, flooding the shadows with bright pink light. The humming increased, sending vibrations through my hand, up my arm and then spreading through my entire body.

I sucked in a sharp breath as I realized whatever was left of her inside that pendant had now merged with me. Her mind to my mind. It was different than before when I merely sensed her. Now she was there, a part of me.

We were one.

CHAPTER TWENTY-SEVEN

After eavesdropping on the general and the chancellor, I headed back to my chamber. I, as both myself and Sheylara, thought it would be difficult to sleep that night with the impending doom hanging over us.

But Sheylara insisted that she had it all in hand and to trust her.

So, I did. I slept that night, at peace for what seemed like centuries. But I realized that was the queen and her thoughts intermingling with mine. I thought at first our merging would be difficult to accept, but it seemed we were much alike. Our fusion was seamless and we were still able to communicate with each other as though we were separate.

The Dalmonii dwelled in Dal Breifna for thousands of years. They were an ancient Fae race with their own language which was the tongue of the ancients.

I awoke shortly before dawn and pushed aside the bedcovers. My bare feet hit the cold stone floor, sending a jolt through me. Gooseflesh sprang up on my arms and legs. I needed no servant to help me dress, for I used the ancient language to conjure my gown.

"Dystra elyneir no'solidar."

My nightgown transformed into a beautiful velvet gown of shimmering deep blue with long sleeves that came to a point on the top of my hands and a high neck. I wore black knee-high riding boots. My long dark hair was swept back into a long braid. A silver circlet crown rested on my head. A matching cloak with a white fur collar rested on my shoulders, a silver clasp at the throat and a hood resting against my back. The glowing pendant was still around my neck, resting against my chest, giving my face an ethereal glow as it shimmered.

I hardly recognized myself in the mirror as I stood before it.

A swift knock on the door and then it opened. The servant woman paused in the doorway, gaping at me.

"I see you're already dressed," she said.

"Yes." I gave her a smile as I turned to her. "I'm ready."

"The High King awaits. I'm to escort you."

"Very well."

I knew what waited for me on the west lawn, that General Gorwin would be ready to arrest me and put me in the dungeon to rot. Sheylara stepped forward as we followed the woman from the chamber down the long hallway. The castle was quiet this early in the morning and I suspected most of the servants were doing the bidding of the High King as he prepared for war with Rovaria.

Leave everything to me, she said.

I allowed my true self to take a step back, but deep inside there was a stirring. Something bright and hot and savage.

It is your magic. Do you feel it?

My mouth went bone dry. *I do.*

I will help you hone that power, she said. *Do as I command and we will defeat these men who think they are better than us.*

Yes, my queen, I said.

We exited the castle and headed across the west lawn where the men had gathered. There was a large company of them, including their horses. The High King, the chancellor, General Gorwin, the man who intended to arrest me, and several others.

Behind us in the east, the sun peeked over the edge of the horizon, lighting the sky from a deep indigo to a burning orange. I clenched my hands into fists, my palms breaking into a hot sweat. And yet I was not afraid. I held my head high and kept my gaze pinned on the general just as he kept his gaze on me. His eyes narrowed as he looked at me and then he gave a nod to two of his men.

They charged toward me. I lifted a hand, gave it a wave toward the first man. He flew backward, landing on the ground and skidding across the lawn, leaving a deep indention in the grass. He groaned as he rolled to his side, unable to get back to his feet.

The second man broke into a run toward me. I waved my other hand at him in the same way. He, too, flew backward and landed on the ground. General Gorwin, in his fury, shouted for his men to take me down by any means necessary.

"You will halt," the High King bellowed. They all came to a stop, unwilling to defy the king's orders. "What is the meaning of this, Gorwin?"

I glanced at him, saw his face pinched and red as he glared at his general.

"Your majesty, forgive me, but this girl is not who she seems," Gorwin said. "She is an imposter and she must be taken into custody."

Several of his men headed for me once again. High King Faelnar stepped between me and his men.

"On whose authority?" the king asked.

Gorwin cut a glance to Corfeis who remained rooted in place, his eyes narrowed into a glare at the general. He shook his head.

"These were not my orders, sire," Corfeis said.

"You agreed to it," Gorwin accused.

"Is that true, Corfeis?" Faelnar pinned his chancellor with his hot glare.

"Your majesty, the general led the vote and the council agreed to it—"

"Silence," the High King snapped. "You attacked an innocent young woman."

"Sire..." Gorwin began. "She has ensnared you in her spell. She is *not* the Stolen Princess."

"Does it matter if she is or isn't?" Faelnar demanded. "She gave us valuable information about Rovaria not even your spies have been able to give us. An attack on her is an attack on me."

Silence descended as the two men on the ground climbed to their feet. They headed back to their respective places.

"Forgive me, your majesty," Gorwin said. "I was only trying to protect you."

"By conspiring behind my back," the High King said. "I cannot allow such treachery in my own court—nay, my own council—by my own general. Corfeis, have him taken to the dungeon. I will decide his fate, and yours, when we return to the Five Towers."

Corfeis's face flushed hot as he ordered the men to take Gorwin away.

"Your majesty—" Gorwin protested, as one took him by the arm.

The High King held up a hand to silence him. "You will not speak to try to proclaim your innocence now."

They led the general away, but the chancellor remained behind with his flushed face. The High King's threat hung over him and he feared retribution.

As he should.

The High King turned to me, looking me over with a critical eye. "You do not look like the Stolen Princess, that much is true. But if you say you are, then I believe you."

A smile creased my lips as I gave him a deep nod. "I thank you, your majesty, for your trust."

My gaze went back to Gorwin, whose face was pinched with fury as they dragged him away. So determined was he to arrest me, he hadn't considered his High King would never allow it.

"Bring her horse," Faelnar said.

"Your majesty, you don't mean to bring her with us?" Corfeis said. "She is dangerous—"

"Aye, and that's why she's coming with us." He glanced at me, a smile evident under his thick beard. "You *do* wish to accompany us, princess?"

I nodded. "I do."

"Good." He turned back to one of his other generals. "Her horse. *Now.*"

Moments later, Peppermint was brought to me, saddled and ready to go. I glanced down at my bare hands and conjured a pair of pale blue riding gloves. The High King gave me a nod of approval as I mounted the horse.

"Open the portal," he said.

I realized with some trepidation he was speaking to me.

But Sheylara expected that. I held my hands up, palms out toward the distant tree line and spoke the ancient language.

"*Valadar anathar.*"

As before, when I came to Kasari, the air flickered in front of us and then an opening formed. It was difficult to know if I was the one creating that magic or the First Queen.

"We ride!" the High King shouted and kicked his horse into a gallop.

Moments later, we were all on the other side outside the Wandering Wood north of the small town of Millhall where the meeting was to take place.

For now, we waited the arrival of King Jeffrey and his men.

The sun was high in the sky by the time King Jeffrey and his men arrived. There was a long line of them heading toward us in the distance. The High King sat on his horse gripping the reins, his jaw clenched tight. His second general, Haemir, was to his left. Lord Corfeis to his right. I remained in position behind them.

Faelnar turned in the saddle, piercing me with his lethal gaze. "Come beside me, princess."

"Your majesty—" Haemir started to protest. A glare from the High King made him fall silent.

The High King waved me toward him. "Come."

I nudged Peppermint forward and paused between the king and the chancellor.

"So it begins," the High King said, his voice low. Then he turned to me. "You will protect me and my men."

"Aye, your majesty," I said with a nod.

"By any means necessary," he added.

I cast a nervous glance toward the approaching company, knowing Simon, the Royal Sorcerer and my father, would be among them. Knowing, too, he was prepared to unleash the Spell of Unmaking, despite it being dark magic.

"Aye, your majesty," I said again.

My gut clenched with the fear gnawing at me. But that was me feeling that way, not Sheylara. She pushed herself to the forefront of my mind, ready to do battle. Ready to exact revenge for everything that had happened to her while she was trapped inside the pendant.

There is something I did not tell you, she said. *Something even your father did not share with you.*

I remained silent as her words floated through my mind, waiting for her to continue.

When you were a child and the pendant broke in half, there was a brief moment when I almost escaped. My essence, if you will, seeped from the broken half. Your mother was dead. I intended to use her as a vessel.

I sucked in a sharp breath. No, Papa did not tell me this when he spoke of the pendant and how it killed my mother.

But your father used his sorcery to put me back inside one half of the pendant. The half he decided to keep hidden in his spellcasting room.

"You lie!" I blurted, startling the men next to me.

The High King gave me a puzzled look with his brows drawn together in confusion. "Princess?"

I do not lie. It is the truth. Ask him and he will tell you.

"I don't believe you." Tears filled my eyes as a sob caught in my throat.

"You don't believe who?" Corfeis asked.

"You're only telling me this now to make me hate him more," I spat.

Sheylara flickered through my mind. *I tell you this now because it is the truth, because you needed to know.*

"Who is she talking to?" Haemir asked. "Has she gone mad?"

Remain silent, she said, her voice hard and angry. *Unless you prefer to live the rest of your days in the High King's dungeon branded as a madwoman.*

I said nothing. I pressed my lips together as a tear ran down my cheek. I understood then what Sheylara had done. She wasn't able to use my mother's body for herself, so she coerced me into using mine. And every minute that passed was another minute with her in control of my mind. Another minute that I was losing my true self. Even now, I felt my own being slipping away, farther and farther and deeper and deeper away from who I truly was.

You have served me well, Violet. And for that I truly thank you. But now, it is time for me to become whole again.

My breath hitched as she shoved me away and then she was all that remained inside my head.

"Princess?" the High King asked.

I, Sheylara, closed my eyes, allowing my true consciousness to take over. I tapped into the girl's untamed magic and brought it forth, letting it spill through me with a bright, pulsing heat as it merged with the power of the pendant. A ribbon formed between the magic and the pendant, giving me the conduit I needed. I shoved the girl named Violet aside and moved into her skin.

Now I had become whole again. Now I was Sheylara again. The Stolen Princess who became a Queen.

CHAPTER TWENTY-EIGHT

The king of Rovaria, his Royal Sorcerer, his Lord Chancellor, his Captain of the Guard, Falkirk, and a few guards rode closer. The rest of the company remained behind them, lined up in perfect lines on horseback waiting for the king to give the word to attack.

They came prepared to fight but then, so had the High King of Dal Breifna as evidenced by his own army sitting in perfect lines behind us.

High King Faelnar gave us a nod and the four of us trotted to the middle of the field to meet them. Faelnar took the lead, pausing mid-field in front of King Jeffrey.

Simon, the Royal Sorcerer, pinned me with his sharp, assessing gaze.

King Jeffrey had his eye on the High King. They each sized each other up. Faelnar lifted his chin a little higher. King Jeffrey puffed his chest out a little more. The two of them were like two peacocks trying to outdo each other.

"I am High King Faelnar Akin'dar, leader of the Dalmonii and High King of Dal Breifna," he said, breaking the silence.

"I am King Jeffrey, ruler of Rovaria. I have come at your behest." His gaze cut to me. "We've come for the girl."

"Yet you missed the deadline by a day." Faelnar shook his head. "The girl belongs to me now."

"No," Simon said. "I do not accept that. She is my daughter." Then his fierce gaze was on me. "Violet, I don't understand what you're doing. This is madness. Come to me, now." He waved me toward him, then held out his hand to me.

I shook my head. "I think not, Father."

That stopped him cold. He dropped his hand. "*Father*?" His eyes narrowed to slits. "You are not my daughter. What have you done with her? Where is she? Where is Violet?"

A wicked laughed bubbled up my throat. "She has given herself to me. She is no more."

Anguish creased his face. "I refuse to believe that. Whoever you are, whatever you've done to her, I will break this spell."

"There is no spell to break," I said, my voice soft and menacing. "For I have broken it myself. I have taken control of the girl. As I tried to do years ago when you stopped me. But fear not, sorcerer, she lives on."

I held up the pendant as it glowed and pulsed pink light. It was a ruse. I no more had the power to put the girl inside the pendant than he had the power to save her.

His eyes widened. "*What have you done?*"

"What you stopped me from doing all those long years ago. The girl's untamed power residing deep within her allowed me to take over. She doesn't know how to control it. She never did, thanks to you."

"Enough of this," King Jeffrey snapped, impatient. "What more do you want of us if you don't wish to return to Rovaria?"

"Revenge," I said. "I have waited a thousand years for it."

"Violet, stop this madness. You—" Simon began.

"I am not Violet!"

He forged on, undeterred by my outburst. "She would never want this. She would never want to hurt her own kingdom. Or me."

"Rovaria is not my kingdom. Dal Breifna is," I replied. "I am Dalmonii as my father before me. And you are not my father."

"And she has decided to remain with us," High King Faelnar added.

"You are not Dalmonii." Fury pinched Simon's face as he glared at me. "I forbid you to stay with them. Come back with me. Let me help you."

"You cannot help me," I said.

"The girl stays with us," Faelnar said.

"High King Faelnar," King Jeffrey began, "do not make us go to war over the life of a silly girl."

At that, Simon's head snapped toward his king. "My daughter is not a silly girl."

"You said yourself she stole the pendant from you," King Jeffrey said.

Faelnar ignored their banter. "It is not over a girl that we go to war. It is over centuries of suffering from your kingdom. We have waited patiently for you to come to us, to offer friendship, and you have not. We have waited for you to make peace with us after your so-called First King stole our princess. You have not."

King Jeffrey scoffed. "That was more than a thousand years ago and I had nothing to do with stealing your princess. Surely you know that. It was the First King—"

"The First King who went to war with my father, Valeth Akin'dar," I said.

Simon's eyes lit with some bit of knowledge. "Yes, Valeth Akin'dar fought the First King on this very ground, didn't he?"

"Fought and died," High King Faelnar said. "He rests in the crypt of the Five Towers."

"But there are others who are buried on this battleground, aren't there?" Simon asked.

High King Faelnar's gaze narrowed. "Aye."

Simon closed his eyes, then, and raised his arms to the sky, palms upward. The sky turned dark and stormy. The clouds rolled in from nowhere, gathering over our heads as he spoke. His words were indiscernible at first and then became clearer as he spoke louder.

"With ancient words and power deep, I bid you rise from eternal sleep, break the chains of time and space, reclaim your form, embrace this place. Turn now to face your new king and fight for him for all eternity."

"NO!" I shouted, realizing what the spell meant.

But it was too late.

All around us, the spectral images of the dead rose from the ground. The very battleground they had fought on so long ago. Their ghostly images were still dressed for battle, bloody swords in their hands as they turned to face King Jeffrey, his men, and his army.

"What is this?" King Jeffrey said. "What have you done, Simon? This isn't the Spell of Unmaking!"

"You bloody knave," Faelnar snarled. "You brought us here to *slaughter* us."

Simon opened his eyes, a smile on his face. "And yet I have raised the dead. The dead who are now in King Jeffrey's control."

How clever the sorcerer was, handing off the power to control the ghost army to his king and thereby dooming him to death by using dark magic. I admired that about him.

I sensed the girl trying to surge forward, trying to pound through the bonds I had around her. I forced her back, shoving her deep into the recesses of my mind.

"Men of the dead, face your new enemy," Simon said, pointing to High King Faelnar. His sad gaze landed on me. "I am sorry, Violet, but you give me no other choice." And then he began to chant. "*By the fire's blaze and spirits' might, I stand before the dark of night.*"

Panic welled deep inside me as I realized what he planned to do. Quickly I dismounted and stepped in front of the horses, placing myself between that of the ghost army and the High King and the others.

"Don't do this," I implored. "You cannot mean to wipe out an entire race. It will not save your daughter!"

"What is she doing?" Corfeis asked.

"Leave her to it," High King Faelnar said.

I faced them head on, their wraithlike bodies turned toward me with weapons raised, though how they intended to defeat someone living and breathing, I did not know.

Simon's eyes glowed bright as he chanted the next line of the Spell of Unmaking. "*With courage strong and facing our foe, their strength shall not deal a final deathblow.*"

"I don't want to hurt you," I said, raising my hands, palm out.

And the third line. "*Let this protect my honored liege from a wild and hostile siege.*"

My pulse throbbed as the rage tore through me.

"Attack them!" King Jeffrey shouted.

The ghost army surged forward.

Simon chanted the next line. "*Now, with this verse of ancient speech, the universe begins to breach.*"

Beneath my feet, the ground rumbled. Behind me, the High King emitted a war cry. Before me, King Jeffrey remained on his horse as his army rushed to meet the Dalmonii on the battlefield.

I needed the girl's untapped, raw magic now more than ever. Digging deep, I pulled the silvery thread of magic. It flooded through me as I pushed it forward through my fingertips and directed it toward Simon. The burst of light hit him square in the chest. He stumbled backward a few steps, the breath knocked out of him. He lifted his head to look at me. Our eyes met and something deep in his connected to me. Something I was unable to deny and I realized that was the girl trying to claw her way up and up and up.

I shoved her back down.

Simon waved his arms in a wide arc as once again the ground rumbled. Around us, the armies collided but the two of us were safe. It was as though we stood inside a protective bubble.

"Release my daughter and I won't finish the Spell of Unmaking."

"You raised an army of the dead. You used dark magic and you will pay for that with your life." The words burst through me without thought.

"I raised the army from the dead, yes, but only to give them life once again. It is King Jeffrey who uses them as a weapon," he said.

I lifted my hands again, ready to strike. As the light pulsed from my fingers, from the pendant around my neck, he put up his hands in front of his face, pushing out his own magic toward me. Magic collided with magic, exploding in brilliant shades of white and pink and blue illuminating the protective bubble we stood in.

Deep inside, the girl's thoughts glimmered against mine, trying to push forward, trying to stop me from attacking her father. But I was in total control of her magic. Despite that, she continued to fling herself against her bonds.

"It's no use!" I shouted to him. "Your daughter is gone."

"Then I will destroy you *and* your people." He took a deep breath, then chanted, "*By words, the threads of fate unwind—*"

"I will not allow it!"

I pushed against his magic with a violent thrust. He flew backward, landing on the ground, unable to complete the spell. But again, the ground rumbled and men cried out with pain as they were slaughtered.

With slow steps, I walked toward him. The center of his chest was singed. Kneeling beside him, I checked for a pulse. A faint flutter was there. He wasn't dead.

Suddenly something deep inside me snapped. I sucked in a sharp breath as my back went ramrod straight.

It was the girl.

Somehow, she had managed to break through the bonds I'd placed around her and now her thoughts rushed through my mind.

You killed my mother. I will not allow you to kill my father.

Her voice filtered through my thoughts. It felt as though she had a strangle hold on my throat. I couldn't breathe. The pendant pulsed and glowed wildly, the stars inside gyrating and swirling as if it sensed her.

"You cannot defeat me, *girl*. I am more powerful."

You are no more powerful than I am. You said yourself I had powerful, enchanting, masterful magic.

I howled with infuriation of her throwing my own words back at me. Deep inside, a punch of magic—hers—sent me to my knees. I pitched forward, my hands breaking my fall. The breath see-sawed in and out of me. My eyes watered.

She was at the forefront of my mind, now, punching her way through with such violence, I had no time to react. No time to gather my strength. No time to fight back.

"You are nothing but a stupid girl!" I shouted.

"She is not a stupid girl." Simon's ragged voice was near me.

I lifted my head to see him on his feet, his face haggard, his clothes singed. Yet he stood with his hands outstretched, his fingers glowing.

"You're helping her!"

"Violet, I know you can hear me," he said, ignoring me. "Fight her. You have the power to do it."

I howled again as a bright hot searing pain went through me. I fell backward, tears clouding my vision. The pendant continued to glow and pulse with furious light and a loud humming against my chest.

"I was wrong to keep you from your magic," he continued. "Come back to me and I will teach you everything I know."

I rolled to my side, my hand fisting clumps of grass and dirt as I pushed upward. "Not if you're dead."

I flung the fistful of dirt toward him with a beam of white, hot magic, but he deflected it easily. He shoved it aside as if it was nothing more than a gnat in his face.

The girl continued to push through my mind. That silvery ribbon of magic I had used earlier was there once again. She grabbed onto it before I could and then suddenly, she burst through my mind.

The burning pain of it all was too much. I pitched forward again, crying out with the pain.

"That's it, Violet! You can do it!"

"Stop. Helping. Her!" I ground out.

But the girl was still there, her magic pulling away from me like the tide pulling away from the shore. As though she was sucking it all away, back into her own self.

She gave me a mighty shove with that masterful magic she had never used but yet appeared to have suddenly mastered it. Pushing me down, down, down and deeper, deeper, deeper until I no longer controlled her and then—

I sucked in a sharp, wild breath, the air around me shimmering with magic. The acrid twang of it filled my lungs as I took a deep breath and expelled it, sitting back on my heels. I glanced around. I was still in Papa's bubble and there he was, sitting on his knees with his hands pushed palms out looking at me as though I was a stranger. His hair was tousled. His tunic was scorched. All around us were the sounds of swords clanging and the metallic stench of death.

Tears blurred my eyes. "Papa?"

Relief flooded his face. He pushed to his feet the same time as I did. He hugged me tight, so tight, like he would never let me go. Then he kissed my forehead.

"You did it," he whispered, then pulled back and held me at arm's length. "Where is she now?"

"She's still there...deep inside. Papa, I didn't mean to release her from the pendant, but—"

He gave me a weak smile. "It's all right, Violet. We can make it right."

"How?"

"Together." He held my hands in his. "A banishing spell."

As the war raged around us, we remained safe in our bubble, and he began to chant.

"By the strength of ancient lore, I cast you out forevermore. The spell is cast, the ties are severed, they will not last." He paused, his eyes glistening as we looked at each other. *"Banished forevermore. So, mote it be."*

As he said the last words, it felt as though she was being pulled from the center of my chest and then a shimmering mist seeped from my skin, forming a cloud over my head. Papa released my hands, using his to catch that cloud, twisted it and make it conform. Deep inside my mind, she wailed her frustration and her anger, her agony at being defeated.

"Remove the pendant, Violet," he said.

I did and watched as he compressed the cloud smaller and smaller until at last it was nothing more than a wisp. Then he used his power and shoved it toward the pendant, putting her right back inside it where she had been trapped for a thousand years.

The light faded from the pendant and winked out. The stars no long swirled or danced. It was nothing more than a plain pink crystal as it had been when I found it. I stared down at it, feeling a sense of loss and yet a sense of utter relief. She was gone. Out of my head.

Even the shimmer to my skin had vanished.

But something remained. That bright ribbon of magic was still there, coiled in my breast. Waiting.

"We have to destroy it," I said, my voice soft. "She wouldn't want to be trapped in there forever."

"We do," he agreed.

I lifted my gaze to his. "Here, on this battlefield where her father perished."

He nodded. "Hold it by the chain away from your body."

I did as he instructed, stepping back away from it as far as possible. In his hand, he forced a small ball of fire. It danced in his palm. He held it close to the pendant and released it. The flame encircled the pendant, heating it up. I watched as it cracked, splintered, and then burst into a thousand tiny pieces. The stars fluttered upward away from the broken pieces as though they, too, had been trapped all this time. Then pieces of crystal rained down to the ground.

A spectral image lifted away from the fragments. It was a woman. Her misty image looked down at both of us, gave us a small smile as though relieved to be released from her curse at last, and then disappeared into the night.

CHAPTER TWENTY-NINE

Papa released the protective bubble around us, then immediately took my hand. We ran away from the fray, putting the battle at our backs. I stole a glance over my shoulder to see High King Faelnar had dismounted from his horse and was engaged in a sword battle with King Jeffrey. I saw neither Lord Chancellor from either kingdom, nor General Haemir or Captain Falkirk. I did not know if they were alive or dead.

Dead men and horses littered the battleground. A pang of panic went through me as I scanned the area for Peppermint. I didn't see him anywhere. Hot tears sprang to my eyes. Despite everything I'd been through, the loss of Peppermint was the ultimate affront. My heart sank to the pit of my stomach. Not Peppermint. I couldn't lose him.

"Peppermint!" I cried out, wanting to weep as panic pounded through me.

Papa yanked on my arm. We had to run for our lives.

As we sprinted toward freedom, a deep, guttural scream ripped through the air. We both halted and turned back to see King Jeffrey had taken a sword to the gut by High King Faelnar. The king of Rovaria fell to the ground, dead.

High King Faelnar tossed his sword to the ground. His chest rose and fell with his heavy breathing as his gaze turned to the two of us. Papa shoved me behind him, but I peeked around him to see the High King mount his horse and charge toward us. And still the war raged on without the High King.

"You," the High King said, pointing at Papa. "You should be arrested and tossed in the dungeon for the remainder of your days."

Papa stiffened at the High King's words. "I am not your enemy, your majesty."

"You tried to use the Spell of Unmaking."

"Tried. But never completed it," Papa pointed out. "And King Jeffrey was the one who insisted I use it to destroy you and the Asheans. He was your enemy."

High King Faelnar cut a glance at the dead king and the ongoing battle. "Can you stop them?" he asked.

"Stop them? Stop the battle, you mean?" Papa asked.

His gaze returned to him. "Aye."

After a long silent moment, Papa gave a nod. He turned to me, gripped me by the shoulders. "Violet, I want you to keep going. Head to Millhall to the south. Wait for me there."

I shook my head. "I'm not leaving without you."

For I feared there would be some treachery and the High King would kill Papa.

"I'm *not* leaving without you," I repeated.

"Give her to me," the High King said. "She will be safe with me." He held a hand out to me.

Papa looked from him to me and back again. "What assurances do I have you will do her no harm and return her to me?"

A long moment passed, then the High King gave a smile. "You have none, but I suppose you'll have to trust me."

"I'll be all right, Papa," I said as I moved past him.

The High King hoisted me onto the back of his horse and then trotted away, back toward the battle. Papa broke into a limping run to catch up. As he approached the edge of the battleground, where the ghost army and the armies of Rovaria and Dal Breifna fought, he halted next to us and raised his hands to the darkened sky.

He chanted, "*As this spell is cast and words are spoken, the sacred link between us now is broken. Go forth with grace and return to the unknown. So, mote it be.*"

As he spoke the last words, the dark clouds broke, and the ghost army flickered away and was gone.

All the fighting stopped. Rovarians and Dalmonii alike dropped their weapons.

"Your king is dead," High King Faelnar said, his voice loud enough for them to hear. "Bend the knee to me and I will let you live."

Papa cut a glance up at the High King. "They will never bend the knee to you," he said, his voice low. "They are loyal to King Jeffrey."

I peered around the High King to see Captain Falkirk step forward. Relief washed over me when I saw he still lived.

"We do not recognize you as our king," Falkirk said. "King Jeffrey has an heir. Prince Philip will ascend to the throne."

"Who are you? Who speaks for the realm?" Faelnar demanded.

"Captain Falkirk, your majesty, and the one left in charge here on the battlefield since the king and the Lord Chancellor are both dead."

A pang of sadness went through me as I thought of Eliza and Jacob. They lost their father, though they did not know yet.

"You wanted us to make peace with you, to offer friendship." Falkirk spread his hands as if in surrender. "Allow those of us left to return to Rovaria and I swear to you, the new king will do just that."

High King Faelnar turned to Papa. "Does he speak true? Can I trust him?"

"Captain Falkirk is an honorable man," he said. "If he swears the new king will make peace, then he will make it so."

Faelnar gave a nod and then said to Falkirk, "Very well. You will return to your kingdom. We will return to ours. I expect to receive this offer of friendship and peace within the fortnight."

"By your command, your majesty," Falkirk said.

He ordered several of his men to pick up the king's body and place it over the back of one of the few remaining horses to take back to the castle. He did the same with the Lord Chancellor's body. Then he gathered what was left of the Rovarian army and headed away from the battleground.

Papa reached for me. I slid off the back of the horse, standing next to him as he looked up at the High King.

"And what of you, Royal Sorcerer? Now that you have your daughter back," he said.

"We are going home to Blackthorne."

Life had changed once again, this time for the better. It was the best answer I had ever heard. I almost cried with relief. To go home, back where we belonged, was a balm to soothe my aching soul.

"No more Royal Sorcerer for you, then?"

Papa reached for my hand and took it. "I think not. I will make my living another way."

"Godspeed to you both."

With that, the High King rode off behind the rest of his men. They gathered at the border. Together, we watched as they opened a portal and sifted through it. In minutes, they were gone.

I glanced around. The area was littered with the dead, an echo of the past battle. I wondered, then, if these souls would join those who had been raised from the dead. Which brought another question to my mind.

"When you used the spell to raise the ghosts, wasn't that using dark magic?" I asked.

Papa's face held a contemplative look as his gaze fixed on the field of dead before us. Perhaps he had the same thought as I did.

"When I raised them," he began as he chose his words, "I made sure to transfer the power of them to the king." He gave me a sheepish glance. "Thereby absolving me of the dark magic."

Shock rolled through me. "You transferred the power to control them to him."

He nodded.

"Because you know the consequences of that," I added.

He nodded again. "Deep down, King Jeffrey was...not a good man though he tried. His greed for power drove him to make terrible decisions. There was a chance he'd survive the battle, but then if he had, he'd forced me to use the Spell of Unmaking."

And we both understood the consequences of that. He would have been turned into a dark sorcerer and the Dalmonii would have been wiped from the continent forever. Papa chose the life of one man versus the lives of an entire race.

"Are we really going home, Papa?" I asked, my voice quiet.

He turned to me, taking me by the shoulders. "Yes. I swear this to you. We will return to the castle, get Sophia and gather our things, and then be on our way."

I couldn't wait to get home.

"I suppose we'll have to walk," I said.

There were no more horses. Papa nodded and together, we followed as the company of men disappeared over a ridge.

But then I heard it. The thunder of hooves on the ground behind me. Turning, I cried out with surprise. Peppermint galloped toward us. He was unscathed and his saddle was still intact. I lost track of him when I dismounted when Sheylara was still living in my skin.

"Well, look at that," Papa said, a smile in his voice. "Your friend has come to save us from walking all the way back to Bellbrooke."

Peppermint halted next to us with a happy snort. He nuzzled my neck. I patted his nose, then hugged him, the smell of horse and leather filling my nose. Tears of joy ran down my face, so relieved was I that he was all right.

"You're a good boy," Papa said as he patted his neck. "Are you ready to take us home?"

As if he understood, Peppermint snorted. We both laughed.

Papa alighted into the saddle first, then held a hand down to me. I climbed up behind him and moments later, we were on our way.

CHAPTER THIRTY

The sun dropped below the horizon, leaving us with no choice but to stop for the night. We found a small village. So small, in fact, it wasn't on any map, called Colkirk. But they had a tavern and were able to feed us and give us rooms for the night.

We left at the first light of day, reaching Bellbrooke by late afternoon. The castle was already in mourning for the loss of their king and their Lord Chancellor. When we arrived at our apartment, Sophia had been pacing the length of it. She halted mid-step when we entered.

"Thank the gods! I've been so worried about you."

She flung herself into my arms. I hugged her tight, so relieved that she was still here and unharmed. When she pulled back, I noticed her face was pale. Dark circles were underneath her eyes. She looked as though she hadn't slept in days.

She dropped a curtsy to Papa. "My lord, I'm glad to see you as well. When I heard the king marched off to war, I feared the worst."

Papa and I exchanged a glance. Then he said, "I'm afraid not all of us returned."

"I know." Sorrow crossed her face. "I know about the king and the Lord Chancellor. The royal family is in mourning."

"What about Eliza and Jacob?" I asked. "Have you seen them?"

She shook her head. "Not since Captain Falkirk returned."

"They must have marched all night." Papa raked a hand down his face. "Sophia, we are going home. I want to start packing our things immediately and leave at first light."

"Home?" She blinked surprise. "You mean, to Blackthorne?"

"There is nothing for me here now," he said. "Have our trunks brought up."

"Yes, my lord." She dipped another curtsy and left to alert the servants.

"I know it's been a long journey so far," Papa said, "and we have longer yet to go."

"Don't worry, Papa." I gave him a smile. "I'm ready to return home and don't mind packing. Even if it takes all night."

"Good, I'm glad to hear. Once we return home, I want to get my affairs in order."

"Affairs? What do you mean?" My brows drew together in question.

"I mean to sell the estate to Cousin Rupert. And then you and I will be leaving the continent."

My heart dropped to my shoes. "Leaving the continent?" I said, my voice faint.

"You can bring Sophia with you, if you wish. But I think we need a fresh start in a new place."

I said nothing as I stared at him in utter shock. Leave Blackthorne, my childhood home? How could I? I was in no position, though, to disagree.

"Where will we go?" I asked.

"There is another continent to the north of us. Ellethor, it is called. A big, wide land with all sorts of new kingdoms to explore."

"I have never heard of this place."

He gave me a small smile. "The world is a big place, Violet."

He brushed his hand over my cheek as he headed off to his bed chamber, not realizing he had just destroyed my entire world. But I thought of Aiden. I had to tell him I was leaving. I had to tell him what he meant to me while I was here. I had to tell him...so much. Had he returned from Whitefell? There was only one way to find out.

I slipped out of the apartment and headed through the castle. All was quiet, even in the great hall. The only place I knew to look for him was in his music room. I had my doubts he would be there this time of night, but hope swelled when I heard the soft music filtering from the room. The door was cracked a bit and I paused to listen.

It was a mournful tune and one I had not heard before. A heavy sorrow shuddered through me.

I pushed open the door and paused there, waiting for him to see me. But his head was down as his hands went over the keys. I moved closer, the swish of my gown and the soft thump of my boots alerting him to my presence. He lifted his head, his face drawn with his grief, but when he saw me, he leapt to his feet and came around the piano.

He took me in his arms, hugging me close. He smelled of leather and horses. I inhaled his scent, closing my eyes and relishing in it.

"By the gods, I'm glad to see you here. When I heard you were taken by the High King, I feared the worst," he said against my hair.

"You heard that?"

He pulled back, holding my hands in his and giving me a small smile. "I am a spy, after all." He looked me over. Question lined his face. "Where is your pendant?"

"I'm afraid that's a very long story," I said with a sigh.

He seemed content to accept that. "Perhaps someday you'll tell me, then. When you're ready."

"What happened in Whitefell? When did you return?"

"That's a long story as well." He led me to the chairs by the cold hearth. I took one of them as he poured tea. "There were, in fact, forces gathering there. But they were not from Dal Breifna, nor did they intend to invade Rovaria or attack Bellbrooke. There was an emissary along with his company from Ashea."

He handed me the tea. The scent of bergamot wafted from the cup, giving me a sense of comfort. "You saw them?"

He nodded as he poured his own cup. "Indeed. I was able to talk to them and find out their true intentions. It seems that King Jeffrey cut off their main water supply. He managed to dam Loch Midlem, drying up the rivers that led from it into Ashea. The Ashean king wanted to discuss this with King Jeffrey.

"Lord Desmond fed the Ashean king other lies to make them want to fight. The Ashean king had his army gathered on the northern border, ready to invade if things did not go well with the ambassador. I spoke many hours with him and managed to talk him out of the invasion, beseeching him to allow me to speak with King Jeffrey and make things right. They have agreed to stand down, especially in light of recent events."

I sipped my tea as I mulled this over. "Why did he come to Whitefell? Why not come north to Bellbrooke?"

"Because Whitefell is the nearest settlement to the Ashean border. He knew no other way. When I received word there was a battle in the north, I returned here at once only to find you gone along with the king, the

Lord Chancellor, and your father." He placed his cup in the saucer and leaned forward. "Were you there, Violet?"

I shifted uncomfortably in my seat as I thought of all that had happened on that battlefield. How I had nearly lost myself. I took a deep breath, expelled it.

"I will tell you the story."

And so, I told him everything that had happened with the pendant. How I found the missing half in Papa's office. How when I put them together, it unleashed the First Queen into me. And how she had tried to overtake me, body and soul. Then I told him about the fight on the battlefield. Everything from the ghost army to hiding in a protective bubble with Papa as I fought to regain control of who and what I was.

"It was strange, really. Like seeing and feeling everything that was happening to me but I was on the outside looking in. She nearly destroyed me." I held the cup of tea closer to my face, the steam warming my cheeks.

"But you fought her and won."

I nodded. "Not without a price, though. We destroyed the pendant. When we did, her spirit was released."

"She's finally at rest, then," Aiden said. "You did the right thing."

"I know. But a part of me...misses her. Is that strange?"

He shook his head. "Not at all. She was in your mind, dominating you."

"Somehow," I said, my voice low, "I think she gave me the strength to become who I am. Papa says he's going to help me with my magic."

"Then perhaps you'll become a great sorceress like you wanted." He gave me a winsome smile. "Something else troubles you, though. What is it?"

I placed the tea cup aside and leaned forward, reaching for him. He placed his aside and took my hands in his warm ones. I stared down at our entwined fingers, trying to memorize this moment, how it felt for him to hold my hands, and how much my heart ached to leave him.

"We are returning to Blackthorne. We leave at first light."

"On the morrow?" There was a bit of alarm in his voice.

"Yes. That's why I really came. I wanted to tell you. I hoped you were here." I lifted my gaze to his and my heart shuddered. "I'm glad you were."

"I'm glad I was, too, but, Violet..." His voice trailed off. "Will I see you again?"

My throat constricted as I shook my head. "My father intends to leave the continent once he sells the estates to my dreadful cousin."

He said nothing, merely squeezed my hands in his as understanding went through his mind. "I see. So, this is farewell, then."

"I'm afraid so."

I looked away, back down at our hands as the tears came. I tried to blink them away, but it was useless. A tear landed on our entwined fingers. I pulled a hand free to whisk them away.

"It's silly, I know. We hardly know each other, but I will miss you, Aiden."

He pulled me to my feet as he rose. We faced each other, and then his hands came up and cupped my face.

"And I you, dear Violet."

He kissed me, then. He tasted like bergamot and honey. His lips were warm and tender yet firm, demanding a response. I returned his kiss with a reckless abandon I had never experienced before, making me shudder. When he released me, I stepped away from him for if I hadn't, I was afraid

I would never leave his arms. The blood pounded through my mind, leapt from my heart, and made my knees weak and trembling.

"I should go," I said, my voice a raspy whisper. Then I cleared my throat and tried again. "I have to be packed and ready to leave by morning."

He reached for my hand, holding it a moment, then kissed the back of it. "Goodbye, Violet."

My breath hitched. "Goodbye, Aiden."

Then I fled his music room with tears running down my cheeks.

CHAPTER THIRTY-ONE

We left Bellbrooke castle before the sun was even up and traveled down the East King's Highway toward home. Despite staying up all night packing, with Sophia's help, and fighting exhaustion and a sense of longing for leaving Aiden behind, I was happy to be on the way back to Blackthorne.

I wasn't able to tell Eliza or Jacob goodbye. They were in seclusion during their mourning period. Prince Kalen was also gone. He had been sent back to Ashea while I was in Dal Breifna. I was glad to hear he safely returned to his kingdom. But I thought of them all. Of our luncheon on the north lawn and our game of Bowls. Of Eliza's effervescent infectious joy. Of Jacob's quiet reserved nature. Of Kalen's kind eyes and his calm demeanor. I missed them.

Somehow, Papa had convinced Captain Falkirk to loan us a flat carriage to haul our trunks as well as several of his knights to escort us. One drove the carriage, two more rode horses alongside me on Peppermint, and Papa and Sophia on borrowed horses from the castle stable.

We rode hard all day to reach Blackthorne by that evening. Seeing it come into view made my heart skip a beat. But as we approached, we noticed several carriages arriving ahead of us.

"What in the gods is going on here?"

Before anyone could answer him, Papa kicked his horse into a gallop and headed off toward the manor. Sophia and I exchanged a surprised look.

"Should we follow?" she asked.

I shook my head because I really didn't know if we should follow him or not. Whatever was happening in the manor, I had a feeling Papa would be displeased. One of the knights trotted forward to keep pace with me.

"What should we do, my lady?" he asked.

"Take the cart to the west side where the stable is. Wait there until further instructions," I said, sounding authoritative and decisive.

The two knights led the carriage to the side of the manor with the stable while Sophia and I trotted up to ensuing chaos. We dismounted and headed toward the front door, but a man dressed as a butler—and not our butler—stopped us.

"Do you have an invitation, my lady?" He gave Sophia, who stood a few paces behind me, a cursory glance.

"I don't need an invitation to enter my own home." I mustered as much of a snooty tone as possible.

His eyes widened a bit as he looked at me, then glanced back at the manor where there were shouting voices. One of them was Papa's. I didn't wait for his reply. I shoved by him and headed for the door.

"Come, Sophia," I said over my shoulder.

She didn't argue. When we entered, we both stopped and stared.

The front hall, the atrium, the parlor, and the dining hall had all been turned into a gambling hall. There were people everywhere, playing cards and dice and spinning a wheel as they placed bets on red or black. I scanned the crowd for Papa, but didn't see him. I did, however, see

Harriet, that harlot, as she sat next to a man wearing a garnet waistcoat laughing at something he said. She fluttered her lashes as she held a glass of champagne in one hand, twirled her pearls in the other while showing off quite a bit of cleavage.

Fury erupted through me as I stared at her, my hands clenched into fists.

Sophia leaned toward me. "Is that—"

"It is," I said before she could get it out. "I knew she was trouble!"

Gods knew what the upper floors looked like. Where had she stashed all the furniture? Furthermore, where was Cousin Rupert and the servants? Because none of these servants were the ones we had left behind.

Papa came from the dining hall then, his hand around Cousin Rupert's elbow as he dragged him through the crowd. There was a furious glint in his eyes, his face was pinched, and his cheeks flushed. He didn't see us, thankfully. He gave Rupert a shove into the middle of the crowd in front of the table in which Harriet sat.

"Tell them!" Papa boomed. "*Now.*"

Rupert twisted his hands together, his face pale as he scanned the crowd. "I'm afraid the party is over. You all have to leave now."

Silence descended as all eyes went to Rupert. Harriet rose from her seat, her eyes narrowed as she bustled around the end of the table and confronted Papa.

"What is *he* doing here, Rupert? You promised me he wasn't coming back."

"You did *what*?" Enraged, Papa clenched his fists and for a moment, I thought he was going to punch him.

I took Sophia by the hand and started to back away, back toward the door to make a hasty exit if we needed to.

Rupert gave Papa a sheepish look, then cast his glance to his wife. "I said he *may not* be coming back, dearest. You misunderstood."

Harriet glared at Papa, then turned her malicious gaze on her husband. "You are an embarrassment to me and my friends."

"Get them out," Papa said, his voice hard as ice.

"I-I'm trying, but—"

"Then let me help you."

Papa grasped Rupert by the collar and dragged him toward the door. Sophia and I quickly stepped aside as he unceremoniously tossed him out. Harriet rushed to the door, her eyes wide with shock. Then she turned on Papa.

"You—"

"You're next if you don't get out," he said.

The blood drained from her face. Then she turned and scurried out of the manor. It took everything in me not to laugh out loud.

"All of you! Out!" Papa bellowed.

One man tried to retrieve a stack of bills on one of the tables. Papa smacked his hand away. "Leave it and get out."

He shooed them toward the door as they all began to file out, one by one with disappointment and confusion on their faces. They likely didn't know who this strange man was who had returned to kick them all out. The gambling tables were the only things left behind.

Rupert made another appearance in the open doorway, the light from the full moon at his back making him nothing more than a shadow. Harriet was beside him, clutching his arm and trying to pull him away.

"You can't keep that money. It's mine," he whined.

"It's *mine*," Papa corrected. "And you are no longer welcome here."

He glanced upward, toward the stairs, as though recalling he had personal items in the bedrooms. "Can we at least gather our things?"

"No! I will have them packed and sent to your home in Lampfort."

Rupert flushed hot. "I...well, I sold our home in Lampfort."

Harriet emitted a high-pitched gasp. "You did *what*?"

Papa crossed his arms over his chest. "You were hoping I wouldn't return. Is that it?"

Harriet punched Rupert's upper arm as hard she could. "You stupid fool!"

Then she took off, leaving him standing in the doorway alone. He spread his hands in an imploring gesture. "Please, cousin. You wouldn't let me be homeless, would you?"

Papa moved toward the door, his face impassive. "Oh, wouldn't I?" Then he slammed the door in his face. "And don't come back!"

He spun away from the door, his hands in fists. Then he saw me and Sophia for the first time. We stared at each other, both of us surprised at his actions. He'd kicked Cousin Rupert and his wife out for good. I was unable to hold in the laugh that bubbled up my throat. Thankfully, Papa laughed, too. When we finally caught our breath, he gave me a contemplative look.

"I have decided *not* to sell Blackthorne to Cousin Rupert," he said, referring to our earlier conversation.

"Does that mean we're not leaving the continent?"

He shook his head. "No."

Relief sputtered through me. I was so happy we were staying but as I glanced around, I realized we had quite a lot of work ahead of us.

"What are we going to do with all this?" I waved to the gambling tables.

He sighed. "Perhaps we deal with that in the morning. I'm exhausted."

And then I remembered the carriage. "The trunks!"

"Bollocks," he swore under his breath. "I'll deal with that. Where are they?"

"By the stable."

He nodded. "You two go to bed. We will worry about the rest in the morning."

I watched as he wound his way around the gambling tables and out through the kitchen. Sophia hooked her arm in mine.

"Shall we go see what they did to the upstairs rooms?"

"I'm almost afraid to see," I muttered.

Together, we trudged up the stairs. All I could do was hope for the best.

When I entered my room, I was relieved to see it was unchanged. I squeaked with joy as I landed on the bed and curled on my side.

"My lady, you're still dressed—"

I waved her away as I fought off a yawn. I kicked off my boots, letting them thunk on the floor by the bed. It wasn't the first time I slept in my clothes. She grinned and closed the door behind her. Moments later, I was fast asleep.

When Sophia and I unpacked my trunks, I came across the two gowns that had been gifted to me by an anonymous suiter I hoped was Aiden. The seafoam one and the lovely sparkly blue one. I gave a wistful sigh as we hung them in my wardrobe, likely never to be worn.

Life at Blackthorne returned to some semblance of normal. Cousin Rupert, at the behest of his dreadful wife, fired all our servants and replaced them with his own. Papa quickly reversed that decision and then scoured the countryside for those who had been loyal to him. He begged them to come back. Only the cook, Miss Morton, and the old butler were the only ones who returned. But at least with them back, it was like home again.

The gambling tables were removed. Harriet had auctioned off some of our furniture, much to Papa's ire. However, he used what money was left behind from the gambling tables to buy new. We heard the gossip from town Harriet left Rupert and married someone else. I wondered if it was the man in the garnet waistcoat. Rupert, however, sent a letter telling us he had found the love of his life in the Port of Dunfail and was sailing away with her to the Quiet Island.

Papa muttered, "Godspeed and good riddance," when he read the letter.

It made me giggle.

I thought of Aiden often as the spring turned to summer and the summer into autumn. Every day, I rode Peppermint toward the East King's Highway in the hopes I would see him again on his black horse heading away from Bellbrooke. I wondered if he still had a job as a spy for the young king, Phillip. His coronation was in a few weeks.

Papa started giving me simple magical lessons. The ribbon of magic deep inside me had come alive. Sometimes I thought of the pendant and wondered if that had anything to do with the awaking of magic inside me. We never talked about it.

One chilly morning, when I was dabbling in the greenhouse, Papa joined me.

"I'm glad to see you back to your gardening," he said.

I added dirt into a small pot and then planted a seed as he wandered over. He peered over my shoulder.

"What are you planting?" he asked.

"Tomatoes," I said. "For Spring."

But I sensed he stood there for a reason other than having an interest in gardening and had something else to say. I wiped the dirt from my hands on my apron and turned to him.

"Did you need me?" I asked.

"Actually, yes."

He paused as he walked down the length of the wooden table, looking at all the tiny pots. That morning, I managed to plant herbs and a few other vegetables. I was looking forward to seeing them sprout. When he turned to me, he had an odd look on his face.

"Violet, I hope you know I only want the best for you."

I didn't like where this was going, but I remained silent as he continued.

"That's why I have found another suitor for you."

"Papa," I groaned.

He held up a hand to stop my complaint. "I do realize Lord Desmond was a dismal choice, however, I hoped you would give this one a chance?"

"This one?" I propped my hands on my hips. "Is he here? Now?"

"He's waiting for you in the parlor."

I huffed out a breath. This was much like before when Lord Desmond came to court me and I rebuffed and insulted him and basically called him a murderer.

"Will you meet with him?" Papa asked.

Irritation chafed me. "It appears I have no choice."

"Sophia is waiting to help dress you." He motioned toward the door.

He had it all planned. He knew this suitor was coming to meet me. He must have waited until I was preoccupied with my pots and seeds to bring him into the house. I sighed.

"Very well."

I removed the soiled apron and trudged through the house, up the stairs to my room where she, indeed, waited. The lovely seafoam dress was spread out on the bed. I stared at it with suspicion.

"That?" I asked.

She nodded. "Since you never got a chance to wear it, I thought this would be a nice opportunity."

"Don't you think it's a bit...grand for such an occasion? I only need a day dress." I headed to the wardrobe.

"Oh, no, my lady. This will be perfect for this occasion."

Something about the way she said it made me turn to look at her askance. "It will?"

She nodded and gave me a bright smile.

I allowed her to dress me in the gorgeous, seafoam silk gown, feeling wildly overdressed. Instead of braiding my long hair, she brushed it out. Then she pulled it all back and secured it with a matching green ribbon at the nape of my neck.

"There! Lovely!" she exclaimed, clearly happy with her handiwork.

I had to admit the gown was one of the loveliest I'd ever seen or worn. Taking a deep breath, I left my room and headed back down the stairs to the parlor. The door was closed. I paused there, remembering the day I overheard Papa telling Lord Desmond he would give my hand in marriage for forty-thousand gold. As I stood there, I heard nothing. No voices.

I pulled the door open and stepped inside the room and came to a jarring halt.

Standing there at the mantle, dressed in white breeches, tall black boots, and a navy waistcoat over a white shirt was Aiden Lockhart.

He turned when he heard the door. His sharp blue eyes lit up as an irresistibly devastating grin crossed his face. I found it impossible not to return that grin, despite the frantic pounding of my pulse. Finally, I found my voice.

"*You* are the suitor?"

He bowed. "In the flesh." He peered at me intently and then gave a nod. "I was right. That color does bring out the green in your eyes."

I flushed, hot and wild. "You sent it?"

"Yes, and the other one. I had hoped to dance with you at the ball, but since the ball was canceled..." His words drifted off.

"And you were in Whitefell."

"I planned to be back for it with the Ashean emissary in tow. But let us not speak of that which is behind us."

Before I could reply, the butler wheeled in a tea cart with tiny sandwiches and lemon cakes. He poured us each a cup of tea and then left, closing the door behind us. I took my cup and perched on the edge of the chair. He did the same. We sat in amicable silence for a moment.

"What should we speak about, then?" I asked.

"About our future." He took a sip of tea as if it was the most natural thing in the world to say.

My heart thundered so loud in my ears it was all I heard for a brief moment. "*Our* future?"

"Yes, of course. Your father wishes me to court you."

"Does he?"

"He wrote to me, you see, while I was still at the castle. I was preparing to leave and head for the Port of Dunfail. Since you were leaving the continent, I saw no reason to stay," he said. "And then his letter arrived and everything changed."

I peered at him over the rim of my porcelain cup. My palms broke into a hot sweat. "It did?"

"Yes. I had a reason to stay on the continent. King Philip has no use for my services as a spy, so I packed up and left. There's a lovely little town call Lampfort north of here that does need my services. As a piano teacher."

I stared at him. My mouth had gone utterly dry. With a shaking hand, I placed the tea cup on the table in front of me and then folded my hands in my lap. My stomach churned acid, revolting at the very thought of tea.

"Do you know where Lampfort is?" he asked, as he sipped his tea.

"I do." I resisted telling him my wretch of a cousin lived there once.

"I rented a flat there," he said. "It's a small place but I was able to secure a position as a piano teacher at the local fine arts school. Did you know Lampfort has a fine arts school?"

He spoke as if he were talking about nothing more than the weather. Stunned, and trying to make my mind catch up with all he was saying, I merely shook my head. I had no idea Lampfort had a fine arts school.

"They teach music and dancing," he went on. "From what I understand, the school is becoming quite popular especially with the gentry. It won't be long before the nobility take notice and begin to enroll their children there. It's a small salary, but with time I believe it will increase. It's enough to make a comfortable living and—"

"Wait." I jumped to my feet. "Why are you telling me this?"

"I thought my intentions were clear." He placed his cup on the table next to mine and slowly rose to his feet. "I intend to marry you, Violet. After a suitable courtship, of course."

A quick breath of utter astonishment escaped me. I was too startled to respond and was struck mute. His eyes were filled with a fierce sparkling as the corners of his mouth lifted in an easy smile.

"I've shocked you." He reached for one of my hands, holding it in his. "I admit, when we parted that day at the castle, I was certain I lost you forever. When your father's letter arrived, I knew I could waste no time getting back to you."

"But...But...I don't understand."

"What's not to understand?" he said with a little laugh. "Ah, perhaps I've gone about this the wrong way." Still holding my hand, he lifted it toward his lips. "Violet, will you do the honor of allowing me to court you?"

My breath hitched as our eyes met. I found I could get lost in the depths of his blue eyes. With a smile, I nodded.

"Yes, I will. On one condition."

His brows rose. "And that is?"

"That I can continue my magical studies."

"Of course, you can, my darling girl. I understand the fine arts school is looking for a new teacher of enchantments." He winked and gave me a sly smile.

My heart thudded hard as I thought of myself as a teacher. I was nowhere near good enough. Yet. But perhaps someday. The thought warmed me.

"I'm glad you said yes," he continued, "otherwise, I just made a fool of myself."

I laughed. "You are no fool, Aiden Lockhart."

He pulled me into a tight embrace, wrapping his arms around me, holding me close. "I'm glad you didn't leave." His voice lowered to a whisper, as though we were trading secrets.

"Me, too," I whispered back.

"I was going to be positively bereft without you."

I grinned, slipping my arm around his waist. "Were you?"

"Indeed," he said.

Then he kissed me. The sweetest, most perfect kiss. A kiss I never wanted to end.

And just like that, life changed once again. This time in the best, happiest way.

Acknowledgements

The cover for this book was purchased prior to me having a story for it. Sometimes, it works that way. It was a pre-made. I didn't even have a title for it yet, but I knew as soon as I saw the cover I needed it. Initially, I thought about including it in my fairy tale retellings, so I did some research in search of one to retell.

I found *The Six Servants*, by the Brothers Grimm, and read through the synopsis. I was intrigued by the idea of having rejected suitors. Well, in the actual fairy tale, the evil queen is a sorceress who beheads the suitors when they fail the assigned impossible tasks. This book is not a retelling of that story. Instead, I took the idea of rejecting suitors and put a different spin on it.

The Sorcerer's Daughter was born. I didn't know there would be a magical pendant until I started writing the blurb. Many thanks to **Erin Dameron-Hill** who creates amazing covers time after time and for inspiring such a fun story.

A huge thanks to **Kathleen Baldwin** who helped me tweak this blurb into its final form. She is not only an amazing author, but a lovely person and I am so thankful for her talent and her time in helping me. She was also kind enough to read the book and give me a cover blurb. If you haven't read her *Stranje House* series, do yourself a favor and pick up the first book, *A School for Unusual Girls*.

Thanks to **Jennifer August** for our endless chats about books and writing at our monthly lunches. She helps me figure out stuff when I'm stuck and gives me great ideas when I'm not sure which direction to go. I love our lunches and look forward to them every month.

To my sister, **Kathy**, who proofread this book for me and found those persnickety typos I missed.

To my beta reader, **Amanda Ryan**, who gave me some great feedback on the direction of this book.

To my sister-in-law, **Nickie**, who gives me unfailing support no matter what.

And, finally, to you, **readers**. Without you, none of this is possible. Your support means the world to me as an indie author. You make it worthwhile to keep writing and publishing.

Also by Michelle Miles

Age of Wizards (Epic Fantasy)

In the Tower of the Wizard King

On the Hunt for the Wizard King

Dragon Protectors (Paranormal Shifter Romance)

Desiring the Dragon Lord

Seducing the Dragon Knight

Tempting Her Dragon Bodyguard

Dragon Protectors Book Collection, Books 1-3

Dream Walker (Urban Fantasy)

Call of the Dark

Blood and Bone

Flame and Fury

Smoke and Ashes

Light of the World

Dream Walker Collection (Books 1-5)

Dream Walker: Origins (Fantasy)

Provenance

Enchanted Realms (Fantasy Romance)

Once Upon a Midnight Clear

Once Upon True Love's Kiss

Once Upon an Enchanted Kiss

Five Towers (YA Fantasy)

The Sorcerer's Daughter

**Ransom & Fortune Adventures
(Time Travel Action/Adventure)**

Highland Fling, Vol 1

Dead of Winter, Vol 2

The Citadel, Vol 3

Lord of the Underworld, Vol 4

Realm of Honor (Fantasy Romance)

One Knight Only

Only for a Knight

A Knight to Remember

A Knight Like No Other

Shadows of the Knight

Realm of Honor Collection (Books 1-5)

Guardians of Atlantis (Fantasy Romance)

Tempting Eden

Seducing Eve

Ravishing Helene

Guardians of Atlantis Box Set

Shorts and Anthologies (Fantasy/Paranormal)

A Dance Among the Faeries, Short Story

Eorwulf, Short Story

The Soul of Sharah, Short Story

Sinfully Sweet, Short Story

Flights of Fantasy: A Collection of Short Stories

ABOUT THE AUTHOR

MICHELLE MILES believes in fairy tales, true love and magic. She writes heart-stopping urban fantasy, epic fantasy and paranormal romance with an action/adventure twist that will leave you breathless. She is the author of numerous series that includes everything from angels and demons to fairies, dragons and elves.

She is a member of Romance Writers of America (RWA) and Science Fiction and Fantasy Writers Association (SFWA). A native Texan, in her spare time she loves reading, listening to music, watching movies, hiking, and drinking wine. She can be found online at Facebook, Instagram, Pinterest and Goodreads.

Your Adventure Awaits

Read more at MichelleMiles.net

www.ingramcontent.com/pod-product-compliance
Lightning Source LLC
Chambersburg PA
CBHW071418200726
48294CB00002B/440